MR CAMPION'S MEMORY

MR CAMPION'S MEMORY

Mike Ripley

**SEVERN
HOUSE**

First world edition published in Great Britain and the USA in 2023
by Severn House, an imprint of Canongate Books Ltd,
14 High Street, Edinburgh EH1 1TE.

Trade paperback edition first published in Great Britain and the USA in 2024
by Severn House, an imprint of Canongate Books Ltd.

severnhouse.com

British Library Cataloguing-in-Publication Data
A CIP catalogue record for this title is available from the British Library.

ISBN-13: 978-1-4483-1108-8 (cased)
ISBN-13: 978-1-4483-1282-5 (trade paper)
ISBN-13: 978-1-4483-1109-5 (e-book)

Typeset by Palimpsest Book Production Ltd.,
Falkirk, Stirlingshire, Scotland.

Praise for Mike Ripley

"Impressive . . . brilliant inventiveness"
Publishers Weekly Starred Review of *Mr Campion's Mosaic*

"Charming, clever, and witty . . . Another delightful mystery"
Booklist on *Mr Campion's Mosaic*

"A cunning mix of silliness and wit"
The Times on *Mr Campion's Mosaic*

"Ripley has a wonderful talent for capturing the voices,
mannerisms and wit of Margery Allingham's original
creations"
MINETTE WALTERS on *Mr Campion's Mosaic*

"One of Campion's most waggish adventures"
Kirkus Reviews on *Mr Campion's Mosaic*

"Ripley again marries a crafty plotline with a persuasive
evocation of Allingham's style and characterizations. Fans of
the originals will be delighted"
Publishers Weekly Starred Review of *Mr Campion's Wings*

"Exceptional . . . Both old and new Campion fans will hope
for many more exploits"
Publishers Weekly Starred Review of *Mr Campion's Coven*

"Ripley spins a head-scratching whodunit while effectively
recreating Allingham's tone and characters. This clever
continuation of a beloved series keeps getting better"
Publishers Weekly Starred Review of *Mr Campion's Séance*

About the author

Mike Ripley is the author of more than thirty books and writes the internationally respected *Getting Away With Murder* column for Shots magazine. His 'reader's history' of the heyday of British action and spy thrillers 1953–75, *Kiss Kiss Bang Bang*, won the H.R.F. Keating Award for non-fiction in 2017.

For Janet and Jim Cohen,

great friends, loyal supporters and very generous hosts

in London, Cambridge and Tuscany.

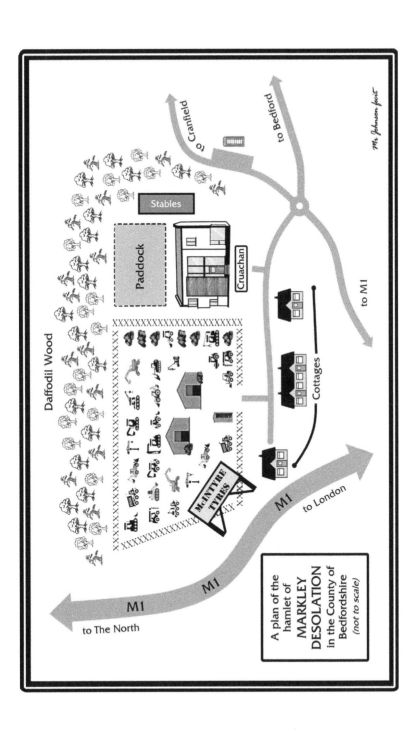

CONTENTS

ONE

A Relatively Simple Request

'Funerals can be so . . . distracting, can't they? They positively disrupt everyday life.'

'That's rather the whole point of them, isn't it?' responded Mr Campion, favouring his nephew with a quizzical eyebrow. 'Every funeral marks the disruption of at least one person's life.'

The younger man shook his head, as if to clear it. 'Sorry, Uncle, I'm not thinking straight.'

'Why should you? The funeral of one's father should be disconcerting; it would be odd if it was not.'

'It is also the funeral of your brother.'

'And? Do I not look grief-stricken enough? Am I wailing too quietly or not dramatically rending my garments? Naturally I was devastated by my little brother Baden's death, and sixty-four is no age for a heart to give out, but I cannot pretend we were close as siblings. You of all people know that your father took the family line where I was concerned.'

At his side, Mr Campion felt his wife Amanda, immaculate in tailored black, lean into him and increase the pressure of her grip on his arm as they walked, surrounded by the pack of quiet mourners back to the church where the vicar, his white surplice shining out like a lightbulb in that palette of sombre colours, waited with a final blessing.

The young man who had threaded his way through the column and was now shuffling along beside the Campions, hands clasped behind his back and his head down, his eyes on the churchyard path, spoke quietly, but firmly.

'My father used to say you disowned the family rather than that they disowned you, and he almost disowned *me* when I adopted the name Campion for professional reasons. I hope you don't mind about that, by the way, but the family name is so cumbersome and I suspect he considered it unsuitable to be linked to a public relations business – or any business or profession, come to that.'

'There were few professions – and no trades – of which Baden approved,' said Mr Campion, 'so I certainly don't blame you for adopting a *nom de guerre* – or should that be *nom de travail*? And Campion has served me very well for fifty years, so I see no reason why you should not continue the tradition. In fact, I'm quite flattered you chose it, and Christopher Campion does have a certain ring to it, positively chiming with professional competence. I agree, the family name is a bit of a mouthful and few successful business ventures start with the letter K.'

'Kraft? Kodak? Kellogg's?' suggested Christopher Campion.

'Krupp?' Amanda whispered in her husband's ear.

'That's not helpful, dearest. This is a funeral and decorum is the order of the day, especially as we approach the vicar.'

'My fault,' said Christopher, 'I distracted you, but I really wanted to ask you something, Uncle.'

'If it is about wills, or graves, or epitaphs, I am not your man. I guess those are the topics of the day, or at least this day.'

'Actually it's not about my father; it's more a professional matter.'

'Professional? Your profession?'

'Yes, mine, but I think also yours.'

'My dear boy,' said Mr Campion, 'I have no profession. Some would say I never had one, but whether I did or not, I am most definitely retired from it.'

'Well done, darling,' said Amanda.

Mr Campion turned his spectacles full on to his wife's heart-shaped face. 'For what?'

'For acting your age,' Amanda replied primly, then turned to the younger man at her husband's side. 'Your uncle Albert is retired, Christopher. Whatever he might once have been, he is now a man of total inaction. His days of derring-do are now derring-done; they are his yesterdays. The only thorny problems he tackles now are presented by rose bushes – and they often get the better of him.'

Mr Campion slowed his gait, as if to refute his wife's rather depressing testimonial, but then caught the sparkle in her eyes, noted the upturned corners of her lips and thought the better of it.

'It was advice I was after, simply advice,' Christopher pleaded in a voice which suggested he had reluctantly put more dangerous options on the backburner.

'On a public relations matter? I can't think how I might possibly be qualified to help.'

'Your memory could.'

'My memory? I wouldn't rely on that. Shaky at best, sometimes downright treacherous, as my wife will testify, especially when it comes to birthdays and anniversaries. I once, a long time ago, even forgot I'd married her, and only really had her word for it.'

'Albert!' Amanda took her hand from her husband's forearm, made a dainty fist and lightly punched him in the ribs, then returned to the arm-in-arm position of the dutiful wife. Only Christopher, in the huddle of mourners surrounding them, noticed the action. 'You had amnesia and it was a temporary condition.' She turned her face, a portrait of pure innocence, towards her husband's nephew. 'At least that's what I let him think.'

'What exactly is it you want me to remember?' Mr Campion asked him.

'Nineteen thirty-two,' said Christopher, glad to be back on track and not embroiled in the domestic banter, albeit affectionate and never petty-minded, for which the Campions had something of a reputation.

'The year 1932? All of it? Were we on the Gold Standard? Who did I vote for? How high were hemlines? What did a gallon of petrol cost? Who won the FA Cup? That sort of thing?'

Christopher, a man to whom quick thinking did not come naturally, and who had considerable experience of not being taken seriously, tried to put some urgency into his request.

'Look, it's something which involves a client of mine, a big client, and it's all rather important – at least to me – and I could really do with talking it through.'

Mr Campion felt a gentle nudge in his ribs, although he detected no visible movement by his wife, even though he was in range of her perfume and her attention was firmly fixed on his nephew.

'I do not think this is the time,' he said, 'and I am sure this isn't the place, Christopher, but I will be in London next week. Perhaps we could meet and chat there?'

The younger man's face brightened and his shoulders rose, as if he had shrugged off a heavy load.

'Thanks awfully, Uncle, that would be very useful.' He pointed a finger towards the looming church porch where, having exchanged solemn small talk with the vicar, the column of funeral attendees was dispersing into the waiting fleet of shiny black limousines. 'Unless, that is, you're coming up to the big house for a drink and some cold cuts.'

Mr Campion shook his head. 'No, we will not be partaking of the funeral meats – a depressing ritual if ever there was one. Our car is nearby, so we will be heading off home rather than calling at the big house.'

'Too many bad memories?' Christopher asked without thinking.

'No,' said Mr Campion. 'Just not enough good ones.'

The church, the mourners and the convoy of black cars had long disappeared from the Jaguar's rear-view mirror before Mr Campion relaxed his grip on the steering wheel and broke the silence.

'I wasn't too curt with young Christopher, was I?'

'Not at all,' said Amanda. 'Asking a favour for his business at his father's funeral may not have been exactly tactful, but it was a relatively simple request and you accommodated him. He could have chosen his timing better, but you know what Christopher's like.'

Indeed, Mr Campion did, and felt a great affection for – and a little affinity with – his nephew, despite having once described him as *that unusual sort of public relations man, the sort who starts fires rather than puts them out.* To be fair, Christopher never intentionally sparked a flint into kindling, but he had shown himself, through a combination of innocence and gullibility, capable of fanning rather than extinguishing any flames smouldering around the public image of a company or business or the private life of a minor celebrity. Thanks to television, there were now more celebrities demanding public relations advice than there were public relations consultants and so, however incendiary Christopher's methods, it seemed unlikely he would lack for clients.

Mr Campion rather admired him for having the courage to set himself up in a profession which was not recognized, indeed ridiculed, by his father and two elder brothers, who all regarded public relations as a trade somewhere below journalism, itself a calling far beneath that of licensed victualler, racehorse trainer and bookies' runner.

Christopher's father Baden – who had been named for the founder of the Scout movement – laid the blame for his son's poor choice of career on a combination of factors: that as the youngest child he had been 'babied' for far too long by his mother, that he had been born too late to fight in a decent war, and that he had never, as a boy, got enough fresh air or spent enough nights under canvas. Baden's relations with his elder brother, Albert, ran on similar lines, although good manners and social conventions prevented him from openly displaying his disappointments, unlike the situation with his son, whom he had humiliated and embarrassed in public on numerous occasions. The nearest Baden had come to criticizing Albert was to express sympathy that his brother had been forced to attend Rugby rather than 'a decent school', and there was no doubt that this was not a joke – Baden's sense of humour was conspicuous by its absence.

The real cause of Baden's dearth of brotherly love – and, in fact, the root of dissension in the entire family – was, of course, the question of the hereditary title which came with the family name. It was a name which Albert had abandoned in favour of the more pastoral Campion in his undergraduate days at Cambridge, immediately after the end of the Great War, which he had seen out as a teenager in uniform, though not in action (another black mark against him in Baden's book, no doubt).

When the eldest son of the family, Herbert, died suddenly and childless in 1940, Albert was in line for the viscountcy but refused to accept it. As there was at that time, more than twenty years before the Peerage Act, no legal method of disclaiming the title, it was considered to be 'in abeyance', as it could not pass to another family member as long as Albert lived. Whether he liked it or not, Albert was, legally, the rightful heir; he simply chose to blissfully ignore the fact.

Elite society may have been shocked by his decision, but the effect was hardly seismic, as by 1940 the upper echelons of society (as well as the lower strata) had become aware of Mr Campion as a resourceful, decent man prepared to right wrongs and defend the oppressed, usually with the full cooperation of the police. Plus, there was a war on and the rejection of a title, however noble, seemed of little consequence in the grander sweep of historical events. Within the family, though, it proved the last straw. Rejecting the family name could have been dismissed as youthful irresponsibility, but refusing the viscountcy when it came his way was beyond the pale. Only his sister Valentine sympathized with Albert's position, even if she did not fully understand his motives.

'Val would have been at the big house,' said Amanda, carefully watching her husband's reactions as he drove. 'She would have wanted to see you.'

'I know. I telephoned her last night and made my excuses. She was much closer to Baden than I ever was. There was only a year between them, you know, whereas I was six when Baden came along, and no bumptious six-year-old boy really has time for a baby brother.'

'Bumptious? You?'

'I was a holy terror by all accounts, and couldn't be packed off to Rugby soon enough. Then it was the army – a brief and thankfully uneventful sojourn – and then Cambridge and a life of footloose fancy until, that is, *you* tamed me. The family did not need me, but other people seemed to. The family had Herbert, who fitted the bill beautifully until he went and died at the ridiculous age of forty-one.' Amanda noticed a change in the tone of his voice. 'Now Baden has gone at sixty-four, which is no age at all these days, and I feel somewhat . . . vulnerable, I suppose, as I have already had my three-score-and-ten.'

'Don't you dare talk like that, Albert Campion. I won't stand for it. You are as fit as a fiddle and I do my damnedest to make sure you look after yourself. You know your food and you like your wine, but you've hardly put on a pound in weight since I first met you. Val and I, and indeed we speak for all women of a certain age, regard your ability to stay thin as a rake as your least appealing feature. It's really infuriating.'

'Nervous hyper-energy is what the masters at Rugby called it, though my grandmother had a more forceful diagnosis and her favourite command, delivered in stentorian tones, was always "Albert, stop fidgeting!".'

'You're not a fidget, you just have a quick and very active mind. Now that is an appealing feature – well, it appealed to me,' said Amanda, carefully stroking the back of Albert's hand so as not to disturb his control of the steering wheel. 'And I've seen other women give you the once-over and comparing you to their husbands who have run to fat and lethargy. I think that's why you keep in with Lugg. Next to him you look like a Greek god.'

'Next to Lugg, a pregnant hippo would look positively sylph-like. Do you remember the "Dance of the Hours" scene in *Fantasia*? Always reminds me of Lugg.'

Magersfontein Lugg, like the recently departed Baden, had been christened at a time when Britain's imperial misadventures dominated the newspaper headlines. But whereas Baden had been named for a national hero, the story went that Lugg's parents had been inspired by the headline in a newspaper 'wrapped around fourpence worth of wet fish' concerning the Battle of Magersfontein which, contrary to the understanding of a proud and patriotic father, had not actually been a British victory.

Mr Campion had long since abandoned any attempt to describe his relationship with Mr Lugg in terms which were fathomable to the man on the Clapham omnibus, or at least the conductor collecting the fares. Even a basic job description – one on which employer and employee agreed – had always proved elusive in all the long years of their association. The designation 'butler' had been dismissed as inappropriate from the outset; if the word was even breathed in Lugg's presence, it tended to provoke a violent reaction. The terms 'valet' and 'steward' were deemed vague, weak and inappropriate, and whereas Lugg's presence was certainly regarded as inappropriate on many occasions, it was never considered weak or vague. Titles such as 'adjutant' or 'aide-de-camp' suggested an air of military precision and discipline, both qualities which would be notably absent from Lugg's curriculum vitae had he possessed such a document. The man himself, if pressed or questioned under caution, would say that he acted as a sort of curator to Mr Campion, whereas Mr Campion had been known to admit that Lugg was both a family retainer – although sometimes in the sense that a cuckoo becomes a retainer to a nest of sparrows – and his 'left-hand man'.

There was no doubt that the two men were close and had shared both adventures and misadventures for the better part of half a century; however, even Lugg, the older of the two, was coming round to the idea of retirement these days. Both relished the epithet OAP, as long as it was explicitly defined as Over-Active Pensioner, and Campion was the first to admit that, given his girth, his huge ham hocks of hands, and a face which had been likened to the portrait of a bulldog painted on to an artillery shell, Lugg was still a formidable figure who demanded respect or at least a wide berth. His physical presence alone was enough to part a stream of football supporters exiting a ground after a four–nil defeat, or attract the undivided attention of a barman, however crowded a pub was. The sight of him had once, by the opening of a wrong door, reduced a boisterous Baptist revival meeting to pin-dropping silence.

'You are quite right, darling,' said Campion, as if he had been considering the matter deeply. 'I should always insist on having Lugg at my side in public, so that I look my best. Unless, of course, there are bullets flying or an angry mob is pelting us with cobblestones or rotting cabbages, in which case I will seek shelter behind his ample form.'

'Well, his form is certainly ample enough,' said Amanda, happy that her husband's mood seemed to have lightened. 'I suppose being a human shield is the one advantage of being immensely fat.'

'There is another.' Campion smiled. 'It makes him very difficult to kidnap.'

Amanda chuckled and allowed the Jaguar to cover half a dozen more miles before she returned, in a circumspect way, to the events of the day.

'Lugg never got on with Baden, did he? I mean, I know the old codger is not good at hiding his feelings, but whenever Baden's name was mentioned, he didn't even try to hide them.'

'You mean the way he always referred to him as "'im 'oo got dropped on 'is 'ead at Eton"?'

Amanda laughed again and clapped her gloved hands in appreciation of Campion's impersonation. 'And did he?'

'Did he what? Did he go to Eton? Good Lord, yes; he never let anyone forget that.'

'Oh, I am aware of *that*. I meant did he get dropped on his head there?'

'Very probably. Most boys were in those days; perhaps they still are.'

'Did him going to Eton irritate you?'

'Not in the slightest. I was closest in age to Herbert and he went there, but it was thought better for the both of us if I didn't follow in his wake, so I went to Rugby. Baden was six years younger than I and, by the time he was ready to be packed off to school, Herbert was the responsible choice to look after the new bug, as we used to call them.'

Campion concentrated on overtaking a rather dangerously shaking lorry, and only when the manoeuvre was complete did he return to the conversation.

'Funnily enough, Lugg has always had a soft spot for young Christopher,' he said airily. Then, with concern, 'You don't think I was rude to him?'

'Certainly not. You'd just seen your brother laid to rest—'

'And his father,' Campion interjected.

'Which makes him wanting to discuss public relations in a churchyard doubly tactless, unless it was something to do with the family.'

'I doubt that very much. Val would have tipped me off if there were problems with the family, and anyway, I cannot believe Baden had any need for public relations advice, even from his son. Perhaps *especially* from his son.'

'Baden did not have much regard for the profession?'

'Baden did not think much of any profession, apart from the army and, at a pinch, the navy. He never trusted lawyers, but then few people do, and he clearly had little time for the advice of doctors.'

Amanda stretched a hand over to Albert's head and flicked his ear, which produced a satisfying yelp of surprise.

'Don't be horrid. Baden had a heart attack which no one could have predicted.'

'He might have shown a little more of his heart to his youngest son.'

'That's as may be, Albert, but there is absolutely nothing you could have done about that, or can do about it now, except to meet with Christopher, listen to him politely and help him if you can.'

'I'll certainly let him take me to lunch – I understand that most public relations get done over lunch – and find out what he wants.'

'He said he wanted to tap your memory.'

'He did, from 1932, which is a long time ago. I don't see how I am going to be able to help him, or his client.'

Amanda slapped out a brief drum roll on the handbag lying in her lap. 'Just remember, Albert Campion is now retired and enjoying a life of leisure. He is not available for any high jinks, dubious shenanigans or public relations stunts of any kind.'

'Your strictures are well noted, my dear, and today of all days I have been reminded of how old I am. But you're forgetting one thing . . .'

'What?' asked Amanda suspiciously.

'The reason you love me: because I never act my age.'

'Not now, nor – I suspect – back in 1932. What were you up to forty years ago?'

'I cannot possibly think that whatever I was up to, it might be of the slightest interest to Christopher and his client, whoever it is.'

'Was Lugg with you back then?'

'Lugg seems to have been around ever since I lost my baby teeth, so yes, he probably was.'

'No good, then,' said Amanda confidently.

'Excuse me?'

'If you were with Lugg, that's what you'd be up to.'

TWO

The Elusive Free Lunch

'**B**ack in the Thirties, this place was condemned as unfit for human habitation,' said Mr Campion. 'Not this restaurant, of course – this is a charming innovation. I meant this courtyard and the back alley.'

Christopher had suggested Giovanni's, a smart Italian restaurant on the edge of Covent Garden, with a frontage on New Row, where two upper storeys of open sash windows, framed by flowering window-boxes, provided the air conditioning. Finding the entrance, however, was a magical experience for the unseasoned traveller, as it was around the corner in Goodwin's Court. This dark cut-through had once been slum housing but now, with their bulging round bay windows, the surviving cottages had taken on the appearance of a row of shops as if designed by a child with an overactive imagination. The shops were there purely to service a dolls' house and its inhabitants, who would be a princess and her prince – so more of a castle, really. The shops would sell everything the child's fantasies required and everything a miniature prince or princess could desire, from saddles for their unicorns to individual sachets of fairy dust and, of course, sweets. Lots of sweets.

Although it was by his invitation and would, presumably, be charged to his expense account, Christopher had handed the wine list to Mr Campion. He deduced, from the selection on offer, that the owner was more than likely to be Sicilian, and ordered a bottle of Nero d'Avola which he assured Christopher was 'a meaty and underrated red'. While his host looked slightly wary, the waiter taking the order approved enthusiastically and assured them they had made a most excellent choice.

Small talk dominated their *antipasti* and main course of veal cutlets. On Christopher's part, this was a far from diplomatic summary of the reaction of his family and assorted relatives to the absence of Mr Campion from the aftermath of Baden's funeral. Mr Campion allowed the reported gossip to wash over him, only acknowledging it with an occasional wry smile and the odd sigh, although his curiosity was sparked by Christopher asking, at least twice, if Lugg (of all people) was in good health and 'still around'.

For his part, Campion followed polite convention, enquiring after Christopher's social life (unmarried, 'between girlfriends', still playing amateur rugby and an enthusiastic member of something called the Campaign for Real Ale), and only when it came to the coffee and *grappa* stage did he finally ask his nephew the purpose of their meeting.

'Have you ever come across Sir Lachlan McIntyre?' asked Christopher, stirring two teaspoons of brown sugar loudly into his tiny espresso cup.

'As in McIntyre's Tyres? I don't know the man, but I remember the advertising campaign and I'm sure his products must have graced the wheels of a car I owned.'

'That's the chap, and he did start off in the tyre business. He picked up a load of army surplus stock just after the war and sold them to garages all over the country,' said Christopher, tinkling a nervous tune with his spoon. 'That's how he made his *first* million, but the real money came when he got contracts to buy surplus equipment from the military, both ours and the American's.'

Mr Campion feigned indignation. 'Good Lord, he's not a gun-runner, is he?'

'Of course not; he bought up heavy machinery . . .'

'Artillery? How careless of the War Office!'

'No, no, nothing like that. He bought construction equipment: bulldozers, cranes, excavators and diggers, the things the Yanks call backhoes, stuff like that.'

'And I assume he did things with them, or was he simply an eccentric collector?'

Christopher choked back a cynical snort. 'He made a lot of money out of them. Once the wartime building restrictions were removed, his machines were in great demand clearing bomb sites and building new housing estates and roads.'

'So McIntyre the tyre magnate became McIntyre the builder?'

'Not exactly. He didn't do the actual construction, he just rented out or leased the heavy equipment to whoever needed them: builders, property developers, local councils, government departments.'

Mr Campion raised an eyebrow. 'So the government sold him the equipment, probably at a knock-down rate, and then rented it back off him? How astute.'

'It did raise a few eyebrows, like you just did, especially when he got his knighthood; and then there were concerns about some of his employment practices and conditions.'

'The big, bad capitalist exploiting the workers? Paying them a pittance? Sending their children to the workhouse?'

Christopher studied his uncle's face, attempting to judge how serious he was being, and concluded not very. 'Actually, he pays his drivers and mechanics very well and they are really loyal to him.'

'But you would say that if you're his PRO. What did that Betjeman poem say about public relations officers? *A man who really ought to know/For he is paid for saying so.* One might ask why, if McIntyre is such a benevolent employer, he needs a PRO at all.'

'Because some of his attitudes produce rather unfavourable comments in the press. You see, he's very anti-union; it's almost a religious conviction with him. He won't allow a trades union in any of his companies, and if he finds a driver, say, has gone and joined one, he sacks him on the spot.'

'Couldn't have made him popular with the last government,' mused Mr Campion, 'though less of a concern to the present one, which seems to find unions as irritating as Sir Lachlan does. I am no expert on industrial relations though and, despite the excellent lunch you have treated me to, I fail to see how I can be of any help with the press.'

'Press relations isn't the problem,' said Christopher, still twirling his spoon in a now empty cup, 'and I can handle them. That is, after all, what I am paid for. The problem is with one particular journalist, a chap called David Duffy.'

'The name doesn't mean anything, I'm afraid. Should it?'

'My dear uncle, given your interest in things nefarious and downright criminal, I'm surprised you didn't notice the reports of the man shot to death in his car near the M1 two weeks ago. I would have thought that would have been right up your street. David Duffy was the man in the car.'

Mr Campion did vaguely remember reading, or seeing on the television news, a report that police were investigating a suspicious death following the discovery of a body in a car parked in a lay-by off the M1. It had, one source said, all the trademarks of an East End gangland killing carried out a comfortably safe distance from the East End, but in truth, Mr Campion had not given the story a second thought. The victim had not been named and it would have meant little to him if they had.

David Duffy, Christopher explained, was of the breed of journalists generally regarded as the most annoying, at least to public relations officers. They went by several shorthand descriptions, ranging from 'persistent' to 'foot-in-the-door' to 'gutter hacks', and although they could not be bought off with a lavish free lunch, they would eat it anyway. The most belligerent of the kind were said to take pride in being members of 'the awkward squad' and often refused to take 'yes' for an answer as a matter of principle.

Duffy had originally approached the McIntyre company in the orthodox manner, through its public relations consultants, for general background information on its activities. Christopher had been assigned to brief him and shepherd the journalist gently towards the truth, or at least a truth acceptable to his client. This meant providing the full 'open house' treatment, showing Duffy around numerous sites where McIntyre's machines were busily chewing up then shovelling the landscape flat, or digging long lines of drainage ditches. Such building sites were usually muddy or dusty, had few amenities and were rarely photogenic, but Christopher had a strategy for winning over visiting journalists by giving them the opportunity to actually drive a bulldozer or a digger; few overgrown boys – for most of them were male – could resist the urge to play with such big mechanical toys.

Duffy, unusually, had shown little interest in opening that big boys' toy box and instead had pressed for more personal information on the founder of the feast, Sir Lachlan McIntyre himself, which Christopher felt was outside his brief. When all other forms of argument, persuasion and several lavish lunches had failed, the reluctant PRO agreed to ask Sir Lachlan to grant a private interview with Duffy. To his surprise, McIntyre, who was normally reticent when it came to personal publicity and public speaking, had agreed to a one-on-one 'on-the-record' meeting. It did not go well.

Christopher had not been present at the interview – on the specific stipulation of his client – but had received a no-holds-barred account of it down the telephone, complete with a lexicon of expletives, within minutes of it ending. Sir Lachlan made it quite clear that to have put him in such an invidious position was not the action of a consultancy hoping to have its contract renewed, or even continued. His temper was not improved by being reminded that it was he who had agreed to the interview, against the best advice of his consultants, but he was slightly mollified when his consultants accepted full responsibility for rectifying the situation, with Christopher being nominated as the leading peacemaker, or possibly the negotiator of an armed truce.

The reason the interview had gone so badly off the rails, like the train at the end of *The Bridge on the River Kwai* was, according to Sir Lachlan, because the journalist had been: (a) impertinent, (b) aggressive and (c) downright personal. Duffy had not seemed remotely interested in McIntyre's contribution to industry and the British economy in general, let alone his copious contributions to charity. All he wanted to pursue, and he pressed the issue really rather rudely, was Sir Lachlan's more youthful years, before the war and before he became a Captain of Industry.

Mr Campion interrupted Christopher's frantic reportage. 'Would that include the year 1932, by any chance?'

'Why, yes, how did you know?'

'You mentioned 1932 at your father's funeral; several times, in fact.'

'Did I? It has been preying on my mind. What could have happened in 1932 that could be significant?'

'Apart from Amelia Earhart flying solo across the Atlantic, I can't think,' said Campion wryly, 'but then I really don't understand the context of the question.'

'You and Lugg were . . . pals . . . back then, weren't you?'

'Please take as read my expression of haughty derision at the term "pals", but it is fair to say that Lugg and I were acquainted back then, though once again I am at a loss to see what that has to do with anything.'

'I'm just as confused as you and Sir Lachlan were; you see, we hadn't done a script for anything that far back.'

'Script?'

Christopher explained that it was professional practice to put clients as important as Lachlan McIntyre through 'media training', where they would stage mock interviews and attempt to predict any banana-skin questions which a journalist might put before them. In preparation for the Duffy interview, Christopher had rehearsed Sir Lachlan personally, concentrating on the post-war rise of McIntyre Tyres, which went on to become McIntyre Consolidated, as the company was now known. That was the 'riches' segment of McIntyre's rags-to-riches story, and they had not expected Duffy to concentrate on the 'rags' preamble, if for no other reason than that it was already public knowledge.

When McIntyre had been knighted, Christopher's agency had made sure that the story of his rise from poverty in the rough Glasgow enclave of Govan to millionaire business magnate with an estate in Bedfordshire, was well-known. It was a carefully tailored narrative, well-*scripted* to strain the heart strings. In the approved version, Lachlan had left school to be apprenticed as a welder in the shipyards which dotted the banks of the Clyde, but he did so on the eve of the Great Depression and soon found himself both unemployed and orphaned when his parents died in a tragic house fire at Hogmanay. As a scrawny nineteen-year-old he had hitchhiked down to London (he had scraped together the train fare but that did not sound so romantic), where he wandered the streets (actually as far as Stepney where he was taken in by a widowed aunt) and found work at the West India Docks. Perhaps prompted by the way his parents had died, he joined the Auxiliary Fire Service as a part-time fireman and acquitted himself bravely during the Blitz after war broke out. It was, he was to say (because Christopher had coached him), the most action he saw during the war as, after being called up in 1942, he saw nothing more exciting than the inside of the quarter-master's stores and nothing more dangerous than a buckled tin of corned beef, his army career beginning and ending with the rank of private.

To complete his personal history, he had married in 1936 and was still married to the same woman, though the union had produced no children to share in the wealth accumulated after the war thanks to McIntyre's business acumen.

'A curious background for a self-made millionaire,' said Mr Campion, 'but there again, perhaps not. A tough Scot with a Calvinist work ethic who had no doubt learned a few tricks from his time working the docks, and a few more fiddles in the quartermaster's stores, was probably just the sort of entrepreneurial chap to spot a business opportunity after the war.'

'Steady on, Uncle. There's never been any suggestion of dodgy practices in Sir Lachlan's business dealings,' said Christopher with a hurt expression.

Mr Campion could not suppress a broad grin. 'Oh, come on, Christopher, you're not on defensive duties now. I'm sure your client's business practices have been scrutinized by journalists and others in the past. He must have had a fairly clean bill of health to get a knighthood. I mean, it is not as if we were back in Lloyd George's day when you could buy one by bunging a few quid into a political party's coffers.'

Christopher looked furtively over his shoulder to reassure himself that no other diners or waiters were within earshot. 'You've actually tweaked a nerve there, Uncle, but that wasn't what bothered Sir Lachlan. He's used to snide comments and sideways looks from snobbish politicians and businessmen who are jealous of his success, and believe me, on that score, he can stand up for himself. He has a temper and sometimes he lets it loose. The thing with Duffy was that the questions he wanted answers to were not about McIntyre the businessman but about his time before the war, in the Thirties after he came down from Scotland to London. The questions were very personal and Sir Lachlan took umbrage at them.'

'Personal in what way?'

'About his political beliefs and his social life, or so he told me. I know that's a bit vague, but he wouldn't go into detail and was still fuming when he told me.'

Mr Campion took off his large round spectacles and polished the lenses on the handkerchief he had eased from the breast pocket of his jacket. 'This Duffy chap – he didn't have McIntyre down as a closet communist or a fellow traveller, did he? It was a very popular calling back then.'

'You must be joking,' sniggered Christopher with a snort. 'Sir Lachlan a communist? It's unthinkable. He has no politics; he's a conservative.'

Now it was Mr Campion's turn to snigger.

'I mean without the capital "C", of course,' Christopher added, 'and he dislikes even talking about politics. Asking him how he voted would be regarded as the height of rudeness.'

'And Duffy was rather rude, I take it.'

'Downright belligerent, according to Sir Lachlan, who stood up and stormed out of the interview. He has sworn never to talk to a journalist again and threatened to shoot Duffy if he ever found him trespassing on his property.'

'Not publicly, I hope,' said Campion severely.

Christopher paled, as if the idea had never occurred to him, and once again his head swivelled rapidly to check he could not be overheard. Just to be sure, when he spoke, it was in a whisper. 'No, thank goodness, though if he put his mind to it, he could certainly do it as he's something of a crack shot.' When he saw the expression on his uncle's face, he continued at speed. 'His passion is hunting deer – stalking, they call it in the Highlands – and Lachlan is a Scot, which probably explains it. His house has sets of antlers coming out of every wall.'

'And you say that Mr Duffy was shot to death, and this was soon after the rather stormy interview with your sharpshooter client, was it?'

'Unfortunately it was.'

'Then your client might be needing a good lawyer rather than a first-rate public relations officer.'

'He has both,' said Christopher with a simpering smile. 'Which is just as well as the police have been all over him, and me too, for that matter.'

'You've been formally questioned about Duffy's murder?' Mr Campion was now totally serious, sitting upright and paying attention.

'Naturally. They found Duffy's notebook and diary, where he had scheduled his meetings with me and with Sir Lachlan, so I told them I had briefed him on the McIntyre operations and offered him every cooperation, with a view to getting as much positive coverage as possible. That was my job, after all, and just at the moment it's more important than ever that Sir Lachlan's image remains . . . shall we say, untarnished. Of course, I couldn't tell the police *that*.'

Mr Campion's eyes widened behind his glasses. 'I'm guessing this might be the nerve I tweaked earlier.'

'I thought you'd guessed when you mentioned Lloyd George and buying peerages. Oh, don't look at me like that, it's not the same thing at all, but it is delicate. You see, Sir Lachlan is being considered for a life peerage in the next New Year's Honours. Of course, that's all strictly hush-hush and under wraps and, before you ask, all above board. There has been no suggestion of political glad-handing or dirty dealing.'

'But a journalist digging up dirt from the past might inhibit his chances of an ermine robe?'

Christopher nodded enthusiastically. 'Exactly. You've put your finger on the nub of our problem.'

'*Our* problem?' Mr Campion tried not to sound like an outraged aunt.

'I was hoping you could help smooth things out; I really do need someone of your gravitas at my side.'

'My dear boy, if I ever had any gravitas it was sold on the white elephant stall at the village fête years ago. I am the last person in the parish to give advice on picking up a peerage.'

Christopher was not to be diverted. 'But with your track record, you're the perfect chap to pour oil on troubled police waters.'

'I'm beginning, as the song goes, to see the light. Let me guess. You have a dead journalist whose last attempt at a scoop ended in a verbal punch-up with your client, who just happens to be the sworn enemy of Bambi's mother and a dead shot. Would it be fair to say that Sir Lachlan McIntyre is a person of some interest to the constabulary?'

'He's their number one suspect,' admitted Christopher gloomily.

'I can see that assassinating an annoying newspaperman might be a hindrance to membership of the House of Lords, though on the other hand, I am sure many of their current lordships have considered just such an action after reading the gossip columns, and may very well welcome a convicted assassin into their berobed ranks. As I have absolutely no power or influence over the award of a peerage, I take it that you expect me to help in establishing Sir Lachlan's innocence with the forces of law and order.'

'That would be just the ticket, Uncle. You've always got on so well with the police.'

'It may surprise you, dear nephew, that my natural charm, my stunning intelligence, my razor-sharp intellect and my dashing good looks, not to mention my modesty, may not go down well with all policemen, especially those working hard on a murder case to which I have no legitimate connection.'

Christopher's eyes widened. 'Oh, but you do. You were on Duffy's list.'

'What list?'

'The police found it in Duffy's notebook and you were on it.'

'I've never heard of the man,' said Mr Campion slowly, 'and until this lunch knew next-to-nothing about Lachlan McIntyre. Exactly what was in this notebook?'

'It was one of those spiral reporter's notebooks and most of the pages were covered in shorthand squiggles. I'm afraid I don't do shorthand and the police wouldn't let me show it to my secretary.'

'But you have seen it?'

'They showed me a clean page, which just had a list of names in plain writing, and asked if I could explain what they meant.'

'And could you?'

'McIntyre's name was on the list and then four or five others which meant nothing, and the heading on the page was "1932", which had been circled in thick pencil, but that meant nothing either.'

'So where do I come in to it?'

'The name Campion was there and the police at first thought it was me, but it quite distinctly said "A. Campion".'

'You are sure that wasn't a shorthand reference to a Campion singular? Perhaps it was a shopping list and he needed to get a Campion—'

'It was clearly you, Uncle. For one thing, I wasn't born in 1932, and for another, the next name on the list was, quite clearly, "M. Lugg".'

Mr Campion sighed and signalled for another *grappa*, having realized that the legendary free lunch had proved as elusive as ever.

THREE
Pilgrim's Progress

'Why can't Christopher get it into his thick head that you are retired? You did tell him that, didn't you?'

'Innumerable times,' said Mr Campion, avoiding his wife's flashing eyes, 'but the lad was quite desperate for a helping hand from a kindly uncle.'

'He's not a lad, Albert, he's a grown man, though I had my doubts when he purloined the name Campion. Was that in homage to you and were you flattered by the hero-worship?'

'I think Christopher borrowed the Campion moniker because he's seen me carry it off, with some style I might add, for fifty years now, and it has proved itself to be a useful buffer against the family name and all the silly expectations which go with it. He's found something he likes doing and seems rather good at it, so – as far as I am concerned – he's welcome to the name.'

'If he's so good at press and public relations, why does he need your help?'

Mr Campion, anticipating Amanda's reaction, had waited until she had picked him up from the station and driven him home before revealing the substance of his London lunch with his nephew. Although his wife could fly a jet aeroplane and a helicopter (which she claimed was the more difficult), Mr Campion still hesitated at breaking bad news when she was at the wheel of the Jaguar driving at speed along unlit country lanes. Once at home and sitting around the kitchen table eating some reheated steak-and-kidney pie, homemade and naturally delicious, with a glass of claret, he had summarized Christopher's dilemma.

'Things have moved out of Christopher's usual sphere of expertise.'

'And into yours? Perhaps once, Albert, but not these days. You don't give a hoot about who gets a peerage – nor should you – and you long since stopped hobnobbing with policemen down the Platelayers' Arms. This is Christopher's problem; let him solve it.'

'I would happily leave this to the public relations experts, darling, but for the matter that my name has been taken in vain.'

'Your name, or Christopher's?'

'This Campion; the one here before you.' Mr Campion pointed his forefinger at his chest. 'My name was one on a list found in the notebook of the murdered journalist Duffy. The police thought "A. Campion" referred to just any common-or-garden Campion, but it was clearly little old me.'

'You are sure about that? Have you seen this notebook?'

'No, the police have it. Christopher only glimpsed it in passing when the police waved it in front of him because they thought it might be him.'

'But why wasn't it him? From the sound of it, he had had dealings with Duffy, whereas you say you've never met him.'

'I haven't; that's what's so strange. Even stranger was the next name on the list, a certain M. Lugg, Esquire.'

'Magers? Then it's clearly guilt by association.'

'Me with him or him with me?'

'Both. Can you explain how you both made the list?'

'Not at all, and even more obscure is that it has something to do with the year 1932, as Christopher indicated at Baden's funeral.'

'Just a minute . . .' Amanda placed a delicate fist under her chin and furrowed her brow in classic 'thinker' pose. 'If you're on this list – a list found in the notebook of a murdered hack – why haven't the boys in blue come calling?'

Mr Campion squirmed uncomfortably in his seat. 'The listing was somewhat vague and the police assumed the Campion in question was Christopher. Rather naughtily, Christopher did not disabuse them of this, which he should have done.'

'And Lugg?'

'They didn't press him on that, and I suppose the Bedfordshire police have wasted many hours trying to trace the mysterious "M. Lugg". They may even have contacted the French embassy to see if they had a Monsieur Lugg on their books.'

'Don't tell me that Bedfordshire is the only county in the realm where Lugg isn't known to the police?' asked Amanda casually, then became more serious. 'You did say Bedfordshire, didn't you? That's where Lachlan McIntyre lives, in a ghastly place called Markley.'

'You know McIntyre?'

'No, but I've met his wife, Lucy. They live quite close to Cranfield and I give the occasional lecture there at the College of Aeronautics as it was, though it's now the Institute of Technology. We sit on some of the same committees: fund-raising, allocating bursaries. Social events, that sort of thing. I don't know her well, but I understand she puts McIntyre money into many a worthy cause.'

'Which would be good for the image of McIntyre Consolidated.'

'Whereas a murder enquiry is probably not so good, especially with a peerage in the offing.'

'Quite,' said Campion, 'though back in history many a lord was created solely on the basis of the number of the king's enemies they had killed. Not that I'm suggesting McIntyre has done anything of the sort. Christopher is confident he is innocent and no charges have been laid yet. It would be awful if Christopher found he had a murderer as a client.'

Amanda looked at him suspiciously. 'And you feel that Christopher needs your help. I know you too well, Albert. You are simply unable to resist getting involved.'

'I do think I have a duty to explain that they may have got the wrong Campion from that list, as wasting police time is a serious offence. Plus, I will admit to a certain satisfaction in being able to report M. Lugg to the police.'

'Do you know anyone in the Bedfordshire police?'

'Not a soul.'

'Then I strongly suggest you have a word with Charlie Luke to see if he can smooth your path.'

She caught the way her husband's eyes dropped from her to his empty plate on the table before him.

'You already have, haven't you?' said Amanda, and there was a touch of frost in her voice.

Despite the heavy workload imposed on him as a senior figure at New Scotland Yard, Commander Charles Luke never forgot a friend, but only a select few were granted the privilege of immediate, or almost immediate, access. When Mr Campion had telephoned him, he had been in a high-level meeting, but his underlings were well-trained, a message was taken and passed on, and Campion's call was returned at the first opportunity with profuse assurances that it was not in the slightest an imposition on a very busy man.

Mr Campion was well aware of the fact that it was and that Luke, apart from his regular duties fighting crime and maintaining public order, was having to deal with an upsurge in IRA activity, militant unions and the internal campaign against corruption within the CID being waged by the new Commissioner of the Metropolitan Police, who had vowed that the force would arrest more criminals than it employed. Feeling guilty at taking up his old friend's time and attention, Campion kept the pleasantries to the bare minimum and asked Luke outright if there was a Bedfordshire colleague 'he could pester' about a case they were dealing with, to which Luke had asked tersely, 'Uniform or detective?' and when Campion said it would be the latter, Luke provided a name – Detective Chief Inspector Stanley Castor – and a proviso.

'Stan is very traditional when it comes to coppering, Albert. Slow and sure, but he gets there in the end. Your usual flannel won't cut it with him; he'd feel more at home dealing with Lugg than with you.'

'He may well have to, as it happens,' Campion had said with a hint of mischief.

'Not that I really want to know, unless I have to,' Luke had asked warily, 'but what are you up to? Are the two of you back in the snooping game?'

'Nothing like that, Charles. Just doing a bit of public relations.'

Mr Campion did not know Bedford well; certainly not as well as Lugg claimed to, for apart from being a connoisseur of the products of the town's main brewery, he never missed an opportunity to boast that he had seen the original Glenn Miller orchestra play there at the Corn Exchange in July 1944. Campion knew that a large portion of Bedford's population was of Italian descent; they regularly bought grapes in bulk from Spitalfields Market in London in order to make their own rather pleasant *vino da tavola*, naturally for personal consumption only. He was also aware that the Puritan John Bunyan had used his time in Bedford Gaol to write his most famous work, though Mr Campion hoped his journey into Bedfordshire would prove less strenuous than the experiences of Bunyan's wayward pilgrim.

His, however, was not a pilgrimage into the unknown, as he was no stranger to visiting police stations; indeed, his London flat, a hangover from his bachelor days, was above one in Bottle Street off Piccadilly. Yet he was on a sort of quest for knowledge, if not truth, and hopefully Luke's nominee DCI Castor would help him avoid any potential sloughs of despond.

Stanley Castor was indeed a policeman of the old school, the sort of copper who, although a pipe smoker himself, always had a packet of ten cigarettes in one pocket of his raincoat and a quarter of Jelly Babies in the other, for the exclusive use or distraction of mothers and children who may have witnessed something germane to his enquiries. Within a minute of being shown into his office, Campion had him pegged as a slow but methodical professional who went quietly about his business, knew every market trader and petty thief on his patch by their first name, and was frightened by nothing bar having to intervene in a domestic dispute. He would be shocked to the core to hear that any of his officers were corrupt or 'on the take', though he would be personally aggrieved not to receive his regular Christmas bottle of Scotch from the town's Licensed Victuallers. His junior, much younger, officers would complain – among themselves – about his lack of dynamism and reluctance to adopt more modern methods of policing, but Campion could see why Charlie Luke would regard him as 'a copper's copper'.

'Thank you so much for seeing me, Chief Inspector.'

'You have friends in high places, Mr Campion,' said Castor, offering a firm handshake.

'I hope that's not a problem.'

'Don't worry, no noses out of joint here. If a man like Commander Luke vouches for you, the least I can do is give you the time of day, so how can I help you?'

'I think we may be able to help each other, or at the very least

I can offer a small amount of information which might dot an
"i" or cross a "t" in one of your ongoing investigations.'

Castor settled himself behind his desk and peered at Campion
over a pile of bulging cardboard files. 'I'm all for tying up loose
ends,' said the policeman, fumbling with a pipe and a brown
leather tobacco pouch, 'especially in the Duffy case. We don't
get many cold-blooded murders round here.'

Campion hid his surprise well and raised a finger as if making
a debating point. 'I'm interested in your use of the term "cold-
blooded", Chief Inspector, and in the assumption that I am here
about the late David Duffy.'

'Well, you are, aren't you? The deceased had written the name
Campion in his notebook, so when a Campion comes calling
. . . well, it doesn't take a Sherlock Holmes to do the
arithmetic.'

'Could it not have referred to Christopher Campion, or any
other reasonably adjacent Campion? Christopher is my nephew,
by the way.'

'We ruled Christopher out as a person of interest early on. For
a start, he had a cast-iron alibi for the time of the murder, and
he was in Duffy's notebook several times, always referred to as
"that bloody PR man", according to the girl here who reads
shorthand. Plus, it was clear that the list had something to do
with the year 1932, and your nephew could hardly have been a
twinkle in his father's eye back then.'

'You are sure it was the year 1932 and not the number one
thousand nine hundred and thirty-two?'

'There are other indications in the notebook which convince
us it was the year he was interested in.'

'May I see the notebook?'

'I'm not sure about that, Mr Campion. It could be an important
exhibit if a case is brought.'

'For that you need a suspect. Have you made an arrest?'

'Not as yet, but I am not prepared to divulge details of our
ongoing enquiries, especially to someone who was named by the
victim.'

Mr Campion made no attempt to conceal his surprise. 'You
mean me?'

'I do need to know your relationship to David Duffy, and we

can talk about that now or as a formal statement under caution with a solicitor present. It's your choice.'

'Oh, I choose you, Chief Inspector. I have no desire to bolster the coffers of our legal eagles. I can tell you here and now that I had no dealings with the late Mr Duffy at all and, until last week, by which time he was safely dead, I had no idea he existed. If you want me to provide an alibi for the time of the murder, I am sure I can, and I will answer any question you would like to bowl at me. Just don't ask me to remember what I was doing in 1932.'

Castor finished packing his pipe and clamped it between his teeth. 'Pity, because that was exactly what I was going to do.'

'My wife insists my memory is a positive sieve when it comes to important things such as what she just said five minutes ago.'

DCI Castor nodded in sympathy, his pipe waggling frantically up and down as he muttered, 'Aye, we've all got one of them.'

'So remembering what I was doing forty years ago,' Campion continued, trying not to look at the dancing pipe, 'would be something of a challenge unless I had some sort of context. Can you give me any context?'

Castor rummaged in a jacket pocket, produced a box of Swan Vesta which he rattled violently to make sure it was loaded, then proceeded to light his pipe. The ritual – and clearly it was a ritual – took a long minute and a half by the mental ticking off of seconds in Campion's brain. He knew the policeman was buying 'thinking time', and was well aware that he was prone to doing the same, although his technique involved the elaborate polishing of the already spotless lenses of his spectacles.

'Come to think of it, you might be able to help me with a bit of context, Mr Campion,' said Castor through a cloud of blue-grey smoke, the smell of which reminded Campion slightly of newly laid asphalt.

'I am at your disposal, Chief Inspector, but pray tell how.'

'You move in rarefied circles well above my social station.'

'I am not sure that is accurate, and I'm almost sure it's not a compliment.'

Castor removed the pipe from his mouth and used the stem to point at his visitor.

Mr Campion felt it was aimed right between his eyes.

'You'll be familiar with the titled strata; you probably know hundreds of lords and ladies socially. Your wife's a lady, isn't she?'

'In all senses of the word.'

'So you'll appreciate the . . . delicacy . . . of this investigation. Sir Lachlan is an important man in this county, with important friends, and he'll be held in even higher regard if he becomes Lord McIntyre of Markley.'

'He's in line for a peerage, is he?' Campion asked innocently. 'I thought those things were all kept hush-hush and under wraps.'

'They are, but I suspect you knew about it on the toffs' grapevine—'

Campion opened his mouth to protest but thought the better of it.

'—and I know about it because part of the process is a thorough police background check.'

'And did Sir Lachlan pass the test?'

'With flying colours. I assume you know him?'

'You assume wrongly. I've never met the man.'

'But you would not object to meeting him?' Castor sucked on his glowing pipe as if he himself was being asked the question.

'Not at all.' Campion smiled genially. 'If there were no police objections to me chatting to a suspect in a murder investigation, I was going to suggest it myself.'

'As long as you keep me fully informed,' said Castor, tapping his teeth with the stem of his pipe, 'I see no harm in it, and you do have a stake in things as you were on that list in the victim's notebook, even though you say you didn't know David Duffy either.'

'You'd better tell me about Mr Duffy, Chief Inspector. Could you start with how he died? I've always found that the very best place to start.'

The body of David Duffy had been discovered slumped over the steering wheel of his ten-year-old Triumph Herald. The car had been parked in an unofficial lay-by, more the muddy verge of an approach road to a junction with the southbound M1 motorway, and DCI Castor had remarked wistfully that had the car been parked on the other side of the motorway, it would have been a case for the Buckinghamshire constabulary rather than

Bedfordshire. That the car was its own crime scene was not in doubt. There was a bullet hole in the rear window and a matching one in the windscreen; only the unfortunate Mr Duffy's head had got in the way to interrupt a perfect trajectory.

Death would have been instant, and Duffy would have had little warning of his impending doom. His assassin – and Castor had no qualms about using that word – had approached the car from behind and fired a single shot. The killing had taken place in the night though the target, Duffy, had been clearly visible, as the car's interior light was still on when the vehicle had been found early in the morning by a passing lorry driver from Bedford.

Scene of crime officers had deduced that Duffy had parked, switched off the car's engine and was writing in or reading from the reporter's notebook which had been found in the footwell by his feet. There were no fingerprints on the Austin's door handles other than Duffy's, and no obvious signs that he had attempted to exit the car. In theory, Duffy could have seen his killer approaching the back of the car in the rear-view mirror had he been looking, but with the interior light on and the night outside dark, that was unlikely. He was almost certainly concentrating on the notebook in his lap when the fatal shot was fired.

As to that shot, it had been fired from a rifle or a very powerful handgun at relatively short range at a slightly downward angle, suggesting that the killer was tall – certainly above average height. The bullet had gone through the rear window, Mr Duffy's head and then the windscreen, but had not been recovered despite a fingertip search of the surrounding rough ground and vegetation.

The on-call police surgeon had estimated the time of death as around midnight, and it was Castor's theory that the killer had approached Duffy's parked car on foot, for surely he would have heard or seen the lights of another car pulling up behind his. There were no clear footprints in the lay-by as the lorry driven by the Good Samaritan who had pulled in to discover the body had inadvertently destroyed any there might have been.

'This lay-by,' Campion had interjected. 'Where exactly is it?'

'It's not a proper one, just a rough bit of land on the verge of a village road which leads to the roundabout to get on to the M1,' Castor had answered.

'Anywhere near the Cranfield Institute?'

'Three or four miles. You know it?'

'My wife does; she's lectured there.'

'That's right, I read somewhere she was in the aeronauticals business. Peculiar job for a woman, that.'

'Oh, I don't know; they get everywhere these days. They'll be making detective chief inspector before you know it.'

Castor's expression suggested that he did not foresee the prospect in the near future. 'Maybe in the Met, but out here in the sticks, I'm not so sure. Anyway, is Cranfield important?'

'Not at all, though I understand Markley is quite close by.'

'It is, and before you ask, it's even closer to the lay-by where Duffy was shot.'

'So would that make Sir Lachlan a person of even more interest to your enquiry?'

'We're not completely stupid round here, Mr Campion, nor are we likely to be swayed by McIntyre's position and influence. He had a motive in that he and Duffy had very public altercations on more than one occasion, and he had the means in that he has a gun room in his house which is more like an arsenal, with enough rifles to equip a militia.'

'I'm sensing there is a "but" coming round the corner.'

Castor fixed Mr Campion with a steely glare which brooked no interruptions as he spoke. 'Sir Lachlan has a cast-iron alibi for the night in question. He was the guest speaker at a dinner of the Royal Town Planning Institute in London, and stayed up there overnight at the Travellers' Club rather than risk a breathalyser by driving back. It all checked out.'

'Other suspects?'

'We are following several lines of enquiry,' said Castor, clearly unwilling to offer more.

'One of those lines being the names on Duffy's list?' Campion prompted.

'We're getting there, but it's the 1932 date that's got us scratching our heads. It may mean nothing, just a random historical reference and nothing to do with what he was working on. By all accounts, he wasn't the most organized of people.'

'Journalists tend not to be. May I see his notebook?'

'No, it's being gone through by our shorthand expert now that

Forensics have finished with it, but I can tell you who was on the list.'

Castor flipped open the top cardboard file on the pile in front of him. Campion could see, upside down, a typed list of names on a carbon 'flimsy'.

'Well, there's you, as A. Campion, and now we know we've got the right Campion.'

Mr Campion held up his hands in mock surrender. 'Got me bang to rights, guv'nor, and that lets Christopher off the hook.'

'I told you, he's off the hook for Duffy, but he still might be on my list for other things because I don't think he told us everything he knows. Withholding information and hindering a police investigation is a serious offence. Now what about this "M. Lugg"?'

'I am tempted to disown him, Chief Inspector, but in all honesty I cannot. Magersfontein Lugg, Esquire, is known to me, and indeed was known to me back in 1932. He is, shall we say, a family retainer and, believe it or not, Commander Charles Luke will vouch for him as long as he's not in the same room.'

Castor remained expressionless and consulted his file again. 'Mary Gould?'

Campion shrugged his shoulders and shook his head.

'Henry Gould?'

'Means nothing, I'm afraid. Siblings? Husband and wife?'

'Walter Lillman?'

'Another blank.'

'Then there's a set of initials, "N.H." and finally "L. McIntyre".'

'I cannot think offhand of anyone with those initials and, as I have said, I have never met Lachlan McIntyre, not now nor back in 1932. What would he have been in 1932?'

'He'd have been nineteen or twenty and he was living in the East End of London.'

'There's a chance, I suppose, that my friend M. Lugg may have come across him in those days. I could ask him, unless you'd like to have him brought in and given the third degree. That might amuse you – it certainly would me – but it would not be a productive use of your time.'

'I'll take you on trust to ask him, though I probably shouldn't. But what I really want you to do for me is something else.' The policeman puffed energetically on his pipe as if he was creating, quite literally, a smokescreen rather than craving nicotine. 'I want you to pay a call on Sir Lachlan. You've got the social skills to talk your way in there and see if he'll let anything slip.'

'Let me get this straight, Chief Inspector . . .' Campion held back a cough and waved a way through the approaching cloud of pipe smoke. 'You want me to invite myself, with no official authority, into the home of your prime suspect, which you have already said has an arsenal of weaponry?'

'But you said you wanted to meet him; virtually volunteered, you did.'

Mr Campion conceded the point. 'I admit I am intrigued by this business.'

'And don't worry about McIntyre's armoury,' Castor encouraged him. 'His hunting rifles are all legally held and have been thoroughly checked by our ballistics expert. None have been fired recently and all his ammunition is accounted for.'

'Didn't you say that Duffy could have been shot with a powerful handgun?'

'McIntyre doesn't own a handgun.'

'That you know of.'

'If he had one, he'd make sure it was legal. Sir Lachlan's record is spotless, not even a speeding ticket. He's very conscious of his public image, especially with this peerage in the wind.'

'Perhaps he's got a good PR man.' Campion grinned. 'So, I've ingratiated myself with Sir Lachlan, perhaps even got myself invited for tea. Then what?'

'Find out what it was Duffy was asking him. He won't talk about it to us, just clams up or loses his temper – and he does have a bit of a short fuse, I'll tell you that for nothing. He won't say anything about why he's on Duffy's 1932 list, but you being on it as well gives you a perfect excuse to raise the subject.'

'I see the logic,' said Campion, 'and I would very much like to know why I was on that list. How do I find Markley?'

'Go past Cranfield and if you find yourself on the M1, you've gone too far. Once in Markley, you can't miss the sign saying McIntyre's Tyres; it's gigantic and almost as much an eyesore as the house he built next door, which' – he peered down at the file before him – 'is called Cruachan for no good reason.'

'Ah, but he did have a good reason for calling it that,' said Campion, who knew because Christopher had told him. 'It's the war cry of some of the Scottish Highland clans, such as the McIntyres.'

'Well, let's hope you don't get to hear it.'

FOUR
Markley Desolation

Cruachan may have been an unusual name for a house in the rolling Bedfordshire countryside, but it was not the most unusual appellation in the village; that distinction went to the village itself, which had been known for several centuries as Markley Desolation. No one was quite sure who or what the original Markley had been, but the Desolation descriptor was generally attributed to the bubonic plague of 1666 and a rich merchant fleeing the epidemic in London inadvertently bringing unwanted visitors in his bedding. All the inhabitants of Markley had become permanent residents and were presumed to have been buried in a mass grave, for the village had not been significant enough to merit a church or churchyard, and surrounding parishes were reluctant to offer any hospitality, so Markley acquired a new, and very accurate, name, for it had indeed suffered desolation. Mr Campion knew of twin villages further east, in Essex, where one had survived the earlier Black Death but the other, only a mile away, had been devastated. They were still known as Black Notley and White Notley, and he wondered idly if there had been a neighbouring village here which had survived the plague and adopted the name Markley Doing-All-Right.

As it was, the road signs, such as they were, pointed simply to Markley, but they were overshadowed and outnumbered by signs directing the motorist to the M1 motorway. As Campion drove into the village – though he thought it no more than a straggling hamlet – he found that even the motorway signs were dwarfed by a giant billboard advertising McIntyre's Tyres. It was weather-beaten and had clearly seen better days, though the fading artwork still showed the famous advertising image of dozens of black tyres of varying sizes rolling in gay abandon down the side of a Scottish glen, as if bowled by an invisible giant hand. Campion had never fully understood how customers were supposed to link repairing a punctured or worn tyre with a cavalry charge of rubber rings down a Highland slope, but the image had been used widely in newspapers and magazines and here, now, thirty feet up in the air, on signage which would be clearly visible to motorists driving on the nearby motorway, at least those heading south towards London. Perhaps those on the other, north-bound carriageway had already equipped their vehicles with McIntyre products, or there might be the mirror image of the billboard on the other side of the six-lane highway if Sir Lachlan had managed to get planning permission. Campion felt, somehow, that McIntyre Consolidated was not a business which had much time for planning niceties, based on the eyesore the billboard advertised.

It was not that the sign marked the location of a concrete and glass office block or a factory from the dark Satanic school of industrial architecture; in fact, no dominant structure was immediately obvious. Such buildings as were there were single-storey prefabricated huts scattered haphazardly across the landscape, in what Campion could only think of as a compound. The whole area, which covered two fields' worth of agricultural land, was doubly secured against attack, firstly by a high-wire fence topped with triple strands of barbed wire and then what seemed to be an even more formidable internal wall of black rubber tyres, stacked to well above head height.

Even from the driving seat of his Jaguar, Mr Campion could see what these defences were protecting: row upon row of motorized machinery, mostly painted yellow or orange, designed to rip, dig and remove earth in every conceivable way without the use of explosives. They were ranked in precise rows, as impressive as a tank regiment lined up for inspection by a passing field marshal, and the perimeter fence was dotted with signs warning anyone who could read that they should keep out and that heavy machinery was dangerous even when standing idle. All that was missing, thought Campion, was advice not to feed the animals, but there was a small guard hut by the gate which marked the

entrance, and the bored-looking watchman next to it was available to shout a warning to anyone who got too close to the
enclosure.

Although the very antithesis of an agricultural scene, McIntyre's
tyre and machinery emporium was not the only blot on the landscape. Had there been a prize for wayward architecture in
Bedfordshire it would have gone to the house in the adjacent
field, which stood in splendid isolation at the end of a long drive,
at the entrance to which was a hanging wooden sign the size and
shape of a surfboard identifying it as Cruachan, the McIntyre
home.

As he nosed the Jaguar up the gravel driveway, he took a long,
slow look at the frontage of the house and mulled over possible
captions should it ever be photographed for *Homes and Garden*
magazine. The best he could come up with was 'box-like functionality as defined by a glass-blower in an opium den', which
he felt was not exactly helpful but was certainly charitable.

Not only did the house look out of place for Bedfordshire,
it had the air of being transplanted from another country. Campion
had seen nothing like it outside of Scandinavia, with every
window stretched to an almost unnatural length, as if desperate
to claim the last rays of a midnight sun. The steel, brick and
glass frontage cried out for the nickname 'The Glass House', but
Campion promised himself never to use that as it begged many
a question about stones and the people living in such dwellings.
For those of his generation, it also had the immediate connotation
of *the* Glass House – common parlance for the military prison
in Colchester.

He knew that Sir Lachlan was younger than him, but the
generation gap between them when it came to tastes in architecture could not be measured in mere years. Still, it was McIntyre's
money and he could spend it as he wished, as he clearly had,
and to hell with what the neighbours thought.

Not that, he discovered, there were many neighbours to worry
about.

Before turning into the driveway, Mr Campion had driven
slowly the length and breadth of Markley, such as it was, regis-
tering only a handful of dilapidated cottages almost certainly

built for farm labourers a century ago. None were remotely suitable, even with considerable renovation, as the home of a self-made millionaire businessman, so it was understandable that Sir Lachlan, who already owned the land, had decided to build his glass palace from scratch. Why he had decided to make it quite so ghastly was a mystery.

The contours of the land and the huge vehicle compound would conceal the house from the prying eyes of motorists zooming by on the M1, though it would do little to combat the noise and dirt from the motorway, let alone the motorized monsters going to and from the compound. It was a curious location in which to build an expensive new house, unless, of course, one wanted to keep a close eye on one's business interests by living next door to them.

Determined not to allow petty snobbery to influence his meeting with McIntyre, Mr Campion parked the Jaguar, strode cheerfully up to the imposing front door and pressed the illuminated doorbell. His heart sank and he gently bit his lower lip as he heard, from inside, the tinny chimes of 'Flower of Scotland', and promised himself not to show surprise if a burly, kilted Highlander answered his summons.

The fact that it was a woman was no less intimidating. Campion judged her to be of exactly the same height and probably the same age as Amanda, but her plain, egg-shaped face ending in a jutting square jaw could not have been less similar to that of his wife's. It was, he hastily concluded, a face which was unlikely to flex in a high wind or crack under the pressure of a smile. She was dressed for riding, a tweed jacket over a white roll-neck shirt, jodhpurs and shiny black boots, and her long blonde hair had been scraped back and twisted into a tight ponytail which dangled over her left shoulder and breast like a tarred ship's rope.

Campion silently blessed his luck that he had a wife who preferred machines to horses, in whose company he had never been particularly comfortable, removed his fedora and, after double-checking that the woman was not holding a riding crop, introduced himself – or tried to.

'Lady McIntyre? My name is . . .'

'Campion, yes, I know. You were expected.'

She said it the way she might have said 'you've come about

the trouble' to a plumber or a man from the Gas Board, then revolved on booted heels indicating that Campion should follow her into the house, as if leading him to the offending leak.

'I hope this is a convenient time,' he said to her retreating back.

'There's no such thing where my husband is concerned,' she said without turning round, 'for Lachlan time is money, and if he's not earning money his time is being wasted, but his press agent or public relations man or whatever he calls himself was really quite forceful about it.'

'That would be Christopher,' said Campion, secretly impressed that his nephew had expressed forcefulness in standing up to his client.

Now the woman did turn her head, with a dangerous swish of her ponytail.

'Yes, another Campion. Now I know three, as I have sat on several committees with your wife. She's a very energetic woman.'

'That I cannot deny,' said Campion, his naturally lengthy stride just about keeping pace with the woman's quick march down a wide, pine-floored corridor which seemed to split the house in two.

'And a sensible one, to marry an older man, as I did, but of course the difference between Lachlan and me is less than two years.'

Mr Campion, unable to see Lady McIntyre's face, could not gauge her intentions behind such a statement, and when she stopped in front of a set of large French windows and turned to face him, her expression was unreadable.

'I will pass on your regards,' he said with restraint and a polite bow.

'Lachlan is in his study,' said the woman, nodding at the door to Campion's left then reaching for the handle to the windows. 'Please remind him he has an important business call to make in half an hour.'

'I will try not to outstay my welcome,' said Campion, but he was talking to a closing glass door as Lady McIntyre had already stepped through, wheeled right on a concrete patio and was disappearing at pace.

Mr Campion pressed his nose against the glass and took in the view from the patio, which featured a positive savannah of neatly trimmed lawn and, to the side of the property, a fenced paddock with low-rise buildings which were undoubtedly stables and the destination of the striding Mrs Lachlan. The paddock ended in a wood which curved round to the right of the Cruachan estate, while to the left a natural dip in the ground almost but not quite hid it from the depot of machinery which had paid for it.

Taking a deep breath, Mr Campion pressed his spectacles on to the bridge of his nose and knocked on the study door of Sir Lachlan McIntyre.

'We never had children. That's why she's adopted horses and we've gone through whole herds of them over the years.'

Sir Lachlan and Mr Campion were standing at the ten-foot-long rectangular window – another architectural incongruity – which offered them a panoramic view over the rear lawn and the paddock beyond. After a perfunctory greeting, McIntyre had ushered his guest to the window. For a moment Campion had thought it was to admire a central stone fountain in an unspecified Oriental style which reminded Campion of the decapitated pinnacle of a Siamese temple, its one saving grace being that it could double as a birdbath, and no doubt a very expensive one. But it was not an opportunity to admire the businessman's taste in garden ornaments; instead, the eyes of both men were drawn to the chestnut-coloured horse galloping in the distant paddock, its rider bent over the animal's neck, her long blonde ponytail flying from her head like a windsock.

'They can be very demanding, temperamental and stubborn, and require constant cleaning up after them,' said Campion. 'I understand horses can cause the odd headache as well.'

McIntyre pursed his lips as though considering whether to smile. He decided not to.

'I'll be straight with you, Campion: I agreed to see you partly because my wife has vouched for your wife, but mainly at the request of your nephew, though young Christopher was not so much requesting as grovelling, and I can't stand grovellers. Exactly how you can help me, I have no idea, but I can give you fifteen minutes. Take a seat.'

His wife had called it McIntyre's 'study', but Mr Campion felt that description far too limiting. It was difficult to imagine how much actual studying went on in there as the room did not possess the requisite necessity (in Campion's mind) of a chaise longue – he referred to his own as his 'fainting couch' – for physical relaxation, and floor-to-ceiling bookshelves for mental stimulation. Indeed, the only books in the room were road atlases and AA handbooks. There was a desk, a ghastly modern thing of tubular metal and plastic pine, on which were three telephones, a cassette tape recorder with microphone, a Xerox fax machine, an 'Out' tray full of papers and an 'In' tray of unopened envelopes, weighted down with a long, thin-bladed letter-opener with an antler handle. Campion suspected that McIntyre did his correspondence Victorian-style, standing at his very un-Victorian desk, dictating his replies into the recorder, and guessed that at some point a secretary would collect the cassette and the Out tray. He doubted that would be Lady McIntyre, as she did not look the type to count typing and filing among her interests.

Sir Lachlan's interests, on the other hand, were openly displayed on most of the available wall space. Campion did not feel the need, nor have the stomach, to count exactly how many hunting trophies, exclusively the heads of antlered deer, had been proudly mounted in a celebration of enthusiastic slaughter. The one section of wall not so decorated was equally distasteful to Mr Campion, but given the circumstances of his visit, was worthy of his attention as he realized he was not only in McIntyre's office and trophy room, but also his armoury.

Protected by locked iron grille doors, further secured with a thick metal chain and a huge padlock, was a gun rack containing a formidable collection of rifles. With a pinch of regret Campion recognized a Steyr Mannlicher, a Browning, a Mossberg and a Merkel RX Helix complete with telescopic sight. Hung beneath the rifles were three finely decorated antique shotguns, any one worth more than the collection of hunting rifles, and Campion had less reservations about recognizing the makers' names Holland & Holland, Westley Richards and Rigby.

Beyond the weaponry and the remains of hoofed ruminants, there were few clues to Sir Lachlan's personality, though when Campion followed Lachlan's invitation to take a seat, he realized that the millionaire's personal taste in furniture was somewhat questionable. The only two seats in the room were Greaves and Thomas swivel egg chairs upholstered in blue fabric, the sort of chair which would give the elderly or infirm the sensation of being on a waltzing teacup funfair ride if they did not plant their feet firmly enough.

Mr Campion did not consider himself infirm, but he was of a certain age, and it was not until he was firmly in place and his long legs braced that he addressed his host, now ensconced in the other blue egg and using his feet to sway him from side to side. If this was how Sir Lachlan conducted business meetings, Campion thought, they would not last long.

'I think it's a case of mutual assistance,' he said when he felt secure if not comfortable, 'as I seem to be involved in your current problem with the police, if only by association. I understand that I was a person of interest to the late David Duffy, just as you were.'

'That bloody scribbler! Who was it that said journalists were almost all reptiles?'

'Josef Goebbels, I think,' Campion replied, 'but I really wouldn't trust his judgement on anything. I understand that Duffy was making a nuisance of himself.'

'You can say that again. The little squirt was a pain in the fundament. Your lad Christopher dealt with him initially—'

'Christopher is my nephew. My son has a far more reputable profession as an actor, mostly unemployed.'

Sir Lachlan refused to be amused, or distracted.

'—and gave him all the background information he could possibly need if he was writing a profile of the company. Bought him lunch in London on my shilling, showed him round the depot here, even let him have a go on one of our bulldozers – that usually impresses the muckrakers. But Duffy wasn't satisfied and kept on and on about how he wanted to profile *me*, tell my story, my humble beginnings, so on, so forth. In the end I agreed to see him, if only to get him out of our hair.'

As if to emphasize the point, McIntyre ran his fingers through his hair and shook his head to indicate frustration.

'The interview did not go well?' Campion asked.

'It was a disaster. The little toad got under my skin from the off, asking very personal questions about what I was doing and who I knew forty years ago, even who I voted for. I didn't start my businesses until after the war, so I couldn't see what that had to do with the price of fish. Even wanted to know where I met my wife, the damn cheek of the man!'

'Did he mention a list?'

'Oh, his flamin' list! The police just won't let that one drop. No, he didn't have a list, or not one he showed me, but he did ask if I recognized certain names.'

'Mine included?'

'As a matter of fact, yes. I recall that because of Christopher, but it couldn't have been him because he wasn't born back in 1932, so I asked him and he said definitely Albert Campion, and I could say, with complete honesty, that I'd never met you back then or since.'

'Did he fling any other names at you?'

Sir Lachlan frowned. 'Two or three. There was Mary and a Henry Gould, which sounded like a married couple, and a chap called Walter Lillman, though none of them meant anything to me, either now or back then.'

'Why was he so interested in 1932?'

'I have no idea. I did ask him and he just looked furtive and gave me a snarky little smile which I felt like slapping off his face. To be honest, I lost my temper with him and stormed out. The whole thing was a complete waste of my time. I don't know what dirt he was trying to dig up, but he was certainly digging.'

'And you cannot think of any dirt he could have found from back then?'

'No, because there wasn't anything to find!' McIntyre's face had reddened in a flash and his egg chair was shaking as it swivelled. Campion sensed a volcanic eruption was imminent. 'I'd come down from Scotland, a young lad without a penny to my name and there was a depression on. I had to work bloody hard to survive in London, but scum like Duffy can make anything sound bad if they've a mind to. I'll wager there'll be things in your past which could be twisted to damage your reputation.'

'Almost certainly,' Campion replied smoothly, 'but I am a person of no significance and even less consequence in the great scheme of things. You are a captain of industry destined for great honour and riches – or that would be how a potential dirt-digger might see it.'

Sir Lachlan glared at his visitor, but the colour was already draining from his face; the volcano remained dormant.

'Are you suggesting Duffy was looking for blackmail material?'

'It's a possibility. Did he talk to any of your employees or ex-employees? They are usually a good source of gossip about their employers.'

'We have a relatively small workforce for both businesses.'

'Both?'

'The two companies based here at Consolidated. The tyre business, which was my first venture, and then the machinery hire business which trades as McIntyre Mechanicals, but they really only need a small staff for maintenance and servicing, as long as they all have HGV licences so we can transport machines to wherever they're needed.'

'The motorway must be very useful for that, hence your location.'

'Absolutely, and you'll see more of them in the future, criss-crossing the country, now the railways are in decline. I like to think I started a ground-breaking business, in every sense of the word. We may not build the new roads but our machines do.'

'Quite,' said Mr Campion, concealing his misgivings about Sir Lachlan's view of the future transport network. 'I can remember the excitement when the M1 opened in 1959. In those days the press said that motorways were about as English as bull-fighting rings or ski-jumps in our green and pleasant land, but everyone wanted to have a go on the first one as there was no speed limit and you could treat it like a racetrack. I got into terrible bother with my wife because an old school chum and I clocked one hundred miles per hour coming from the Rugby end in a Triumph TR7. She was appalled I was doing such things "at my age", whatever that means.'

'Petrol was only four and threepence a gallon back then,' reminisced McIntyre, 'and the motorway was a source of national pride. Did you know that McIntyre Tyres sponsored a *Guide to Using a Motorway*? We gave it away in petrol stations; it was very popular.'

'And probably a collectors' item by now,' said Campion, 'though certainly a good piece of public relations at the time.'

'It was good for business, that's for sure. You could say I owe my success to the M1, which is why I settled here with my workers.'

'Your staff live here?'

'Not here in Cruachan.' McIntyre spoke as if explaining crossing the road to a particularly stubborn child. 'In Markley. When we acquired the land here, it came with four farm labourers' cottages. The farmworkers were long gone before the motorway came, and the cottages were in a pretty rundown state, so we did 'em up. Lucy and I even lived in one whilst this place was being built, but now we use one as a sort of rest house for our drivers, and the others are for the depot manager, our senior mechanics, our nightwatchmen, and there's young Carl Spivey who looks after the wife's horses.'

'I have to admit I didn't realize there were any other inhabitants of Markley. I thought it was . . . well, desolate.'

'Oh, so you know the old name, do you? Then you shouldn't be surprised nobody wants to live here.'

And that, thought Campion, has nothing to do with having a motorway in your backyard and the constant rumble of bulldozers and mechanical diggers passing your front door.

'Would it be possible to talk to your chaps, the ones who live on site, that is?' he asked.

'I'll pass the word down the line that it's all right to talk to you and you are welcome to go and knock a few heads, but I doubt it'll be much use. The police had words with them all and none of them ever spoke with Duffy, though they may have seen him being shown round by Christopher wearing his press relations hat.'

Remembering what Christopher had told him about McIntyre's labour relations, Campion asked if they had been with him long.

'Two or three have been with me for nigh on ten years; others come and go. If they're not happy with me or the job, they move on and seek greener pastures elsewhere, like I did. I know what you're thinking, though, and no, I knew none of my current workforce back in 1932. I'd only just hitchhiked down from Glasgow' – Campion noted that his host was sticking to

Christopher's script – 'and didn't know a soul in London. Couldn't make myself understood for the first year because of my Scottish accent.'

'Something you have successfully disposed of in the intervening years.'

'Had to; only way to get on in life down south. Couldn't stand being called "Jock" by all and sundry, so decided to do something about it, even though I couldn't change my name.'

'Yes, Lachlan is a bit of a giveaway, but you did keep some connections to the old country.' McIntyre frowned in puzzlement, so Campion airily waved a hand towards the wall of stags' heads. 'Your trophies – stalking is a popular Highland pastime, so I understand – and the name of this very house has a certain Scottish resonance, I believe.'

'You can stalk deer in southern England well enough, but it's not the same as crawling through the heather in the Highlands, and I'm proud of my Scottish heritage.'

Campion smiled. 'What's the old saying? Scots by blood, Scotch only by absorption.'

'Ah, well, there I differ from the majority of my countrymen as I do not drink. Nor do I smoke, and I have never craved boiled sweets.'

'But you do go back to the old country?'

'On business, of course, and for the occasional stag. We throw a pair of guns and the tent in the back of the Land Rover and head north. The weather's always foul, but we love it.'

'Your wife accompanies you?'

'She's always loved the outdoors and a night under canvas, plus she's a damn fine shot.' He pointed at the trophy wall. 'Half of those are hers, plus at least a score of foxes over the years, and they've all been clean kills. She never left a wounded animal to suffer.'

Mr Campion averted his gaze, not wishing to meet the lifeless eyes of the McIntyres' victims, and settled on the equally disturbing gun cabinet. 'You seem to be armed well enough.'

'Those are our favourites,' said McIntyre casually, 'and those rifles have served us well. The shotguns are more for decoration than anything.'

'They look antique, and valuable,' said Campion.

'They are if my insurance premiums are to be believed. I take them out and clean them every so often, but they're never fired.'

'I understand the police checked your guns after Duffy was . . . found.' Campion put it as delicately as he could.

'They had a specialist come and check the rifles as a matter of procedure, or so they said. I told them they hadn't been used for a couple of months and their chappie bore me out. In any case, the police seem to think Duffy was shot with a large-calibre pistol, and I do not own a pistol; never have.'

Campion stretched his long legs and made to stand up, negotiating his exit from the swivel chair with care. 'You've been most open as well as hospitable, Sir Lachlan,' he said as McIntyre rose as well, 'to put up with my interrogation.'

'Was that an interrogation? I hardly felt a thing.'

As McIntyre stood before him, Campion recalled what the detective in Bedford had told him: that the shot which killed Duffy had done so at a downward angle, suggesting a tall assailant, although McIntyre was no more than average height and shorter than Campion himself.

'Well, that's good,' he said as they shook hands. 'I prefer to leave no impression rather than a bad one. I will continue to nose around and try to find out why the late Mr Duffy was interested in the both of us. If I discover anything, I will of course let you know. I will also stay in touch with Christopher.'

'You do that. He's still on my payroll and ought to earn his corn. Let me show you out.'

Campion made a mental note to tell his nephew that for the time being his supply of birdseed was secure, but as he turned towards the door, he caught sight of a magazine balanced on top of the papers in McIntyre's 'Out' tray. It was some sort of American sporting magazine, open at a full-page advertisement for Remington firearms and ammunition. The advert's tagline in bold type read: *Why would anyone want a bullet that travels at 4,020 feet per second?*

Why indeed? he thought.

FIVE

Pressing Matters

'**M**cIntyre's house is perfectly ghastly, isn't it? Almost as ghastly as his wife.'

Mr Campion was surprised by his wife's opening salvo and relieved that it had been delivered down the telephone.

'I agree with you on the first,' he said carefully, 'but as to your second rather sweeping statement, I am in no position to pass an opinion. I had only the briefest of meetings with Lady McIntyre. She opened the door, showed me in, then mounted her favourite stallion and galloped off into the sunset.'

'Well, darling, you do have that effect on women, but I would count that as a lucky escape. I take it you made it to Bottle Street in one piece.'

Campion automatically glanced around the flat which had once been his 'bachelor pad' in the current terminology, but which now served as a useful base for London excursions, being scrupulously maintained, in his spare moments (when he had them, as he was not slow to point out), by his faithful retainer Magersfontein Lugg.

'Just got here safe and sound and Lugg has done his usual five-star servicing. The brasses have been polished, the stained-glass windows cleaned, there's a new rota for flowers and the level in the font has been refreshed.'

'I take it by that you mean that the drinks cabinet has been fully stocked, or should that be quickly re-stocked?'

'You, my dear,' said Campion with a grin, 'have a suspicious mind. You should know by now that I lack for nothing when Lugg is quartermastering for me. I'm betting the kitchen cupboards are groaning with victuals.'

'Tins of Spam and jars of pickled eggs, knowing Lugg,' said Amanda down the line.

'You do the old boy a disservice. He has some sort of arrange-
ment with the caterers at Brewers' Hall and, after one of their
feasts, he often turns up with sides of smoked salmon, barons of
lamb and haunches of venison which he claims were surplus to
requirements.'

'I'm surprised your visit *chez* McIntyre hasn't put you off
venison for life.'

'It almost did. They do seem to revel in all that stalking-through-
the-damp-heather stuff. Lachlan told me his wife likes nothing
better than a night under canvas on a Scottish mountainside.'

Amanda let rip a throaty laugh. 'You know what I'd say, Albert,
if you ever suggested we did that. I would point out that in my
dictionary, camping is spelled d-i-v-o-r-c-e!'

'Your fears on that score are groundless, though they did strike
me as an odd couple who had little in common, except perhaps
stag hunting. But I'm being unfair because I had only the briefest
contact with them.'

'A couple with very odd tastes in architecture – that house
really is an abomination, yet they are gruesomely proud of the
fact that they designed it themselves. They have a lust for
the modern, or rather the worst of the modern. Did they put you
in one of those horrid egg chairs?'

'My spine is still feeling the experience.'

'Here's a tip, especially if you're wearing a short skirt: perch
on the very edge, plant your feet flat on the floor and lean forward
as if you're taking communion.'

'Your advice, as always, darling, is most welcome, even if it
comes too late for three of my vertebrae.'

'Oh, don't be such a softy. Did you turn up anything to help
Christopher?'

'No, not really. I will have to find out more about the late Mr
Duffy and I have made a few enquiries on that score already. It
will mean staying in London for a day or so, I'm afraid, but I
have Lugg to look after me.'

'Perhaps he can remember a connection to Lachlan McIntyre
back in – when was it – 1932?'

'I doubt that very much. The old boy's getting on, you know.
Seems to have terrible trouble remembering when it's his round
down the Platelayers' Arms.'

'We are all getting old, Albert. Just remember there's been a murder, so you be careful and always remember to hide behind Lugg when the shooting starts.'

'Wise advice, darling, but hark! I think I hear his elfin tread on the stairs as we speak.'

Although now beyond the accepted age of retirement, Magersfontein Lugg proudly boasted to anyone who would listen, apart from officials of Her Majesty's Inspectorate of Taxes, that he held not one, but two full-time jobs at a time when he really should be putting his feet up. Those who knew him would be sceptical that his role as beadle at the Brewers' Hall, home of one of London's ancient guilds, could in any sense be classed as hard labour for a man like Lugg, who was surely born to the task, even if the ceremonial robes had needed letting out. His second job, he would insist, was equally important and even more demanding, if lacking in pomp and ceremony, and that was to continue to 'look after' Mr Albert Campion. Consequently it was not unusual to find him wielding a tipstaff and demanding that visitors to the Brewers' Hall, from the lord mayor downwards, had better be upstanding for the loyal toast if they knew what was good for them of a morning and then, in the afternoon, with a tightly stretched butcher's apron protecting his pinstriped trousers, guiding a vacuum cleaner around the flat at 17A Bottle Street, Piccadilly.

He received no specific instructions as to his housekeeping duties, partly because no one would dare issue them and partly due to his unwavering certainty that he knew everything there was to know about looking after a young man about town, even if the man in question was no longer young and, these days, only occasionally in town. When the flat was unoccupied, Lugg would pay regular visits, for even though it was situated above a police station, there were treasures within upon which a careful eye needed to be kept. The Rembrandt etching and some haunting wartime sketches by Paul Nash, along with certain nineteenth-century first editions were clearly valuable items, but there was also a long, fifteenth-century Italian dagger mounted on the wall which had great sentimental value for Mr Campion, ever since he had liberated it from the house called Black Dudley in Suffolk.

It was a source of pride, though never overtly admitted, that Mr Campion's bolthole (or 'London residence', depending on who he answered the telephone to) could be ready for occupation at a moment's notice: crockery clean, glassware sparkling, sheets aired and the levels on bottles of gin and whisky suspiciously similar to the owner's last visit; allowing, of course, for natural evaporation.

The innocent bystander would have found it impossible to reconcile an image of a house-proud Lugg not averse to donning bright yellow washing-up gloves with the reality of meeting him on the street or, heaven forfend, in a dark alley, as he was a physical presence which inspired awe if not trepidation.

Once described as 'wide for his height', Lugg's gargantuan appetite had resulted in an impressive girth and he was, he admitted, several stones and three collar sizes above his 'fighting weight'. With head down and a firm step, he could force his way to the bar of the busiest pub on cup final day with the ease of a hot knife going through butter. In anger and at full speed, he was a juggernaut which few locked doors could resist, and hands the size of generous hams, plus a bald planetary orb of a head, added to his fearsome appearance. He had once sported a thick white walrus moustache which someone had said made him look like a film star. When it emerged that the cinematic icon in question was Colonel Blimp, all facial hair was henceforth immediately removed.

For a man who was a snug fit, even without the aid of luggage or a winter coat, for the narrow staircase leading up to the door of the Bottle Street flat, only the creak of a rogue floorboard gave away his presence before he inserted his key in the lock. It was enough for Campion to end his call to his wife, swipe a book from a shelf and dive into an armchair, stretching out his long legs and crossing them at the ankles, to give the appearance that he had been in that relaxed state for some time.

'Thank goodness you've finally turned up,' he said without turning, his face buried in the book he had grabbed, which he had discovered was A.J.P. Taylor's *Origins of the Second World War*. 'I was going to make a cup of tea but found I had quite forgotten the recipe.'

'It's a sign of age,' snarled Lugg. 'Don't strain yerself; I know where the kettle is.'

'What is a sign of age?' asked Campion, tongue firmly in cheek. 'I am happy to acknowledge your seniority in such matters.'

'Forgetting fings,' Lugg pointed a sausage-like finger at the book Campion was pretending to study, 'like 'oo started the war. Refreshin' yer memory, are yer?'

'This?' Campion feigned surprise. 'This is purely an academic exercise to keep the brain cells ticking over and running smoothly. You should try it sometime – reading a book, that is.'

Lugg's growl turned to a grunt. 'Pah! It wasn't me wot got the h'amnesia back when the war kicked off. Thought you might be looking for clues as to what you got up to back then.'

Mr Campion silently acknowledged that Lugg had a point. At the start of the Second World War, Campion had stumbled into a conspiracy which threatened Britain's economy and very survival. 'Stumbled' was entirely accurate for having taken a solid blow to the head in a vicious brawl; Campion had suffered severe amnesia alleviated only by the tender ministrations of the young and resourceful Amanda. The few who knew the details of the adventure referred to it as the case where Mr Campion had lost his memory but found a wife.

'Actually, you may have a point.' Campion's admission to Lugg's back as he waddled into the kitchen made the fat man pause and cock his head to one side. 'Given that my memory is somewhat sieve-like, you may be able to help. They say elephants can remember.'

'An' they don't forget an insult either. What 'ave you lost?'

'Nothing except perhaps a few marbles.' Campion tapped his forehead with a fingertip. 'Let me see how many you still hold. What were we doing forty years ago in 1932?'

'Blimey! That's going back a bit. What's it for? They've not got you pegged for *This Is Your Life*, 'ave they? That'd be a larf, mind you.'

'Nothing so vulgar,' scoffed Campion. 'I always thought that a most presumptuous programme. If someone jumped out at me with the words, "This is your life", I would have to tell them,

"It can't be, I haven't quite finished with it yet". No, this is a riddle I've been posed and it's niggling me.'

'An' now it's got to niggle me, has it?' said Lugg in a hurt voice from the kitchen. 'Can't you consult your Girl Guides' diary for 1932?'

'You know I don't keep a diary; it would be far too incriminating – for both of us – so put your thinking cap on. Let the years roll back to when we were young, or at least younger; when I was a carefree bachelor-about-town and you had the agility of a cat.'

Lugg let out a snort and rattled crockery and cutlery far more than was necessary at Campion's sideways reference, not without justification, to his youthful career as a cat burglar.

'Don't know about the toff-about-town label; I never had you pegged as a *boulevardier.*'

'Pity, I would have liked to have had that on my passport under "Occupation", but you're right. My hanging around stage doors or waltzing down the Strand days were behind me by then and I hadn't knocked a bobby's helmet off since I was at Cambridge.'

'You 'ad too many chums on the force by 1932,' said Lugg, returning with a tray containing a teapot, cups and a Battenberg cake cut into slices well over an inch thick, 'so you 'ad to behave yerself. Not too sure you was the footloose and fancy-free bachelor then either. Wasn't that when you ran into the Lady A. out at Pontisbright?'

'That I do remember, of course, though it wasn't '32 and she was a mere girl back then. It was several years before we were married.'

'That's as may be, but she 'ad her eye on you from the off.'

'Well, I always knew she had impeccable taste.'

'And you can count yerself lucky she had a lot of patience too.'

'Oh, I do. We made quite a few trips to Suffolk in those days, I seem to recall.'

Lugg held his cup and saucer with a ridiculous daintiness and slurped tea loudly enough to immediately dispel the image. 'There was that business up at Sanctuary with the gypsies and that 'aunted tower and that crazed horsey woman,' he suggested.

'No, that wasn't in '32 either but, oddly enough, I met another horsey woman this morning, who might well be crazy if she put the effort in.'

'This business, whatever it is that's worrying you – and it must be worrying you because you've asked for my opinion – has it something to do with Suffolk?'

'Not that I know of, but then I don't really know what it does have to do with, other than that a dead journalist by the name of David Duffy was interested in me – and you – and it was to do with something that happened in 1932.'

'A dead newshound? Probably sniffing too close for his own good,' said Lugg, showing little concern and spilling not a single drop of the milk of human kindness. 'What's it got to do with us?'

'I have no idea, but I've thought of a way to find out.'

'Do tell. I can see you're dying to.'

'I'm going to have lunch with another journalist tomorrow; see if they know what the late Mr Duffy was up to.'

Lugg looked at Campion over the rim of his teacup. 'You think one muckraker will dish the dirt on another?'

'Certainly,' said Campion with confidence, 'if they think there's a story in it.'

The word *odalisque* came to mind as Campion turned the book of matches over between his fingers, but decided that the half-naked lady portrayed on the cover was probably not a concubine or an eroticized servant girl. It was simply an attractive lady with a flamboyant hairdo who had dressed carelessly in a toga-like garment which displayed her right breast to full effect. The rear cover of the matchbook declared that the matches, if not the lady illustrated, came with the compliments of the Presscala luncheon club of Hood Court, Fleet Street.

Lugg had not concealed his envy when Campion had revealed that his meeting with one of Fleet Street's finest was to take place in the Presscala. It was an establishment Lugg had great respect for, being firmly in the belief that any licensed establishment which opened one minute after the pubs closed at lunchtime and closed one minute before the capital's pubs re-opened for the evening session was a boon to mankind. Plus, he admitted, he had a soft spot for the crispy-skinned lamb chops served cold there, to be eaten like lollipops after dipping in a vinegary mint sauce.

Adopting his favourite tactic of arriving ten minutes early when meeting a stranger, Mr Campion had claimed a table and a glass of wine and was idly fumbling his complimentary book of matches when his host arrived, although he was in doubt who would be picking up the bill.

Ron Lay-Flurrie, one of the more notorious denizens of Fleet Street, a thoroughfare where notoriety was easily earned, had insisted on meeting at the Presscala, as it was near to his newspaper's office and would be relatively quiet at three thirty in the afternoon. If an emergency required him to return to his desk, it would also not be the first place to which his employers would send a search party: that would be El Vino's.

From what Campion had heard, Lay-Flurrie's absence from the newsroom he ruled with a rod of iron would not be overly missed, as the reporters and photographers working under him were likely to be glad of an hour's respite from his strict surveillance. It had been many years since Lay-Flurrie had been a roving reporter, aggressively door-stepping shady politicians, ghost-writing sensational confessions from vacuous celebrity sportsmen or hanging around the bars and clubs of Soho to pick up titbits of gossip from, or about, the Vice Squad. His dogged determination – many called it mulish stubbornness – to follow up every lead, hint or snippet of gossip, with absolutely no concern for the sensibilities or vulnerability of those involved, had earned him a reputation for abrasiveness and having a skin twice as thick as the average rhino. Lacking most social skills, and with no concept whatsoever of man-management, he was a natural for promotion to the position of news editor on a popular national newspaper.

So much Campion had gleaned from his network of friends, some of whom had felt themselves badly done by in respect of Lay-Flurrie's paper, but the physical presence behind the ferocious legend came as something of a surprise. He had expected a bull-like figure, possibly balding and certainly red-faced, with a beer gut straining both belt and braces, a dirty raincoat flapping behind him like a cape, and a battered trilby perched on the back of his head, with a card saying PRESS tucked into the hatband.

The reality was far less clichéd. Lay-Flurrie was a small man, not much over five feet tall, with a head of white hair slicked with Brylcreem and a neatly trimmed white moustache. He wore a tweed jacket with a quiver of ballpoint pens in the breast pocket, a light blue shirt and a lime green bowtie. When he spoke there were undertones of a northern accent, possibly one which refused to be exorcized no matter how long he had lived 'down south', and when he offered a hand to shake, Campion noticed the index and middle fingers were deeply stained yellow with nicotine. Within seconds of the introductions being complete, and before he sat down, the journalist had produced a packet of Capstan Full Strength and was offering one to Campion.

'No, thank you,' said Campion, offering him the book of matches he had been toying with, 'I gave up when I discovered what was good for me.'

'Health warning, was it?' scoffed the journalist, lighting his cigarette and pocketing the matches.

'Of a sort. The threat of imminent death at the hands of my wife was a very persuasive factor.'

Lay-Flurrie settled himself across the table Campion had chosen, in a corner well away from the handful of other late lunch-takers, and said with genuine concern, 'I never thought a man with your reputation would be browbeaten by the little woman.'

'I am surprised to hear I have a reputation of any sort in Fleet Street, for I have never sought one and feel rather guilty if I am taking the place of any of the thousands who actively strive for one. As for my wife, you clearly don't know her, and she has had full browbeating privileges for more than thirty years now with my blessing.'

The journalist blew a mushroom cloud of smoke and gave a resigned shrug, clearly thinking that his dining companion was a pricklier character than he had expected. For his part, Campion was of the same opinion, but he had not been surprised.

'But thank you for agreeing to meet with me.'

'You came highly recommended,' said Lay-Flurrie, barely concealing a sneer. 'When the word came down from our blessed proprietor in his ivory tower that I should, I didn't think I had much choice.'

'I am sorry if you feel there has been some string-pulling.'

'No need to apologize to me. If you've got strings, pull 'em, that's what I say. Just remember that if we do you a favour, you owe us one. The story belongs to us.'

'Understood,' said Mr Campion, 'though I am far from sure what the story is, apart from the fact that I seem to have been caught up in it somehow.'

Perhaps it was the word 'story' that had acted as a trigger, but Lay-Flurrie's demeanour changed. He leaned forward over the table and lowered his voice conspiratorially. 'How much did Duffy tell you?'

'Not a thing; I never talked to or met him. Until I was told of his death, the name David Duffy meant nothing to me. I cannot even recall reading anything written by him.'

'That doesn't surprise me. His best scoops went out under a fake by-line, what you might call a pseudonym or pen name.'

'May I ask what that was?'

'Trotsky. He always signed his exclusives Trotsky.'

'I'm surprised,' said Campion genuinely, 'I didn't notice that in your newspaper, given its political leanings.'

'Oh, Duffy didn't just write for us.' Lay-Flurrie raised his head, suddenly alert. 'Shall we order some wine?'

'Certainly,' Campion agreed, 'and we should ask for a menu.'

The Fleet Street veteran shook his head. 'Don't bother. I can't trust a man who eats with his lunch.'

The late David Duffy did not work for the national newspaper that Lay-Flurrie represented – at least, he was not on any official payroll. He had been a useful freelance, employed from time-to-time to cover specific stories or certain shifts when regular reporters were ill or on holiday. He was therefore ranked as a 'casual' or, by the proprietor, as a 'pay-bob' – an expression Campion recognized from his wartime years, meaning a junior supply officer on temporary assignment, a position from which little was expected or was usually achieved.

As news editor, Lay-Flurrie had often commissioned Duffy to work on certain projects, but he had chosen the assignments carefully, as Duffy had come with a reputation for abrasiveness when dealing with anyone daring to disagree with his firmly held socialist convictions. Campion had expressed surprise that such a reporter would have been employed even on a casual freelance basis by Lay-Flurrie's newspaper, given its own political persuasion as it reflected the views of its proprietor. The journalist gave a sly chuckle and told him that Duffy was used sparingly. He would never, for example, be despatched to interview a titled toff such as Campion.

'I do not hold a title,' Campion had objected, 'unlike your proprietor.'

'But you could have had one,' Lay-Flurrie had countered smugly, to prove he had done his research as a good newspaperman should.

Duffy's political beliefs had not impinged on his work on the national papers, because when writing for them he had been nothing but scrupulous in assembling the facts of a story. His copy, Lay-Flurrie asserted, was always clean, readable and, above all, accurate; the paper's highly paid lawyers made sure of that, hovering hawk-like over every comma.

Lay-Flurrie lit yet another cigarette and answered Campion's unasked question, explaining that Duffy's alter ego 'Trotsky' did not appear in the hallowed columns of his esteemed organ of news, but rather in a series of 'alternative' publications, such as the satirical magazine *Private Eye* and other 'left-leaning scandal sheets', which even regarded *Private Eye* as part of the establishment. It was there that Campion would find Duffy writing as 'Trotsky', and he almost certainly would not approve of what he found.

Mr Campion disagreed with the journalist's assumption and rather surprised him when he claimed to be a regular reader of *Private Eye* and regarded its satirical stance, admittedly sometimes tasteless, as an attempt to purify the establishment rather than destroy it. His main concern, however, was why Duffy was investigating the self-made millionaire Sir Lachlan McIntyre, an investigation which had caught Campion in its crossfire.

Lay-Flurrie clearly had no idea, claiming that Duffy had not been following any story on his instructions which could conceivably involve McIntyre, and certainly had not tried to claim any expenses – something Duffy had always been prompt to do – in such a context. In fact, and the news editor had checked before leaving the office, Duffy had spent a lot of his time 'off the clock' as it were, in the newspaper's archive, or 'morgue' as it was known internally. Ironic, then, that Duffy had ended up in a real live morgue.

'What was he researching?' Campion had asked.

'Historic stuff, most likely background for a feature he was planning, though he hadn't pitched any specific idea to me. Maybe it was for a bit of muckraking under his Trotsky by-line.'

'So you thought he was a muckraker?'

'Aren't we all, you included, in your own way? The difference between us is that I turn over stones expecting to find creepy-crawlies, while you go looking for the good in people and, from what I've discovered about you, there have been times when you've conveniently rearranged the stones you've shifted.'

Mr Campion studied the journalist carefully but could not decide if Lay-Flurrie was by nature antagonistic or whether he was following an agenda Campion was unaware of.

'I am interested in discovering what story Duffy was pursuing, as I seem to have played a part in it,' he said at last.

'I thought you said you'd never met Duffy,' Lay-Flurrie snapped accusingly.

'I never met or talked to him, but I am told that my name is on a list he made in his notebook.'

'Have you seen it?'

'I have had it read to me.'

'Not the list, the notebook.'

'Not physically, no. It is currently being examined by the Bedfordshire police.'

'Busybodies! They won't know what they're looking at. If I got hold of it, it might give us an idea of the story he was working on.'

'A story which could be the reason he was killed,' Campion pointed out.

'Which means it could be a *good* story, getting Duffy on to the front page for once.'

'Perhaps not in the way he would have wanted, but I am sure there is a story in there somewhere. Would it help if I asked the police to let you see the notebook?'

'You think they'd go for that?'

'Technically it might be evidence, and Detective Chief Inspector Castor, who is handling the case, could probably use an expert journalistic eye. They'll insist on hanging on to it, but I'm sure I can persuade him to let you have a look if you can pop out to Bedford.'

For the first time, Lay-Flurrie's expression softened as he reached for another cigarette, making Campion appreciate the abundant supply of promotional matchbooks scattered around the Presscala.

'The quid-pro-quo,' said Lay-Flurrie through another cloud of smoke, 'being that I tell you exactly what Duffy noted about you.'

'If you wouldn't mind. The only context I have, so I've been told, is that my name crops up in association with the year 1932.'

Lay-Flurrie flicked his cigarette in the vague direction of a brimming ashtray. 'That would make sense. On his visits to the morgue – our morgue, that is – he was rooting through back copies of the paper from the Thirties, looking for stuff on British fascists – you know, Mosley's Blackshirt mob. You weren't—'

'Good grief, no! I most certainly was not whatever it was you were thinking. Are you sure?'

'The archivist was positive. Duffy even asked him to recommend an expert he could consult, some history professor from the university.'

'This couldn't have been simply intellectual curiosity on Duffy's part?'

'He was a reporter looking for facts to hold up a story; he wasn't taking an Open University course.' Lay-Flurrie scoffed at the idea in a tone which suggested that Fleet Street reporters, even freelancers, were not in need of further education. 'He was definitely on to something, according to the archivist, because he had another strange request for material from the morgue.'

'Not about me?'

'Don't flatter yourself, though there is a thin file of cuttings on you down there. Duffy wanted any police reports from the period which mentioned the London Silver Vaults.'

For the first time since he had entered the club and sat down, Lay-Flurrie ignored the cigarette between his fingers.

'What's up? You look like you've seen a ghost.'

Mr Campion removed his tortoiseshell spectacles and produced a white handkerchief to polish the perfectly clean lenses. 'The ghost of a memory perhaps,' he said quietly.

SIX

The Legacy of the Galloping Major

Mr Campion's Memory 1: London and Northamptonshire, 1932

I would occasionally indulge myself with a breakfast fantasy where a frock-coated butler would cough discreetly to divert my attention from a freshly ironed copy of *The Times* and offer a silver salver containing the morning's post for his master's perusal. I did not, however, enjoy the services of a professional butler, rather a far-from-deferential employee who preferred the title 'Gent's gent' and who was unlikely to have left any silver salver un-pawned.

'Second post's come, an' you still in yer silk jim-jams,' snapped Magersfontein Lugg, skimming a single envelope towards me like a conjuror flicking playing cards into a top hat. It landed slightly north of my plate, having narrowly avoided splashing down in my teacup.

I could hardly ignore such an unprovoked aerial attack and so picked up the square, off-white missile and examined it at arm's length.

'A missive from a lady, judging by the handwriting,' I observed.

'An elderly one is my guess, out of town and frugal too,' sniffed Lugg.

'Explain your deductions, young Sherlock,' I challenged him.

'The younger females in your social circle use the telephone these days and I just 'ope for your sake that the operator's not listenin' in. Ladies of a certain standing send a footman round, just occasionally a Beefeater or a Grenadier Guard. Only an elderly lady living in the country would post you a letter and

use a three-halfpenny stamp commemorating the British Empire
Exhibition. I bet she's had it in her purse for twenty years. Like
I say, frugal; on her uppers even.'

'Your observational skills are spoiled only by your poor grasp
of mathematics, old fruit.' I paused dramatically in order to slice
open the envelope with a clean butter knife. 'The Empire
Exhibition was 1924, no more than eight years ago, but you
wouldn't remember, would you? You missed it because you were
away at college. Parkhurst Polytechnic, wasn't it?'

'I may 'ave been on me summer 'olidays,' he admitted
grudgingly.

'Anyway, is that an unreasonable amount of time to hoard a
stamp? Perhaps *Cassandra, Lady Drinkwater* does not corres-
pond with too many people.'

'Who's she when she's at home?'

'I have no idea.'

'You mean you've forgotten.'

'No, genuinely no idea. She says so in her first paragraph,
listen: *My dear Mr Campion, you don't know me . . .* You see,
my feather-filled memory is innocent for once.'

'And what's the "but"? There's always a "but".'

'Dead right. *My dear Mr Campion, you don't know me but I
am the cousin of the late Percival Barrick. I do not believe you
knew him either . . .*'

'Strewth!' muttered the big lump. ''Ere comes anuvver.'

'*. . . but he served for a time as chaplain to your uncle the
Bishop of Devizes, who spoke of you most highly, even if other
members of your family did not.*'

'Well, she hit that nail smartly on the head.'

'Quite.' I ignored his blatant familiarity and continued to
read. '*It is about a family matter which I wish to consult you
and I would be extremely grateful if you would call upon me
for a confidential discussion, within the month. I am loath to
put too much in writing and am no longer connected to the
telephone exchange; therefore I must prevail on you to visit me
here. I realize this is an imposition but it is a matter of great
importance and some urgency.* Those last bits are underlined,
and you know I cannot resist an underlining. We must ride to
her rescue.'

'I'll saddle the white horses, shall I?' said Lugg wearily. 'Any clue as to where we're going?'

'You didn't note the postmark? A bit slipshod for a Sherlock. Lady Drinkwater resides at *Butcombe Manor, Husbands Butcombe, Northants*, according to her rather unusual headed stationery, which has a Butcombe telephone number crossed out. Look.'

Lugg took the single sheet of paper between finger and thumb with extreme delicacy considering the size of his ham-hock hands and sausage-like digits. He perused it briefly then held it to his nose. 'She don't get out much, this Lady Drinkalot,' he sniffed.

'Drinkwater. What were your nostrils expecting: a whiff of opium or incense?'

'Wiv yer elderly ladies – an' I'm guessing Mrs Drinkalot is of a certain age – there's always a whiff of lavender or lilacs, occasionally camphor, but this just smells of must. Her note-paper's even older than her stamps.'

'Well observed, Moriarty, but does nothing else strike you, preferably using your eyes rather than your nostrils?'

'Well, 'er 'andwriting is a bit florid. Neat enough, though, like she was taught well, h'educated.'

'Not the handwriting, the printing. Look at the heading – the address. Have you ever seen a typeface like that? I certainly haven't. It must be personalized, specially commissioned.'

'What's the point of that then? So, at some time, this Lady Drinkwater had a few bob to spend and got herself some person-alized stationery knocked up. Then she fell on hard times, ran out of people to write to and stuffed a box of it in a damp cupboard until she felt the need to scribble a few lines to you. Mind you, if I lived at a Butcombe Manor, I'd have some fancy notepaper done up. You've got to have a decent address to get on in life, and if you've got a manor, you should flaunt it.'

'Sound advice from someone whose professional address is care of the Platelayers' Arms.'

I removed my glasses and began to polish the lenses with a blindingly white napkin, making a pretence of being deep in thought, knowing that this always irritated dear old Lugg.

'It's comin' to yer, ain't it? You've just remembered her. Did you do her wrong in a previous life?'

'I am almost positive I did not,' I insisted, 'but I do hear a faint bell tolling somewhere in the dusty attic of my memory. Got it! The Drinkwaters of Husbands Butcombe made the popular press once, just after the war I think, either 1919 or '20. I think I might have still been in uniform.'

'A juicy murder in a country house, was it?' He made an appalling slobbering noise.

'No, stranger than that. There was a son in the story and Lady Drinkwater was accused of . . . no, it was too ridiculous.'

'Accused of what? You sure it wasn't murder? It usually is in those country manor houses. Proper death traps, they are.'

I replaced my spectacles so I could peer over the rims, giving him my best 'disappointed schoolmaster' expression. 'If you must know, Lady Drinkwater was accused of selling her son to the gypsies.'

Lugg's pallid face contorted as he assimilated the information, but his response was totally predictable. 'Did she get a good price?'

I knew little of Northamptonshire, other than the fact that some of my brother's more boisterous friends regarded it as decent hunting country, and that it contained battlefields from civil wars, whether between white and red roses, or between Royalists and Roundheads, possibly both. Of the village of Husbands Butcombe, I knew nothing other than that it was, according to the fingerpost at a crossroads, two miles from Little Butcombe, which made it, according to a grumpy Lugg in the Bentley's passenger seat, 'just about as far from the sea as you can get in England, and for an island race, that's uncomfortable'.

I doubted both Lugg's sentiment and grasp of geography, knowing full well that his idea of being near the coast or the sea was living within a bus ride of Billingsgate fish market, but it did seem that Husbands Butcombe was several miles from anywhere interesting. The overriding impression was that it was a village which had been demoted to a hamlet for bad behaviour and had both its church and pub confiscated.

There was a manor house, however; one which was difficult to miss from the road, despite the efforts to hide it by the unruly hedges and brambles which cordoned off its grounds. I steered the Bentley through gates which appeared to be permanently open, the two halves of its metal railings hanging precariously from their hinges, and the car crunched up a gravel drive dotted with emerging weeds before slowing to a halt at the front door.

Almost before I had switched off the engine, the door had opened to reveal a diminutive elderly lady wearing an ankle-length fur coat, fingerless black gloves, a brown wool balaclava and wellington boots.

'Strewth!' muttered Lugg as he levered himself out of the passenger seat. 'Must be the scarecrow's day off.'

'Manners!' I rebuked him, then removed my fedora and stepped towards the advancing figure which, I admit, did remind me of a rather bedraggled cat walking unsteadily on its hind legs.

'Lady Drinkwater?'

'You must be Campion,' said the woman, declaiming as if to an angry mob. 'I'm not expecting anyone else. Unless you're the tallyman. You're not the tallyman, are you?'

The tallyman would have found slim pickings at Butcombe Manor, judging by the dusty outlines of pictures long removed from the entrance hall and the bare minimum of surviving furniture in the drawing room into which we were shown. A cold fireplace containing a substantial pile of ash suggested that many a stick of furniture had been sacrificed on that particular altar, though it had only appeased the gods of draught and damp temporarily. Other than four rickety dining-room chairs arranged in a circle, the only surviving piece was a free-standing cabinet or wardrobe, over which a grubby dust sheet had been thrown, making it appear like a lonely ghost looking for a house to haunt.

'I would offer you tea,' said Lady Drinkwater, after we had settled in three out of the four mismatched chairs, the one Lugg had chosen squeaking in protest, 'but I'm afraid the cupboard, like most of the rooms in this house, is bare.'

I fought the urge to reach for my wallet out of charity, but managed to restrain my benevolence, opting instead for befuddled innocence. 'Lady Drinkwater, I'm at a loss—'

'*You're* at a loss? Look around you, Mr Campion, I am an encyclopaedia of loss! I stand before you a penniless widow, decimated by death duties and the gambling debts of a feckless husband and robbed by an ungrateful son.'

Lugg rolled his eyes and flexed his bull neck so that his head jerked suggestively towards the door. 'You have my sympathies, dear lady, but I do not understand—'

'Of course you don't, because I haven't told you the facts yet. If you will allow me to get a word in edgewise, I will inform you fully of my predicament.'

I saw Lugg's right hand down by his side twitch, his thumb and forefinger rubbing together in the universal sign for paper money.

'Firstly, Mr Campion, let me disabuse you of two misconceptions. I am not properly Lady Drinkwater, though I still use the name because I like it and it can be useful. My husband Alfred died in 1899 in South Africa, and I remarried in 1910 to a wastrel named Edward Gidney. Being a dashing captain in a cavalry regiment, Edward put his faith in his knowledge of horseflesh and his strongest characteristic – his stubbornness – to earn a living in civilian life courtesy of the nation's turf accountants. Unsurprisingly he failed completely in this ambition, but not before he had squandered all our liquid assets and disposed of the family silver. Edward finally did the decent thing by dropping dead of a heart attack during the inaugural Cheltenham Gold Cup in 1924.

'Before then, as you may recall from the popular press if you admit to reading such drivel, I lost my son Lancelot, the son from my first marriage, that is, in 1919.'

'In rather unusual circumstances, I believe.'

'The gutter rats of Fleet Street preferred to call them scandalous and outrageous, suggesting that I had sold my son to the gypsies. Preposterous! How ridiculous! To even think such a thing! I did not sell Lancelot to the gypsies; he ran away to join them, taking a sackful of the family silver with him.'

Lugg, sitting quietly, bowler hat resting on a shelf of his thighs, pursed his lips and allowed his eyebrows to rise a good quarter-inch.

'And how old was the boy when he ran away?' I asked.

'Thirty-two,' snapped Lady Cassandra, 'and before you ask, he was unmarried, unemployed and, being charitable, slow in the head.'

'So his behaviour would be out of character?'

'Of course it was! A five-year-old boy might dream of running away to join the circus, but a grown man with a substantial home he would one day inherit, tramping the countryside with a gang of unwashed, illiterate tinkers? Intolerable!'

'For you and Mr Gidney perhaps, but clearly not for Lancelot if he went voluntarily. May I presume to ask if the lad . . .' I faltered, realizing that the decamped son and heir must be at least a dozen years older than I was, '. . . if Lancelot . . . had a happy home life?'

'Honestly, Mr Campion, he did not. He was only twelve when his father died and he never got on with my second husband, who resented the fact that Lancelot insisted on retaining the Drinkwater name. Edward refused to adopt him legally, so he never became a Gidney, and he taunted him mercilessly, thinking him weak and muddle-headed, which he was, but then Edward was a bully and bullies know a victim when they see one. You must think I was a terrible mother for allowing this to happen. Well, you would be perfectly correct; I was a perfectly horrid mother.'

I was saddened and appalled in equal measure by the old woman's confession, yet not absolutely sure it was a confession. Lady Cassandra did not give the impression she was seeking absolution.

'What was Mr Gidney's reaction to Lancelot's exodus?'

'Oh, Edward thought it gloriously funny. Best laugh he'd had in years, he said, but when he discovered Lancelot had helped himself to some of the family silver, his mood changed and darkness descended as with the flicking of a light switch. There was much talk of horse-whipping the boy if he ever came home, but of course he never did, and five years later Edward met his Waterloo at Cheltenham, leaving me with a sheaf of IOUs from numerous bookmakers, a ream of unpaid bills from tradesmen and the inquisition of the Revenue.'

'Interesting,' I said quietly so only Lugg could hear. 'You've mentioned family silver three times now, which makes me think it has some significance.'

'I do not wish to sound mercenary,' said Lady Drinkwater, 'but it has the utmost significance. My first husband, Alfred, left me a fine collection of silver. My second husband, Edward, sold or pawned most of it to cover his gambling debts. When Lancelot ran away, he filled a pillowcase with some of the few remaining pieces and the rest went to support Edward's filthy habits, and then death duties claimed the last of it. Let me show you what I am reduced to.'

Lady Drinkwater rose and moved to the one piece of furniture in the room, the free-standing cabinet or bookcase covered by a dust sheet. With the air of a reluctant magician, she pulled off the sheet to reveal a battered and scratched glass-fronted display cabinet containing, on its top shelf, a single silver tankard.

'The cupboard looks bare,' muttered Lugg before he was put in his place by a withering look from the lady of the house.

'It is ironic, is it not, Mr Campion, that the only piece of silver on the Drinkwater estate actually belonged to Edward Gidney – a beer mug from his regimental mess in 1910. He was supposed to have it engraved with his name and rank, and it should have been left behind the bar as part of the regimental silver, but Edward kept it instead.'

'We had a similar tradition at Cambridge. It was called the Plate of Ale: every student bought a tankard, duly autographed, which he used whilst there and then left it to the college on graduating.'

Lugg was shaking his head slowly from side to side.

'You have something to say?' the lady of the house asked him.

Lugg's shoulders produced a seismic shrug of indifference. 'Never inscribe silver; makes it difficult to pop.'

'I beg your pardon?'

'Forgive my plebeian friend, Lady Drinkwater, but I think he means that the . . . er . . . retail value of silver is diminished by personal engravings should it come to a visit to a pawnbroker or to attracting the attentions of a burglar.' I glared savagely at Lugg, but the big man totally ignored the implied barb.

'That piece . . . that mug . . .' Lady Drinkwater pointed at the lone tankard occupying the shelf as if she was accusing a heretic. 'That . . . pot . . . was indeed taken to the pawnbroker's, in 1920, just in time for a fruitless wager on the 2000 Guineas. I never expected to see it again, but here it is, back to haunt me and remind me of my late ne'er-do-well husband, as well as taunting me about what I have lost.'

The old woman took a deep breath to calm her shaking body. 'Come with me.'

The cellar reeked of damp and, faintly, turpentine, and was as cluttered with objects as the upstairs rooms were devoid of furniture. Light was provided by a single lightbulb, dangling on a yard of flex, and a begrimed rectangular window high up one wall.

'Forgive the mess,' Lady Drinkwater said with a hollow laugh, 'but it's the servants' day off, as it has been since 1924.'

'A positive Aladdin's Cave,' I whispered as we descended the stone stairs.

From behind, Lugg muttered, 'If Aladdin was a rag-and-bone man,' and I had to agree with his assessment, for the contents of the dim, and dusty room were a cornucopia of discarded objects, either unloved or damaged, ranging from rolls of stagnant carpet to an armchair whose stuffing had been harvested for bedding material by mice, an ancient cylinder lawnmower flaking rust, tea chests overflowing with books, their covers iced with mould, a small wall of boxes containing sheets of blank paper, glass flagons full of dark liquids and, saddest of all, a rocking horse with one of its marble eyes missing. Pride of place, in terms of volume of space occupied, was an iron contraption, partly covered with an old blanket, bits of it extending to the height of a man and, on one side, a large flywheel. In outline it could have been mistaken for a mangle or a machine salvaged from a laundry, but I recognized it for what it was.

'My goodness, a printing press! That explains your unusual stationery.'

'Unusual?'

'I should have said distinctive. I found the typeface attractive, but I couldn't place it.'

'My husband – my first husband, Alfred – designed it himself and even gave it a name, *Badinage*, which I think is a joke of some sort. Printing was a silly passion of his, and when he was a boy Lancelot helped him out. Of course, Edward had no time for it, unless it could print ten-pound notes, so the machine was sent down here to rust.' Lady Cassandra waved a hand vaguely at the piles of cardboard boxes. 'Alfred believed in keeping a good stock of notepaper, as you can see: there are reams and reams of the stuff. I have been using it for thirty years and the pile doesn't seem to get any lower.' She leaned over one stack of boxes and reached behind another. 'But this is what I wanted you to see.'

With some difficulty she pulled a large, framed photograph from its dusty hiding place and held it up to her visitors. The photograph showed a woman in a wedding dress, clearly a twenty-years-younger Lady Drinkwater, and, either side of her, a stocky man wearing military uniform and sporting a waxed moustache over a forced grin, and a tall, thin, gangling young man wearing thick spectacles, a Sunday-best suit and a wing-collared shirt and tie.

'A wedding photograph?' I asked politely, though it clearly was.

'An unpleasant memory,' said Lady Cassandra, 'which is why it is filed down here as NWOVOL.'

My confused expression must have negated the need to ask the obvious question.

'Not Wanted On Voyage Of Life,' she explained. 'But never mind that – look at the background.'

The three figures forming that far-from-happy family grouping were posed in front of a vast, bow-fronted glass display cabinet, an impressive piece of mahogany furniture that was the rich relative of the humbler version with its single exhibit now residing in the living room above. And this cabinet was the very rich relative, as it was crammed to bursting with silverware. Lugg let out a soft, low whistle, which I hoped went unnoticed by our hostess.

'All gone now,' said the lady of the house, 'either sold or hocked, all except for that stupid pint pot upstairs, the one piece I was really glad to see the back of.'

'I'm sorry, but I'm confused,' I admitted. 'The tankard, you say, was pawned to finance a wager in 1920 and now it's back in your cabinet. Presumably, then, you redeemed it from somewhere?'

Our hostess positively quivered with indignation. 'Me? I have never crossed the threshold of a pawnbroker's in my life! The tankard was returned to me.'

'By whom?'

'By the gypsies, of course. That's why I wrote to you. Have you not been paying attention?'

'A regular failing of mine,' I agreed, then indicated the hovering Lugg, 'which is why I always bring along an extra pair of eagle eyes, but in this case, please humour me. The tankard upstairs . . .'

'That one, far right, middle shelf . . .' Lugg enthused, jabbing a sausage finger at a point on the photograph, careful not to touch the dusty glass and, out of instinct, leave a fingerprint, '. . . was here in this picture in 1910.'

'But left your possession in 1920,' I said, picking up on Lugg's cue, 'the year after your son ran away with the gypsies. Now, twelve years later, it is sold back to you by gypsies. The same gypsies, or different ones?'

'I have no idea, and I did not buy it back, it was presented as a gift. I was hoping you would find out if it was . . . well . . . legal for me to have it. That's the sort of thing you do, isn't it? The man who delivered it said his name was Shadrach Lee and he and all his relatives are still camped in Little Butcombe. You should catch him there; they won't move on until the harvest's in.'

As I steered the Bentley down the drive and out on to the lane, Lugg let out a long, loud snort of derision which almost drowned out the growl of the engine.

'Unimpressed?' I ventured.

'It's a liberty, that's what it is. Dragging us all the way out here in order to run an errand two miles away. Thinks she's posher than you, though not by much.'

'Did you keep your eagle eyes peeled as I told you?'

'Yeah, spotted it as soon as we went into that cellar.'

'You did? Oh, well done.'

'First thing I noticed was the window,' he said proudly. 'The 'andle had been forced from the outside, round the back of the 'ouse. Piece of cake to get in that way.'

It was not what I hoped he had noticed, but it was useful intelligence all the same.

'Do you think dear old Cassandra knows she might have been burgled?'

'I very much doubt it, and what was there worth pinching down there? Mind you, she's sharp, the old bird. Got a tenner out of you, didn't she? Saw you coming, she did.'

'Of course she did, dullard; she wrote to me asking me to come, and the tenner was a sort of deposit on the mysterious tankard, an advance on what she might get for it if Shadrach Lee's story checks out.' I jerked a thumb over my shoulder, indicating the parcel wrapped in old newspaper sliding around on the back seat. 'We have to discover how he acquired it, establish its provenance, as it were. The proud Lady Drinkwater could not risk going to the pawnshop with stolen goods now, could she?'

'So we find this gypsy feller and ask him where he got it from?'

'More to the point, old fruit, we ask him why he brought it back.'

SEVEN

Rude Mechanicals

M r Campion had waited politely until two minutes past nine before he telephoned DCI Castor, on the assumption that the Bedfordshire policeman would, by then, have reported for duty, taken his coat off and drunk his regulation cup of tea at his desk.

'I'm sorry to disturb your morning, Chief Inspector, as I am sure you have quite enough on your plate,' he said after he had been put through, 'but I needed to ask a favour about David Duffy's notebook.'

'You're a bit late,' came the rather gruff answer. 'I've already had your Fleet Street chum on about it. Said you'd be ringing to vouch for him; chap called Lay-Flurrie.'

'I would hardly call him a chum, but I did promise I would ask on his behalf, as he might be able to decipher more of Duffy's notes than you or I. He is a newspaperman and they pride themselves on being able to read each other's scribbles.'

'You might be right there,' admitted Castor. 'My girl who was trying to decipher it has good shorthand, but it's Pitman's, and Duffy used some other sort she couldn't make head nor tail of.'

'I think it must be what they call T-line and it's quite new but very popular with journalists because it's faster. I'm sure Lay-Flurrie would help with that, but also he could isolate which jobs Duffy was on because he tells me Duffy often had several irons in the fire.'

Campion heard Castor's deep sigh of resignation.

'I suppose that might be useful, but . . .'

'I know it goes against procedure, if the notebook is being held in evidence, but surely it is vital to assess its value as evidence; plus, technically, a sharp lawyer might make the case that the notebook is the newspaper's property.'

'Let's keep sharp lawyers out of this as long as we can, but I can't release the notebook, not yet anyway.'

'But might you permit Lay-Flurrie to come and look at it? Under supervision, of course.'

'I might, as we're not supposed to antagonize the press, though it always seems to be open season for them to have a go at us.'

'Was Lay-Flurrie a tad difficult when he rang?'

'You might say that. He demanded – demanded, mind you – that we fax all the pages to him.'

'That was a bit rude.'

'Rude? It was ridiculous. By the by, what *is* a fax machine?'

Campion had taken up Christopher's offer of a visit to the beating heart of McIntyre Consolidated, 'the full public relations experience' as he put it, on condition that his guided tour followed the exact path of that given to David Duffy. There would be one difference, though, as Campion intended a short side-trip to visit the scene of the crime, something he had deliberately not mentioned to DCI Castor. Nor, indeed, to his nephew Christopher, who was to act as his chauffeur as he had for the late David Duffy.

Christopher collected his uncle from the Bottle Street flat in a bright red Reliant Scimitar GTE, a two-door shooting brake which was proving popular with the county set and certain branches of the royal family.

'Nice car,' said Campion, pleased that his long legs could be comfortably accommodated in the passenger seat. 'Is it new?'

'Spanking; I decided I needed a treat,' answered his driver. 'It's got the three-litre Essex V6 engine, overdrive, and can do over 110 miles an hour. Cost me the best part of two thousand pounds.'

'Public relations pays well, it seems. I hope Mr Duffy was impressed.'

'David Duffy wasn't my client. Sir Lachlan McIntyre was – is – and he wouldn't have employed a PR man who turned up in a clapped-out Triumph Herald, which is what Duffy drove.'

'Drove to Markley and his death,' Campion said quietly. 'What was he doing out there?'

'I've no idea, and at that time of night as well. He certainly wasn't coming to meet me, and McIntyre wouldn't give him the time of day, let alone suffer a surprise visit.'

'And McIntyre wasn't there the night Duffy died. According to the police he was in London with a perfect alibi. So what drew Duffy to Markley and his personal desolation?'

'The only other thing is the McIntyre Consolidated compound, but that would have been locked up for the night.'

'You call it a compound too? That's exactly how it struck me when I first saw it. There is definitely something of the prison camp about it; all it needs are a couple of watchtowers, some searchlights, and at least three tunnels being dug frantically towards the wood.'

'McIntyre doesn't like the word compound, he prefers "depot", but I know what you mean. It is a prison, but a prison for machines, though they are unlikely to stage an escape. If they did, though, they could do it easily; the diggers could tunnel under the fence and the bulldozers could go through it.'

'Has anyone attempted to steal one of McIntyre's mechanical monsters?'

Christopher laughed out loud. 'That would be hysterical! Can you imagine a very slow getaway chase down the M1? Those beasts are not cars where you could change the number plates or give them a quick respray and, even if you did all that, the only place you could sell them would be back to Lachlan McIntyre. Where would you hide a bulldozer if you stole one?'

'On a construction site amidst a lot of others, perhaps? But I take your point – they are unlikely to be pilfered, so why all the wire fences and nightwatchmen?'

'Actually, spare parts and tyres are highly pilferable, but mostly the fences are there to keep children out. They look on it as a bit of a playground with all those giant Dinky toys, but there are plenty of sharp edges in there to chop off inquisitive little fingers and toes. And that would be very bad public relations for Sir Lachlan.'

'Indeed, it would. Was Duffy excited when you showed him round?'

'Not especially; he seemed more interested in McIntyre's house and grounds than in the depot, even though I arranged for him to drive a bulldozer, which is surely every boy's dream after a steam train, isn't it?'

'Well, I certainly hope I get offered the chance on my guided tour,' said Mr Campion, with his best boyish grin.

Christopher managed to restrain his obvious pride in his new car through north London, and only put it through its paces once they had picked up the start of the motorway, producing a gentle reminder from Mr Campion that there was now a seventy miles per hour speed limit. His chauffeur complied sulkily and promised a longer, 'decent' run at some point in the future when the junction for the Markley turn-off was reached with disappointing promptness.

The turn-off could hardly be missed, announced as it was by the gigantic advertising hoarding for McIntyre Tyres; once they had looped under the motorway, they were instantly on to the small roundabout where the larger signs pointed out the roads to Bedford and also Cranfield. A smaller fingerpost, almost an afterthought, advised a sharp left turn to Markley, should anyone have missed the dominating poster depicting tyres rolling down a hill. Anyone who had missed the McIntyre Tyres signage, thought Mr Campion, would certainly have failed the eyesight test required by the driving test and, since its desolation, there could surely be no other reason for visiting Markley.

'Duffy was killed just over there,' said Christopher, pointing a finger at the road to Cranfield. 'There's a sort of lay-by place where he parked up.'

'So he was not actually on McIntyre land?'

'No, and he wasn't even spying on McIntyre property. From where he was parked, he couldn't see anything of the house or the compound or anything much of Markley.'

'And presumably no one in Markley could have seen him; not that it seems a humming and vibrant metropolis.'

'You're not kidding.' Christopher grinned. 'In the next half-hour I will be introducing you to the entire population.'

From what Campion had already seen, he felt it perfectly possible that he could meet all the inhabitants of Markley within thirty minutes, given that he had already met its two most prominent citizens. What surprised him was that the rest of the populace were all in one place, and the meet-and-greet Christopher had planned would take much less than half an hour.

'That's Nick Andrews,' said Christopher, acknowledging the small, middle-aged man in a blue boiler suit who was opening the wide main gate to the compound. 'They call him "Old Nick" because he has devilish luck at cards. The other lads warn visitors not to play three-card brag with him.'

'I'll make a note of that,' said Mr Campion, nodding politely, as one always should, to Old Nick. 'Just how many "lads" are there in this card school? More specifically, how many were on duty on the night Duffy was killed?'

Christopher steered his car carefully between the massed ranks of much larger, more violent mechanical beasts, which had been lined up as if providing a guard of honour for the visitors. 'Technically, only Old Nick was on duty as he was nightwatchman that night. There are only two others living on site, as it were, or at least in the Markley cottages, both mechanics – Andy Todd and Frank Green. Todd was in Markley that night, but Frank Green was up north, servicing one of the bulldozers that was out on hire. They've all been questioned by the police.'

'And nobody else lives in Markley other than the McIntyres?'

'Carl Spivey has one of the cottages,' Christopher said casually.

'And he is . . .?'

'Lady McIntyre's stable boy, except he's long past boyhood.

We think he may be a retired jockey and he has to have a cottage to himself because he pongs to high heaven.'

'An occupational hazard,' said Campion slyly, 'just as all public relations men have a whiff of gin-and-tonic around them.'

'I'm sure I don't know what you mean,' said Christopher huffily, as he pulled the Scimitar into the metal valley between two parked bulldozers. 'Be careful how you go, there are a lot of sharp edges around here.'

Campion – eyeing one of the raised bulldozer blades which loomed over him as he climbed out of the car – could not but agree.

Both men turned their heads when they heard a voice announce, 'Doin' all right, Mr Campion?'

Christopher acknowledged the greeting from the man who had opened the gates for them. 'Oh, hello, Nick. This is my uncle Albert, here to have a look round – with the blessing of the boss, of course. Is the kettle on?'

'Always is,' Old Nick said proudly.

'Perhaps we could join you later after I've taken the guided tour,' said Mr Campion.

Old Nick shrugged his shoulders, muttered, 'Suit yerselves,' and shuffled off back towards the cabin by the gate which no doubt served as the compound's office, the nerve centre of its security system and its staff's refreshment room.

Christopher indicated that Campion should follow him down the first corridor of parked vehicles and, when the older man looked dubiously at the rough, churned-up ground, he assured him it was uneven but dry, as McIntyre had invested heavily in making sure the field was supremely well-drained before he had sited the depot there. After all, it wouldn't do if someone wanted to hire earth-moving equipment, but it was stuck in a muddy field. Mr Campion observed that most of the machines seemed very capable of digging themselves out of trouble, as he took in the blades and buckets with jagged teeth, presented almost in salute as he walked down between two lines of machines. There were bulldozers and small dumper trucks with metal front baskets, huge 'tip-up' lorries with massive tyres, caterpillar-tracked pipe-laying cranes, excavators and loaders, some with biting hydraulic jaws called 'grapples', which gave them the appearance of metal dragons. As he picked his way carefully over the rough ground, Mr Campion had the distinct impression that he was walking through the modern equivalent of a dinosaurs' graveyard.

He listened patiently, but not carefully, to Christopher's explanation of what each machine did and how important regular maintenance, cleaning and lubrication were to ensure the continued efficiency of McIntyre's fleet. By the time they reached the end of the row and faced the prospect of a similar lecture down another line of parked monstrosities, Mr Campion viewed the distance back to the main gate with dismay and suggested they follow the line of the fence which cut the compound off from the paddock and woods at the rear of McIntyre's far-from-stately home.

Campion was curious to get another view of Cruachan and wondered if, even at this distance, McIntyre's impressive gun collection could be seen through those floor-to-ceiling windows, but he told Christopher that he wanted a view of green fields, as walking through those canyons of metal made him quite claustrophobic.

'I could fire up one of the bulldozers and drive you back to the gate in style,' said Christopher cheerfully, 'or even let you drive it.'

'I'm not ready for a wheelchair yet, dear nephew, and certainly not to be shovelled along with the topsoil. Despite everything to the contrary, this is the countryside, so we really should stretch our legs and admire the flora and fauna.' Campion waved a hand towards the row of tyres, double-stacked well above head height, along the length of the boundary fence. 'Such as it is.'

They set off, the fence on their left, the long bulwark of piled tyres on their right, with Christopher giving a running commentary on their various dimensions (huge) and value (also huge) and Mr Campion reluctantly admired his nephew's professional enthusiasm for a subject in which he could not possibly have any real interest. Such was the lot of the public relations man, but Christopher bore it stoically and earned his corn in doing so.

Mr Campion's attention soon wandered to the view to his left. Through the mesh of the chicken-wire fencing, made more daunting by the triple strands of barbed wire which topped it at an angle, he could see the rear aspect of Cruachan, with its veranda and huge windows and the garden they looked out on. He could now make out the building – tacked on to the side of the house like a suburban garage – which he had guessed correctly was a stable, now with its doors wide open, and the paddock beyond it. Through an open five-bar gate, there was access from the paddock to the nearby field, and therefore the small wood which provided a protective cape around the shoulders of Markley Desolation.

As if he had been waiting until he was sure he would be seen, a man emerged from the woods, leading an unsaddled horse so much bigger than him that it seemed capable of sending him flying with a flick of its head, should the mood take it. Man and horse walked into the field, aiming for the paddock behind Cruachan, only a few yards from the two Campions on the other side of the fence.

'Morning, Carl!' yelled Christopher.

Mr Campion assumed he was addressing the groom rather than the animal, and it was the human holding the rope halter who answered.

'And you, Mr Christopher. Playing with your toys again?'

Christopher gave a polite laugh. 'I offered my uncle here a ride on a 'dozer. But he wasn't keen.'

'I've seen him drive a car,' joked Mr Campion, 'and anyway, they are terribly noisy beasts and I wouldn't want to frighten Lady McIntyre's handsome horse. My name is also Campion and you must be Carl Spivey.'

'That's right, but don't you worry about spooking old Buckland here.'

To prove his point, the small, bow-legged Carl Spivey – almost certainly a retired jockey – slapped the neck of the horse with the palm of his hand, producing a dull, thudding noise, but there was no obvious reaction from the victim.

'Well-trained, is he?' Campion asked through the mesh of the fence.

'He is, but not by me. Buckland was demobbed from the Royal Military Police Mounted Troop down in Aldershot, replaced by a younger model, though there's plenty of life left in him. Lady McIntyre gets all her horses from there.'

'I do believe he is pushing out his chest in pride at the very mention of the words Military Police,' said Campion, 'and if I was a squaddie who had gone AWOL and he was chasing me down, I would certainly be glad to see the inside of the guard-room. I take it he's been trained not to react to heavy army vehicles; tanks, armoured cars, Bren gun carriers if they still have them, that sort of thing.'

'Oh yes, full de-sensitivity training, including firearms.'

'Really?'

'Comes in useful when Lady M. goes shooting in Daffodil Wood.' Spivey jerked his head at the clutch of trees from which he had emerged. 'Sometimes she bags a muntjac. Sir Lachlan is quite partial to a bit of muntjac; does the butchering himself.'

'Has Lady McIntyre been out hunting this morning?' Campion asked, though he had noted the absence of a saddle on Buckland, who remained standing to attention and thoroughly bored throughout this exchange.

Spivey shook his head. 'Not today, she's out with Sir Lachlan somewhere. I'm just taking Buckland for a walk to stretch his legs – and mine.'

'You don't ride him?'

'My riding days is over and he's a big lad is Buckland, a long way to fall if you come off. At our age, you've got to think of things like that.'

It took Campion a moment to realize that Spivey was referring to him, and not the horse, when he said 'our age', and wondered just how old the small man was. His wizened, sun-weathered face gave no definitive clues, and any white hair was hidden under a flat cap the size of a dinner plate.

'So the McIntyres are not at home.' Campion looked concerned. 'Pity. I was hoping to have a word. Perhaps you could help?'

'What about?'

'Sir Lachlan asked me to look into the recent death of a chap called David Duffy.'

'Oh aye, the chap what got shot,' said Spivey without overt interest, 'and brought the police down here to Markley for the first time in years.'

'I am not the police, so perhaps you could tell me if you saw anything that night.' Campion thought his plea may have lost some gravity having been made through the wide mesh of the security fence. Buckland certainly looked unimpressed.

'Didn't see a thing, didn't hear a thing. I finished up at the stables, went home, had a bath and cooked myself some supper, watched a bit of telly and was in bed and the land of nod by nine o'clock as per usual.'

'You're an "early to bed, early to rise" sort of chap, are you?'

'Have to be. The boss likes to go for an early morning hack before the milkman delivers, so the horses have to be groomed and saddled while there's dew on the ground.'

'The boss being Sir Lachlan?' Campion suggested meekly.

'Oh aye, he's the boss of all that lot,' Spivey nodded towards the piled tyres and machinery on Campion's side of the fence, 'but the horses is Lady M.'s business. She's the boss of the stables.'

'Does she have many horses?'

'Three at the moment, though Buckland here is her favourite, especially for the dark winter mornings. He likes the going soft.'

'So you were up and about when Mr Duffy's body was discovered? That was early morning, so I believe.'

'Must've been, but I didn't see anything. I couldn't have.'

'Forgive me, but why not?'

Spivey pointed down the length of the fence to the depot gate and, beyond that, across the road, to the cluster of brick cottages which formed the last remains of Markley Desolation. From their front doors, the inhabitants would have an unenviable view of Lachlan McIntyre's army of mechanical monsters, whilst their rear aspect would have the equally unappealing vista of the giant embankment which carried the M1 motorway. Mr Campion rapidly concluded that – whether in front or back bedrooms – the inhabitants would need to be heavy sleepers.

'I live in the end house,' said Spivey, 'so I just walks up the road to Cruachan and lets myself in to the stables round the side. That Duffy chap was found parked round on the Cranfield road, off the roundabout.' He waved his arm to his left, indicating a site over and beyond the McIntyre house. 'I had no reason to go that far, and you can't see the road from the stables 'cos of the trees. First I knew about it was when I heard the ambulances coming from Bedford.'

'Did you ever meet David Duffy?'

Spivey shook his head. 'Not likely! He was a snooper, wasn't

he? Sniffing around for gossip on the McIntyres. If he thought
he'd get any dirt out of me, he would've been very disappointed.
I've got a good job here, working with horses, which is the only
work I like, and at my age I'm not looking to join the queue
down the Labour Exchange. I saw him when he was here with
Mr Christopher and they were driving one of them bulldozers
up and down like big kids, but I was told to stay clear of him,
so I did.'

'Told by whom?' Campion asked gently.

'Sir Lachlan. He values his privacy; doesn't like visitors unless
they've made an appointment through his missus. I sometimes
think he'd be happier if nobody knew where he lived.'

Mr Campion's eyes flicked towards the massive sign advertising McIntyre's Tyres and he felt that perhaps Sir Lachlan had
not thought this through. Buckland pulled gently on his halter
and gave a low whinny, as if in agreement.

Near the main gate of the depot was a prefabricated building not
much bigger than a garage, which had almost certainly once had
the descriptor 'temporary', but which had survived the ravages of
time so well that replacement had no doubt seemed an extravagance.
It had windows and a farmhouse-style half-door to which drivers
or visitors could report, and Mr Campion concluded that this was
what Christopher called the security office, but what Sir Lachlan's
workers would almost certainly regard as the tea-break room.

Before they entered, Campion put a hand on Christopher's arm
and moved to the gate so he could get a good view of the cottages
across the road. There were four dwellings in total, two small,
detached ones either side of a semi-detached pair. All were of a
basic late-Victorian design and intended for use by farm labourers.

'This road,' said Campion, 'does it go anywhere?'

Christopher shook his head. 'Not any more; it's just the
access road for the compound. I think it has been declassified,
if that's the word, and is now a private road. Only McIntyre
vehicles use it.'

'I am guessing that it was once the main street of Markley
before the desolation, and that whatever else was left standing
is now under the motorway.'

Christopher raised his voice above the steady roar of the traffic flowing along the man-made horizon facing them. 'Could be. It's rather difficult to ignore, isn't it? Can't say I'd want to live here.'

'Which one is Spivey's again?'

'The detached one on the left.'

Campion stepped out of the gateway and turned his head to the left, confirming that Spivey could not have seen anything beyond the frontage of Cruachan, as Christopher continued, 'The other lads share the semi and the spare cottage is used as an overnight stop for drivers collecting or returning machines.'

'Cooks, cleaners?'

'They mostly look after themselves, but Sir Lachlan sends in a firm of cleaners once a fortnight to make sure they haven't trashed the place. Surprisingly, they keep things pretty neat and tidy and do a lot of the running repairs themselves.'

'I hope that's acknowledged in the rent they pay.'

'Oh, they don't pay rent. The accommodation comes with the job; makes them grateful and loyal.'

The three loyal and appreciative employees, who between them comprised half the remaining population of Markley, were sitting on a variety of second-hand chairs around what could have been a third- or fourth-hand kitchen table, each clutching a mug of tea. There were clipboards holding sheaves of papers hanging around the walls from rusty hooks, each with a pencil dangling from a string which would, at a pinch, qualify the hut as the site office.

Campion had met 'Old Nick' Andrews, and so Christopher's introductions were limited to Andy Todd, the depot's chief mechanic, and Frank Green, also a mechanic, who could drive anything with wheels or caterpillar tracks so far invented.

They seemed, on the surface, to be a trio of regular working men, men who had worked outside and were not afraid of hard labour. Their arms, all decorated with tattoos of the traditional kind expressing adoration of a loved one, a mother or Tottenham Hotspur, were brown and muscular, and they all appeared physically fit, although Frank Green was developing the paunch common to many a long-distance lorry driver. All three nursed hand-rolled cigarettes.

They proved willing to answer Campion's questions about the night of Duffy's death and all, as far as Campion could tell, answered honestly if not helpfully. Frank Green had been 'up north' fixing a digger which had broken down, whilst Todd admitted to consuming the better part of half a bottle of whisky that evening and had fallen asleep in front of the television. Nick Andrews had been on nightwatchman duty that evening, which had involved a brisk walk around the inside of the compound fence, once at nine p.m. and then again at eleven p.m. to make sure everything was secure before turning in. Like Andy Todd, he had seen and heard nothing.

Mr Campion had not expected to elicit much from the trio, who would have been more closely questioned by the police, but there was something curious about them and he chanced another question. 'And there was nobody else in your digs that night? No wives, girlfriends?'

Three middle-aged male heads shook in unison and three deep male voices muttered that there were no females in Markley.

Once outside, Christopher asked, 'Learn anything?'

'Nothing I was after,' admitted Mr Campion. 'I was hoping one of them had seen or heard Duffy's car on the night in question.'

'Do you want to see it?'

'Yes, we might as well walk round to where it was parked.'

'No, I meant do you want to see Duffy's car?'

'What?'

'It's here, in one of the sheds. The police didn't have room for it in their pound in Bedford, so when they'd done their forensic, they asked us to look after it.'

You might have mentioned that, thought Mr Campion. But he just smiled and said, 'Lead on.'

EIGHT

The Death Car

M r Campion did not feel guilty about having missed what Christopher called 'the sheds' on his perambulation around the McIntyre compound, for he doubted if he could have spotted them with the aid of aerial reconnaissance.

They were two large, corrugated-iron, prefabricated garages, painted the same bright yellow as most of the massed machinery, sited back-to-back in the centre of the depot, flanked by aisles of parked vehicles, which successfully camouflaged them from anyone not sitting high up in the driver's seat of a cab.

A man on foot could squeeze between two parked diggers to gain access, but to put a car in one of them had involved, according to Christopher, some 'nifty parking manoeuvres, a bit like the fairground dodgems' on the part of Todd, Green and Old Nick to clear a path.

The police had been grateful for the offer of a near empty shed in which to store David Duffy's car once it had been searched, fingerprinted and cleaned, and after having, thankfully, removed the body. It was not an ideal solution as it was, after all, a murder scene, but it could not remain at the side of a public road, albeit a minor one, especially when the scene was visible to drivers on the M1 (assuming they had good eyesight and were not paying attention to the road in front of them). With no space currently at the police pound in Bedford, the offer of storage space as a temporary solution was well-received. Duffy's car would be off the road, out of sight and secure.

Christopher led the way, side-on, between two caterpillar-tracked excavators, breathing in to avoid getting oil or grease on his double-breasted suit jacket, with Campion, who had less need to tighten his stomach muscles, following.

'Who else has a key?' Campion asked as his nephew fumbled with the padlock securing the doors of the nearest shed.

'Old Nick has one and that policeman, Castor, has another.'

'Why do you have a third?'

Christopher looked mildly startled by the question. 'This one was for Sir Lachlan. I was supposed to give it to him, but he wouldn't accept it. Said he didn't want anything to do with Duffy, dead or alive.'

Mr Campion was still contemplating that as Christopher pulled the creaking shed door open to reveal the rear end of a Triumph Herald, which he could tell from the number plate was six years old. It could have been any saloon car abandoned in a lock-up garage to gather dust, were it not for the starred bullet hole in the rear window on the driver's side.

Carefully, he eased himself along the side of the Herald, thankful that the interior of the car was in shadow just in case the forensic clean-up had not been thorough enough, but he did realize that if he wanted to see inside the car, the interior light might come on as he opened a door, exposing any lurking horrors. Only when he had seen the exit hole of the fatal projectile, in the windscreen a few inches above the rim of the steering wheel, did he take a deep breath and reach for the driver's door handle.

The internal light flickered on and a strong whiff of cleaning fluid escaped from the car as the door opened with an ominous squeak. There was no blood or gore and, apart from a dark stain on the driver's seat and the hole in the windscreen, there was nothing untoward about the car's basic interior. Campion mentally checked off the steering wheel, the gear lever, the handbrake, the faux veneered dashboard with speedometer and various pull-button controls surrounding the open, but empty, ashtray, and then realized he had been holding his breath.

'Anything interesting?' Christopher asked as Campion withdrew his head and shoulders and exhaled with relief.

'Interesting that the ashtray is empty,' he said as he straightened up and exhaled. 'It's clearly been used.'

'Is that significant?'

Campion turned and looked at his nephew over the rims of his glasses with the expression of a disapproving owl. 'I am not, nor do I pretend to be, Sherlock Holmes. I have never written a monograph on the analysis of one hundred and forty, or however many it was, different types of cigarette or cigar ash, and wouldn't know where to start. All this suggests to me is that the police might have cleaned out the ashtray because they spotted something in there.'

'You mean like a joint? A marijuana cigarette?'

'I know what a joint is.'

'You do?'

'I read, nephew, and I certainly wasn't born yesterday. I couldn't detect any herbal odours in the car, not like you can in a house, where the smell always clings to the curtains, but then I do not have Sherlock's refined sense of smell. Anyway, it is probably not important, though it is comforting to see the police being so thorough. I doubt there is anything left in here for us to find, but we might as well try the obvious.'

'The obvious?'

'The glove compartment, of course. That's the first place I would stash a notebook if I was driving or waiting to meet someone.'

'He was waiting for someone?'

'Why else would he be sitting in his car in the dark out in the depths of the countryside? If he was going anywhere, he would surely have been on the motorway.'

'But there's nobody in Markley *to* meet!'

'Apart from the owners and employees of McIntyre Tyres, who have all been questioned and, as far as we know, cleared by the police.'

A stunned Christopher recoiled in horror. 'You're not suggesting they *all* did it?'

Mr Campion could not suppress a giggle. 'Goodness gracious, no! You've read too many fantastical detective stories, but then, in my time, so have I. One thing I learned from them is that once you have ruled out the ridiculous, whatever is left, however preposterous, must provide an explanation decent enough to convince the village idiot if not a jury. I'm paraphrasing, of course.'

'So what exactly are we looking for?'

'A clue,' said Campion ruefully, 'because at the moment I do not have one.'

He leaned back inside the Herald and reached over the driver's seat to pull open the small glove compartment built into the dashboard fascia. There was only one item inside, a small, dark red book, which an excited Campion removed with a trembling hand. Only when he had it outside the car and was holding it up to read the printing on the cover did his expression sour and his hand stop shaking.

'I knew it was too good to be true,' he said, speaking mainly to himself. 'It was stupid of me to even wish for it.'

'It's not Duffy's notebook, is it?' asked Christopher hopefully.

'No, it is not. The police have that, which I very well knew, so I had no right to get my hopes up. This is a *Bartholomew's London Pocket Atlas*, an old one.'

'Like the A–Z street guide? Everyone has one of them in their car.'

'If they live in London, or they drive a black cab, but then real cabbies do not need one; they have memorized it.' Campion examined the dusty book, its cover simply illustrated with the shield of the City of London showing the cross of St George with the sword of St Paul. 'This looks like the edition produced just after the war, not exactly up-to-the-minute stuff.'

'Goodness knows how old my A–Z is; I've had it for ages. London doesn't change much.'

'Oh, it does, all the time; you just don't notice. I know they stopped publication of this atlas sometime in the Fifties. It must have meant something to Duffy, though the police thought it innocent enough, but perhaps it is best for you to avert your eyes, dear nephew.'

'Why?'

'Because technically, removing something from a crime scene without the permission of the police or a coroner is a crime, and I would hate to see you in court testifying against your favourite uncle.' Mr Campion smiled beatifically as he slipped the book into his jacket pocket. 'Shall we go to the actual scene of the crime?'

'Have you finished here?'

'I think so.'

'Have you learned anything?'

Campion shuffled along the car to stand next to Christopher at the boot. Taking a step back he extended his right arm, making a two-finger gun with his hand and aiming directly at the hole in the rear windscreen.

'A bullet went in there and came out the front. David Duffy, unfortunately, was in the way. That is the lesson here, and from the angle of entry, the gun was fired downwards by a very tall person.'

'You can deduce that?'

'Very easily, my dear Watson, since the police told me as much and I'm happy to take them at their word. Let us see if we can learn anything from where the car was found.'

'You don't want to talk further with the workers?'

'I don't think so, though they're an interesting bunch.'

'They are all very loyal to Sir Lachlan.'

'I am not surprised,' said Mr Campion casually. 'Jobs which include a place to live are not that easily come by for ex-cons.'

They were out of the depot and walking along the access road which had once been the main street of Markley, pre-desolation, towards the entrance drive of Cruachan, before Christopher spoke again.

'How do you know that? About them being jailbirds?'

'I want to say it was elementary, but an educated guess would be nearer the mark. They all had tattoos, non-military and very amateurish ones, typical of incarceration rather than regimental pride, which brought the words "prison ink" to mind. Then they were used to doing their own cooking and laundry and seemed resigned to living without female company, and in accommodation which was provided for them, so they don't have to face the rigours of the rented property market or worry about repairing the plumbing. Also, no neighbours to complain about living next to reprobates.'

'It never occurred to me,' Christopher said, whilst gazing at the façade of Cruachan in case it offered an answer, 'though I did notice that none of the lads are ever invited into the house and Carl Spivey seems to stick to the stables.'

'I'm not surprised, given the number of lethal weapons McIntyre keeps in there.'

'Yes, his rather impressive gun room.'

'It's more of an arsenal, and I would think the local police firearms officer has had words about security if Sir Lachlan wants to keep his gun licences.'

'They're pretty tight on security,' Christopher conceded. 'Nobody is allowed into the house unless they have an appointment, and the locks on the doors and windows – plus the burglar alarms – are all state-of-the-art. Not that they have many visitors, and strangers would be quickly noticed in a desolate place like Markley.'

'Duffy wasn't.'

'Fair point, Uncle, but Old Nick and Andy Todd – even Carl Spivey – would have recognized him if they'd seen him, as they all saw me giving him the guided tour.'

'Which is possibly why he parked so far away,' observed Mr Campion.

The McIntyre house was behind them now, and on their left was the edge of Daffodil Wood which curved in a defensive semi-circle protecting the McIntyre empire.

'The trees here are younger than the ones up by the compound,' said Campion. 'Did McIntyre plant them?'

'I'm sure he did; he has a long association with the Forestry Commission and he's a big supporter of this new charity, the Woodland Trust, though he could have had to do it as part of getting planning permission. The neighbours might have objected to having a huge garage of diggers and lorries on their doorsteps.'

'But there are no neighbours.'

'True. Perhaps he expanded the wood to provide a habitat for the animals he shoots.'

'Or to screen his private life from prying eyes. His business side, the depot, is clearly visible from the M1, not least because of that garish advertising board, but the house is quite difficult to spot unless one is down at this level, looking at it head-on.'

'Significant?'

'Probably not, but I think Lachlan McIntyre may be a man who values his privacy highly.'

'You can say that again. He was very particular about what biographical information I could put in any press release we put out. I certainly got the impression that Duffy knew more about him than I did.'

'That was Duffy's job – he was supposed to be an investigative journalist. The question is what exactly was he investigating? According to his fellow scribbler, Mr Lay-Flurrie, he was doing some serious research into the Thirties and had even consulted an academic at King's College. Did Duffy drop any hints when you were with him?'

'I told you he seemed obsessed with the year 1932, and I told *him* that Sir Lachlan would have been a penniless teenager then, orphaned, unemployed, and walking the streets in a different country in the middle of a great depression.'

Mr Campion looked askance at his nephew. 'Spare me the official public relations biography, Christopher – you've already let on that McIntyre left Glasgow on the train and found lodgings with a relative in Stepney, then a job in the West India Docks. I appreciate times were hard, but many had it much harder than he did. Are you sure there is no guilty secret from back then that McIntyre didn't want an investigative journalist to investigate, especially one who occasionally wrote for *Private Eye*?'

'I didn't know about *Private Eye*,' said a subdued Christopher, 'or I would never have let him do that one-on-one interview with Sir Lachlan.'

'Which did not go well, I believe.'

'It did not, and that's an understatement. To be honest, Uncle, I am rather surprised to be still working on the McIntyre account.'

Mr Campion bit his lower lip and changed the subject. 'Is this the place?'

They had reached the roundabout, at the end of what had been the main street of Markley in the days when it merited a street. Had the village still been a going concern, an imaginative estate agent could have pointed out that Markley had almost instant (perhaps too instant) access to the modern super-highway which would, eventually, offer access to both London and all points north, or at least Leeds. A more conservative, perhaps cleverer, agent might have stressed to potential house-buyers that the roundabout had effectively blocked off the village from all the dirty, heavy and noisy traffic heading for the M1. It was ironic that the only reason Markley still existed was as a depot for extremely dirty and noisy heavy vehicles, but as the village population had been comprehensively desolated, the point was moot.

To their right was the exit leading directly to the motorway, to their left the minor road to Cranfield and, across the sparsely grassed roundabout, the Bedford road into and from which most of the day's traffic flowed.

'It was just round here,' Christopher said, leading the way signposted to Cranfield, 'in a lay-by on the other side of the road.'

It was not a planned or official lay-by, rather a chunk of missing verge, the packed earth being wide enough for a car to be safely off the road, and long enough to take no more than three vehicles before it ended abruptly in a bright red public telephone box.

Possibly the urgent need to use the telephone had resulted in motorists pulling off the road, creating a *de facto* lay-by.

It did not take the Campions more than a few seconds to cross the Cranfield road and walk the entire length of the lay-by, eyes on the ground, as if trying to spot a dropped wallet or appear as a pair of concerned citizens on a voluntary litter patrol.

'Duffy's car was up this end,' said Christopher when they were near the telephone box, 'facing towards the roundabout, so he'd either driven from Cranfield or come off the M1 and turned round here so he could make a quick getaway.'

'Or he knew there was a phone box here and needed to make a call.'

'Long way to come to make a phone call.'

'Unless you were planning to meet someone here. How many telephones are there in Markley?'

Christopher thought carefully in case it was a trick question, which in a village that had not been desolated, it might have been. 'The McIntyre house has two lines – one business, one private; there's one at the depot, and one in each of the houses where the staff live. Sir Lachlan had them put in years ago and pays the bills on them as a perk for his workers, even though Spivey says he doesn't need one. It seems he doesn't like to talk to anyone except horses.'

'So, if Duffy was ringing someone in Markley that night, given that Sir Lachlan was in London and the mechanic chappie – Frank Green – was away up north, it would have been Lady M., Old Nick, Spivey or Andy Todd.'

'I don't know that he'd ever met Lady M.' Christopher grinned idiotically. 'That makes her sound like Lady Macbeth, doesn't it, and I can't think why he'd call Andrews or Todd other than to get into the depot, and he wouldn't be doing that, not in the dark. At that time of night, the place would have been locked up.'

'He might have rung someone not in Markley,' admitted Mr Campion. 'Or not even used the telephone at all, or perhaps he was *waiting* for a call.'

'That's a little far-fetched, isn't it? Driving up from London to sit waiting in a country lane for somebody to ring a call box. Sounds a bit cloak-and-daggerish to me.'

Mr Campion nodded in agreement. 'Perhaps something in his notebook will give us a clue, because for the life of me I cannot see any others here.'

'Really? I thought the scene of the crime would be right up your street when it came to clues.'

'I think, dear innocent nephew, you have me confused with somebody you read about in your youth, possibly by torchlight under a blanket in your dorm. I will not suddenly produce a magnifying glass, sink to my knees and start looking for footprints or tyre tracks. I am too old; my joints are too stiff, and the ground is far too damp for that. If there was anything to find here, the police would have found it. Although . . .' He paused. 'They didn't find the one thing they really wanted to find: the bullet that killed our friend from the Fourth Estate.'

'I never really understood that expression, which I suppose is an admission for a public relations man. Is there a Fifth Estate?'

'I do hope not,' said Campion. 'Four are quite enough.'

'So there's nothing to be learned here?'

'One thing.' Campion looked at the trees across the road. 'No one in Markley could have seen Duffy's car parked here, especially at night. Similarly, though, Duffy could not see anybody in Markley.'

'Which means what?'

'That Duffy was not spying on anyone, nor was he on what I think is popularly known as a stake-out. He was waiting, possibly for a phone call, possibly for an assignation.'

'With whom?'

'His killer, obviously.'

'So, are we any further forward?' Christopher asked whilst piloting the Scimitar back towards London.

'Well, I now have the lie of the land, so to speak,' said Mr Campion, 'but little else. Until we know what Duffy was really after and how I, and Lugg, are connected to it, I fear we'll still be in the dark. There's quite a lot riding on what Ron Lay-Flurrie finds in his notebook.'

'Duffy's editor friend? Can you trust him?'

'As much as one can, or should, trust a journalist. He definitely smells a story in this whole business – plus, I think he might take Duffy's murder as an affront to his profession. If it goes unpunished, it could be open season on journalists.'

'There are some who might think that isn't a terrible idea.'

'And those are exactly the people we should be afraid of. Lay-Flurrie is a dedicated newspaperman, but I think he genuinely wants to get to the bottom of this. It was he who triggered a distant memory from my cottonwool-filled brain.'

'About Duffy?'

'Not directly, but perhaps about something Duffy was interested in, from a long time ago, in 1932.'

'Which involved Lachlan McIntyre,' offered Christopher, suddenly excited, looking at his passenger rather than the road ahead.

Mr Campion raised a finger to point at the windscreen, hoping to divert his nephew's gaze back into the stream of traffic. 'Not at all. I was completely unaware of that name back then. No, but it reminded me of a bit of business Lugg and I were involved in that year, and it started with a letter from a rather bizarre woman in Northamptonshire . . .'

Campion decanted the memory of his commission from Lady Drinkwater and, to his credit, Christopher listened without interruption, though from his occasional grimaces and frequent sighing, Campion could sense his nephew's frustrations as to where the story was leading, if, indeed, it was leading anywhere.

'I'm sorry if this is sounding like a shaggy dog story,' Campion said eventually, 'but there is a point to it all, I hope. Please bear with me.'

'Very well, I will. Is this where I ask you what happened next?'

'It is, but I must ask you to contain your anticipation until we get to Bottle Street, because the next instalment requires Lugg to be at the telling. He was present at the time and may be able to add some fine detail to the fresco I am trying to paint, or at least make up something almost credible to fill in the gaps.'

NINE

Negotiations by the Vardo

Mr Campion's Memory 2: Northamptonshire, 1932

I t was not difficult to find the gypsy encampment in Little
Butcombe; there was not much of Little Butcombe to search
and the gypsies were not exactly hiding. They had camped
in a field of rough grass beyond the church, their wagons in a
semi-circle around an open fireplace marked out with large stones.
Across that lay a large round griddle frame on which steamed a
battered copper kettle and a blackened iron cauldron. There were
six traditional horse-drawn Vardo wagons, the ponies which
pulled them busily cropping the grass; two road-weary lorries,
and two relatively new Eccles caravans with their canvas tent
awnings extended.

Lugg volunteered to stay with the Bentley, 'So yer won't 'ave
to count the wheels before we leave.' I admonished him for his
intolerant attitude whilst complimenting him on his suitability,
and similarity to, a loyal guard dog, and then set off across the
grass, the newspaper-wrapped package under my arm.

I soon found myself fording a stream of curious children
heading towards the Bentley, all entirely unconcerned about the
immobile Lugg, who had pulled the brim of his bowler hat down
over his eyes to add to his air of inscrutability. He remained
static, even when the numerous dogs of uncertain breed – which
ran with, almost herded, the children – began to sniff enthusiastically at his boots and the turn-ups of his trousers.

Because it seemed only polite, I doffed my fedora and bent
to ask a passing child for the whereabouts of Mr Shadrach Lee.
The grubby-faced, lank-haired girl fixed me with large brown
eyes, judged me worthy of a response, and pointed silently to
the Vardo nearest to the smoking fire.

Sitting on the wooden steps, his back against the caravan's

brightly painted door and perfectly framed by the horseshoe shape of the Vardo, was a middle-aged man with a head of thick black curls, wearing the jacket and trousers from two different suits, a vest that had once been white and a bright green neckerchief knotted over his Adam's apple.

Approaching him, I again removed my hat and he in turn removed a glowing, long-stemmed churchwarden pipe from between clenched teeth.

'You hiring or promoting?'

'I think neither,' I said, 'though I am not awfully sure what you mean. It is Mr Lee, Shadrach Lee, isn't it? My name is Albert Campion.'

'I'm sure I be pleased to meet you, Mr Albert Campion, but if you're looking to hire workers, we're already pledged to the farms round here.'

'Well good for you, what with so much unemployment. They must know good workers when they see them.'

'That they do,' said Shadrach, puffing proudly on his pipe, 'and we're here every year when we're needed. Question is, why are you here?'

I glanced around and spotted two elderly women eyeing us, or probably just me, with suspicion. They were the only other obvious residents of the camp, apart from the children and the dogs, which had suddenly, from nowhere, doubled in number. One of the women, now ignoring us, approached the fire pit clutching a large wooden spoon, which she plunged with enthusiasm into the bubbling cauldron, stirred with muscular determination while the other woman looked on clearly with disapproval. When the pot had been sufficiently agitated, the first woman withdrew towards one of the Eccles caravans, licking the spoon. Once she was inside, the second woman strode up to the fire and took a fistful of herbs from a cloth bag strung from her belt and flung them into the stew.

'Rabbits,' said Shadrach Lee in response to my unasked question. 'Those two are in charge of cooking whilst the rest of the family's working the fields, but sometimes their recipes don't exactly coincide. Pity they don't talk to each other.'

'That happens, in families,' I said, using it as my cue to take the package from under my arm and remove the newspaper wrappings, 'and sometimes complete strangers are called in to settle disputes. For my sins, I have been asked by the lady at Butcombe Manor to establish the provenance of this shiny mug.'

I offered the last surviving piece of the Drinkwater-Gibney hoard to Shadrach Lee like a knight presenting his lady with a favour, but he remained impassive and made no move to touch the object.

'It's not *choray.*'

'I know it's not stolen, Mr Lee, at least not by you. It would be a poor thief who returns his swag, which is what you did.'

'And got little thanks for it.'

'I think perhaps you took the lady by surprise. It was an object she had not seen for a dozen years. May I ask what you were doing with it?'

'Returnin' it, as I was asked to.'

'Returning it to anyone in particular, or just Butcombe Manor?'

In answer Shadrach reached into the top pocket of his jacket, produced a small square of folded paper and proffered it. Unfolding it carefully, I discovered it was the top third of a sheet of roughly torn headed notepaper, bearing the professionally printed address of Butcombe Manor in an oddly familiar typeface.

'May I ask who gave you this address – and the tankard?'

'You can ask,' said Shadrach, tapping the stem of his pipe against his teeth for punctuation. 'Don't mean you'll get an answer. Don't know who you are, for a start.'

'There is no reason why you should, but would it satisfy you if I said I am merely someone who is trying to help an elderly lady who seems uncommonly distressed by this souvenir of her family history? I assure you there is no ulterior motive behind my involvement in this matter.'

'Never trusted a do-gooder. Not much good ever got done, least not at our end.'

I felt the urge to reach for my wallet and was immediately somewhat ashamed that the very thought of such crass rudeness had crossed my mind.

'Is there anything I can say which would make you trust me, other than I am generally thought to be of good character, have no anti-social vices I can think of, am politically inert and always try to help people in the hope that help will be offered to me when needed? I am no quoter of scripture, but I believe there is something in there about not being afraid to entertain strangers as you may be entertaining angels unaware.'

'He told me not to tell the old lady,' said Mr Lee through a series of clacks as pipe hit teeth.

'I am not Lady Drinkwater.'

'That much' – *Clack! Clack!* – 'is true. Still, I gave my word and my word's worth something.'

'I am sure it is and I would not want you to break it. Might I suggest a compromise? Let me hazard a guess at a name and you tell me, honestly, if I'm wrong. Fair enough?'

The tooth-clacking was accompanied by a severe but decisive nod of the head.

'Was it someone called Lancelot?'

'I don't know anyone by that exact name.'

The expression did not change, but the clacking stopped.

'How about a name not so exact? Lance, for instance?'

'That sounds familiar,' said Shadrach, the pipe now clamped and silent.

I made a show of looking around the camp, scrutinizing the semi-circle of vehicles and then turning to view Lugg and the Bentley, both now completely surrounded by curious children and inquisitive dogs. 'Would this Lance person be in this camp today, or out working nearby?'

'No, he's not with us.'

'That sounded distressingly honest. May I try my luck with a direct question: where were you when you were given the tankard and that address?'

'Kent, a little place called Sturry outside Canterbury.'

'Hop-picking country.'

'That's right.'

I re-wrapped the tankard in its newspaper coverings and offered to return the piece of headed notepaper, but the older man waved his pipe, indicating that I should keep it.

At the Bentley, I tossed the package on to the back seat and told Lugg that another road trip was in the offing.

'Where now?'

'Into darkest Kent, but via Chancery Lane. We need to visit the Silver Vaults.'

'That journalist, Lay-Flurrie – he told you Duffy was interested in the Silver Vaults!' Christopher was so excited his hand shook and whisky spilled on to his knee. 'You were following a clue! Well, perhaps it wasn't a clue back then, but if it's jogged your memory, it could be a clue to what happened to David Duffy.'

He and Mr Campion had returned to London and joined the 'pre-show' restaurant crowd for an early dinner, then retreated to the Bottle Street flat to wait for Lugg to join them over a fine malt whisky, which would hopefully cut through the fog of memory.

'I am not too sure about that, but it might be a clue as to why my name was in Duffy's notebook,' said Mr Campion, 'and it was the second one. I missed the first.'

Christopher stared at his uncle wide-eyed. Lugg merely fumed, and as loudly as possible.

'The first?' Christopher asked.

'When the Bedford policeman read me the names they'd found in Duffy's book, it just didn't register.'

'What didn't?'

'The initials. There were names, mine and Lugg's included, and a set of initials, "N.H.", which I couldn't place. It was when Ron Lay-Flurrie mentioned that Duffy had been sniffing around the Silver Vaults that the curtain went up, slowly at first, on my memory banks.'

'So who is N.H.?'

'Nathan Hirsch,' muttered Lugg. 'I'd've remembered 'im if only you'd asked.'

'And who is – or was back in 1932 – Nathan Hirsch?' Christopher leaned forward in his chair, positively shaking with excitement.

'Whoa there, Nellie, hold yer horses!' boomed Lugg, his face going purple as he turned on Campion. 'That's not how it happened. You ain't told little Christopher the best bit of the story of that gypsy camp.'

Mr Campion adopted an air of submissiveness and smiled

sweetly at the big man whilst Christopher asked timidly, 'The best bit?'

'My bit!' Lugg's voice reached parade-ground volume. 'I suppose I'll have to tell it meself.'

TEN

Taking His Lumps

Mr Lugg's narrative

H is Nibs here has missed out the bit where I saved the day, as per usual, because that old gypsy king wasn't going to give up anything without naming his price. It was me who had to step up and prove we were a party to be reckoned with.

When we got there, Shadrach asked, straight off, if Mr C. was hiring or promoting. Now we weren't looking for farm labourers or fruit-pickers, so the old fox, eyeing this smart young buck in his Savile Row duds and with a big shiny Bentley, must be there to do a bit of promoting – boxing, fisticuffs, the noble art of pugilism; the gypsies have produced some fine fighters and it would have come as no surprise that Shadrach had a stable of lads he was training for the ring, maybe the amateur circuit or for exhibition bouts at funfairs. Some of them earned good money that way and, back then, when times was hard, you couldn't begrudge them.

I could see him eyeing me up from the moment we got there, the way he might size up a horse for the three-thirty or a farmer might judge whether he would get his money's worth out of a prize bull. He may have been conversing with his distinguished visitor, all polite and respectful, but the old devil never took his eyes off me. I knew from the off that he wouldn't give us anything for nothing, unlike some other more trusting souls I could mention . . . no names, no pack drill, as we used to say in the Boy Scouts.

Fair enough, he gave Mr C. the name Lancelot, or at least he didn't deny it, but he knew he had another trump card to play 'cos he knew where this Lancelot could be found but, *contrary to some accounts*, he didn't come out and say Sturry down in Kent just like that.

Oh no, he ignores Mr C., looks straight past him and nods in my direction. 'That bruiser you brought is a heavyweight for sure.'

'And then some. He may not be running to fat. But he's ambling that way,' says a certain person, rather cheekily if you ask me.

Of course I was busy glaring at all them children, making sure they didn't wipe their sticky little fingers on the Bentley, and discouraging the dogs from doing worse on the hub caps with the end of my boot, but gentle like, as I don't believe in mistreating dumb animals – not as a rule, anyway. Pity some folk don't feel the same way about humans.

Anyway, old Shadrach and young Albert go into a whispering confab and then the gypsy reaches behind him and knocks on the door of his Vardo. Like a jack-in-the-box, the top half of the door flies open and a lad with more curly hair on his chest than his head appears. Then I gets the call from His Nibs to come over and meet him.

I'm not keen on leaving those kids hanging around the car, but I trudges over with all the dogs sniffing round my ankles like I was a prisoner under escort, until I was introduced, formal like, though I didn't take my hat off to him and he never offered to shake hands.

'Mr Lee has an interesting proposition for us,' said you-know-who. 'He has some information we require' – I made a note of that "we" but let it pass – 'but is only willing to divulge that information once his nephew Manfred here has had his daily training session. I believe it's called "sparring" in the boxing world, and clearly I am unsuited to such activity, being of fragile and delicate sensibilities more suited to tripping through a meadow greeting the trees and flowers.'

Or something like that, but the nub and crux of it was that this Manfred fancied himself as a bare-knuckle boxer and wanted a workout, no doubt providing some amusement for the kids and the dogs on a slow day in the camp.

The kids who had been studying their reflections in the

Bentley's paintwork realized there was something going on and came at the charge to surround us, all the time chanting 'Manfi, Manfi', which I'm told is short for Manfred, which means 'man of peace' in some lingo. *That* was all the helpful advice I got from my trainer or second or promoter, whatever he liked to call himself. That, and the whispered instruction in my earhole to 'go easy on him'.

Well, I can tell you, by that time I was in no mood to go easy on anyone, what with the kids shouting and the dogs yapping at my ankles. Plus, the lad Manfred, though no more than a welter-weight, looked like he knew what he was about. He stepped down from that Vardo, fists clenched and stripped to the waist, and started to do a little skipping jig whilst rolling his shoulders to loosen up. He was fit, I'll give him that, and didn't look like he'd been through any sort of wringer. His nose was still straight and his ears showed no sign of growing like cauliflowers. I'd seen more fat on a butcher's pencil.

There was no way I could back out of things of course, though I wasn't pleased – not a happy bunny at all. Still, it made a change for Mr C. to have to stand there and hold my hat and coat, along with my tie and shirt, because I knew who'd be the one to have to wash and iron that if it got soiled.

When I was down to braces over vest, which thankfully was clean on that day, old Shadrach bestirred himself, put one hand on my shoulder and one on Manfred's, and went through the usual rigmarole about wanting a good, clean fight with no eye-gouging or fibbing – that's grabbing a handful of your opponent's hair, if you didn't know it. Then he looks down and sees that Manfred is barefoot and I've still got my best boots on, which I had no intention of taking off, what with all the dogs and ponies there'd been in that field. So Shadrach says there's to be no shin-kicking or stamping on toes either, and I tells him that he's just disqualified all my best moves, but he doesn't crack a smile because he's heard that before.

Then he leads us like a pair of pit ponies away from the fire-place into a bit of space, picks up a stick and draws two lines about a yard apart in the dirt. We both know what to do and we toe the line and come up to scratch – and yes, that's where those phrases come from.

Young Manfred might have had a name saying he was a man of peace, but I could see in his eyes, right then and there, that peace talks were the last thing on his mind. The lad couldn't have been much more than eighteen and he was a lot lighter than me, but he had height and, by the looks of it, a good long reach. He was handsome in a boyish way and I didn't want to mark his face to spoil his chances with the girls. That, plus the instruction from my 'management' to go easy on him, didn't leave me too many options.

I went defensive, fists up to my chin, elbows tight in over my ribs, and decided to let him take the first swing. Well, by crikey he did, and strewth, was he quick. He'd landed two to the head and one round the corner, goin' for the kidneys before I realized nobody had rung a bell or even shouted 'Ding! Ding!', and Shadrach had forgotten to tell me who was timekeeping, how long the rounds were, or even if there were any.

All of them kids didn't help either, with their shouting and screaming and chanting for their boy Manfred, though I can't blame them for that, but I was worried about tripping over one of them, or one of the dogs who'd decided to join in on Manfred's side and was nipping at my heels.

Manfred's bare feet didn't merit the same attention from the dogs as mine because he was moving them too fast. A proper dancer was Manfred, could've been on the stage; beautiful mover he was, real light and dead quick. It was my mistake to get taken in watching his footwork, and that meant he got in more slugs to the head, but that was always my least vulnerable spot.

I reckoned that Manfred's strategy was to keep dancing and throwing shots as fast as he could, buzzing around his opponent like a swarm of midges: annoying but not fatal, going for any target available, not necessarily the best one. Snapping away like that would provoke his victim into dropping their guard in frustration and swinging out, exposing himself.

But I wasn't going to give him that satisfaction and I was getting fed up with the whole stupid situation, so I planted my feet and hunkered down even more, even bent my head as an offering. He couldn't resist and I won't deny that pretty soon there was a ringing in my ears.

When he realized he was hurting his hands more than my

head, he switched down low and went for my stomach, but I was ready for that and let out a squeal like he had really caught me.

Naturally, this encouraged him and he went for the old bread basket again, with some relish. 'Course to do that, he left his chin exposed and that's when I threw my first – *and only* – punch, catching him smack on that sweet spot on the jaw. It was textbook, I tell you, pure textbook, and young Manfred took off backwards, out like a light.

'I thought you were never going to move,' said Mr Campion. 'You just stood there taking your lumps . . .'

'I was waiting for the opportune moment.'

'To put your head down and charge that poor boy like a raging bull.'

'Poor boy?' scoffed Lugg. 'The poor boy who'd been beating the retreat on my skull for ten minutes?'

'It was more like two minutes; I was the official timekeeper.'

'You were, were you? Were you going to shout for the end of round one then?'

'Eventually I might have, but Manfred seemed to be aiming for your head, so I knew he wasn't causing any real damage. Did you have to hit him so hard?'

Lugg glared at his accuser and spoke through gritted teeth. 'I 'it 'im just hard enough. He wasn't hurt, picked himself up soon enough and shook hands. He'd had a workout, learned a valuable lesson, and old Shadrach told us to head for Sturry, so job done all round.'

'Uncle Albert,' started Christopher, who had been listening open-mouthed, 'are you telling me that you put Lugg into a bare-knuckle boxing match just to find this chap Lancelot who ran away with the gypsies?'

'It does sound slightly mercenary when you put it like that,' Campion admitted.

'We weren't breaking no law,' insisted Lugg. 'Bare-knuckle boxing was never illegal in this country.' He looked at Mr Campion who nodded his agreement.

'But I'm at a loss,' Christopher wailed, 'as to what all this has to do with David Duffy.'

'I told you,' Mr Campion said patiently, 'the initials in his notebook, "N.H.", and his interest in the Silver Vaults, could only mean Nathan Hirsch, the very man we went to see at the vaults before we went to Sturry.'

'And that,' added Lugg enigmatically, 'was when we had the second fist fight of the day.'

ELEVEN
St George Be Our Guide

'It was good of you to make time to see me,' said Campion. 'Not at all; it is always a pleasure to talk about my pet subject and, in this case, something of an honour.'

Sabin Danvers – 'No, it's not hyphenated, merely unusual' – was ridiculously young for a professor in Campion's experience. He was no more than forty, whereas Campion remembered from his undergraduate days that professors were, by law, white-haired, snaggle-toothed ancients, many of them confined to bath chairs.

Danvers did share one traditional trait with all professors of the liberal arts, in contrast to neat and orderly scientists, in that his place of work resembled the aftermath of an explosion in a library. Books spilled over the ends of overcrowded shelves, and wire in-tray baskets, straining with papers and magazines, covered the surface of his desk, leaving only room for a telephone and a dimpled glass mug advertising Harp lager, but now filled with pencils and ballpoint pens rather than beer.

His office was in King's College's new Strand building, and Campion thought it only polite to ask how the professor was settling in.

'It's rather a brutal slab of a building,' said Danvers, 'but needs must given the growth in student numbers, though I suspect it is something of a culture shock for you being a Cambridge man.'

'I was at St Ignatius, which hardly counts as proper Cambridge. I do hope that my scraping a degree there by the skin of my teeth fifty years ago is not the reason you regard my visit as something of an honour.'

'Not at all.' Danvers laughed, showing perfect white teeth under a ginger Zapata-style moustache. 'I just meant that historians so rarely get to meet people they have researched in the flesh. The majority, of course, being long dead.'

'Well, I am sorry if I am a surprise, or a disappointment, but I stand before you astonished, not to say slightly nervous, that I am a person of any historical interest. I was given to understand that your field of historical research was British politics in between the wars.'

'It is. My speciality is the origin and rise of British fascism, its interaction with and admiration for contemporary European models.'

'My goodness! I have to admit I was very much alive at that time, but I was blissfully unconnected to anything political, and certainly not that sort of politics.'

'Yet your name cropped up in an official record.'

'Now you have me worried, Professor Danvers. I did suffer a bout of amnesia round about 1940 but I hope I would have remembered donning a black shirt and jackboots and marching with Mosley's mob of hooligans. In fact, I distinctly remember taking up arms and fighting people in jackboots. Did I really turn up in your research?'

'Not mine, Duffy's.'

'Duffy? You mean a journalist who works for *Private Eye* has linked me to the British Union of Fascists in the Thirties? I am horrified. My late mother would be having the vapours at the very thought. In fact, I think I am having the vapours right now.'

'Please do not distress yourself, Mr Campion,' Danvers said quickly, clearly anticipating a heart attack in his white-haired visitor, 'the connection was not with Mosley's BUF but with the Imperial Fascist League.'

'And how on earth does that make things sound better?'

'I suppose it doesn't.' Danvers looked thoughtfully at the ceiling as if he had never considered the point before. 'Not that Duffy, and certainly not I, was suggesting you were a member or an acolyte or a fellow traveller, but you were involved with them.'

'Involved how? Was my name found on their Christmas card list? Did someone ask my collar size so I could be fitted for a black shirt, even though the colour doesn't suit me?' Campion grinned inanely. 'It clashes with my cerulean eyes.'

Sabin Danvers revised his opinion about a pending heart attack. Either his visitor was using flippancy to shield his nervousness, or he was a genuinely cool customer.

'I said you were connected to a fascist movement, more specifically some active fascists, not that you were a member of any organization, and I can assure you that connection was from the side of law and order. You might say you were on the side of the angels.'

'My favourite team. I have been a loyal supporter of them for years, but what exactly is this connecting link which you say Duffy found?'

'He had been researching legal records – magistrates' courts and Crown Courts – for a particular year.'

'Let me guess,' Campion interjected, '1932.'

'Correct; have you seen his notes?'

'Sadly, no, or at least not yet, though I am hoping that access is imminent. The police have them at the moment.'

'Ah, of course. Then I had better fill you in.'

Although he had not been asked for his credentials, Sabin Danvers felt obliged to point out, almost apologetically, that he had read history at Oxford under H.R. Trevor-Roper (and was slightly derailed when Mr Campion murmured that he had known him 'during the war' and that any man whose middle name was Redwald could be forgiven almost anything, even a loyalty to Oxford). For his doctorate, Danvers had made a detailed study of anti-fascist leaflets and booklets published in the late 1920s and early 1930s by the Labour Party, and distributed by the National Union of Railwaymen in an attempt to counter the propaganda of far-right groups, which were attempting to emulate the activities of Signor Mussolini in Italy. Indeed, the earliest manifestation of such had called itself British Fascisti, in honour of their Italian hero, one of the original members being William Joyce ('better known to my generation as Lord Haw-Haw', Campion had offered).

It was not surprising that unhappy, unemployed veterans returning from the Western front and finding a land unfit for heroes had been attracted to such political movements, just as they were in Europe. The professor had asked, as delicately as he could, if Mr Campion had seen active service in Europe during the Great War as he must have been – just – of an age. Campion had admitted that he was, in late 1918, a commissioned junior, very junior, officer but he – and here he chose his words carefully – had not seen action *in Europe*, confident that if caught in a lie, he could argue that Archangel in 1919 did not count as the Western front.

The organization Danvers was particularly interested in was a curious splinter group called the Imperial Fascist League, founded in 1929 by the even more curious Arnold Leese, then living in Guildford, a disillusioned army veterinarian who had practised in India and in Somaliland and had become something of an authority on the diseases of the one-humped camel. (Mr Campion had resisted the urge to ask whether the dearth of camels to medicate in Guildford had led him into politics.)

The IFL was never a very big organization, and probably had less than a couple of hundred devoted members at any one time, and it was strident in its anti-Bolshevism and anti-Freemasonry. It had initially been much inspired by Mussolini's Blackshirts but, following a meeting in Germany with the emerging Nazi Party and one of its leading lights, Julius Streicher, the IFL adopted the half-baked ideas of Aryan racial purity and became vociferous in its anti-Semitism. It screamed about a 'Jewish stranglehold' on all aspects of life, so that both international capitalism *and* international communism were Jewish conspiracies, an illogical not to say utterly bonkers theory, unless one was simple-minded. Unfortunately, it was a theory which did appeal to simple minds in search of a conspiracy.

Anti-Semitism became a key plank of the IFL, coupled with a twisted sort of patriotism; they had a newsletter called *The Fascist*, a flag which was a Union flag with a swastika in the middle, and their slogan was 'Saint George Be Our Guide'. By the time the much better-known British Union of Fascists, the BUF, was founded in 1932, the Imperial Fascist League was set in its ways and convinced it was right, so much so it refused to amalgamate with the BUF because it wasn't anti-Semitic enough!

The league had its own contingent of bully-boys, a paramilitary unit called the Fascist Legion, but it was Mosley and his Blackshirts who took all the headlines with mass rallies and uniforms and his tub-thumping speeches, which had a certain amount of appeal to women, as it was Blackshirt policy to praise women for their vibrant health, physical attractiveness, charm, quick-wittedness, and for being sober and tenacious.

The Imperial Fascist League doesn't seem to have held the same attraction for women, and faded from politics in the shadow of the BUF, apart from a notorious case in 1936 when they accused Jews of ritual child sacrifice, no doubt to further their aims of world domination through either, or both, capitalism and communism.

There was no love lost between the IFL and the BUF, and the BUF would break up league meetings with violence and often inform on them to the police. The leading lights in both parties were thankfully detained at His Majesty's pleasure during the war years, but it was doubtful that confinement had softened their views.

'And all this was Duffy's chosen field of research?' asked Campion.

'Being a journalist, I am sure he was interested in many things, but fascists in London in 1932 was what he wanted to hear about from me. Not that I was his first port of call. He had done his homework and had made copious notes already.'

'Was his research accurate? I got the impression from one of his colleagues that he was reasonably reliable professionally.'

'I was very impressed with his detailed knowledge, for an amateur historian,' Danvers said without condescension, 'and I was able to confirm several things for him from sources I had used, including two names he was particularly interested in.'

'Was one of those names mine?'

'Good Lord, no. They were names I found on a membership list of the Imperial Fascist League. I have them to hand . . . somewhere . . .' Danvers began to scrabble at one of the trays piled with papers. 'Pulled them out when I heard about Duffy's death.'

'His murder.'

'Quite. I thought the police might be interested, but you have beaten them to it.'

'They are still examining Duffy's notebook, but I have been informed of some of its contents.'

'Here we are.' Danvers pulled a typewritten sheet from the pile like a card sharp drawing an ace. 'Walter Lillman and Mary Gould. Mean anything to you?'

'Nothing, other than they are in Duffy's notebook, or so I have been told. You found them for Duffy?'

'No, he came to me with the names. I merely found them on an IFL list.'

'For 1932?'

'Yes and, if it's of interest, also for 1931 but *not* for 1933.'

'That does seem to narrow down the year in question,' murmured Mr Campion. 'Did Duffy ask about any other names?'

'Not specifically. I showed him my source material, but he didn't pick out any other names.'

'And if needed, you could provide me with an affidavit to say my name was quite definitely not on one of those membership lists?'

The professor made no attempt to hide his surprise. 'But of course, my dear fellow – in the highly unlikely event of the need arising, which it won't. You're not worried about the police asking inappropriate questions, are you?'

'Not the police – my wife. Oh, and could you check for the name Lugg: Magersfontein Lugg.'

Danvers relaxed his face into a smile. '*That* name is certainly not on any IFL documents I've come across. I would surely have remembered such a distinctive moniker.'

'The owner of said moniker will be cock-a-hoop to be thought of as distinctive.'

'The name is familiar?'

'Far too – familiar, that is.'

'But not Walter Lillman or Mary Gould? Those were the names Duffy was interested in.'

Campion shook his head. 'I cannot recall either, I'm afraid. I don't suppose Duffy asked about anyone else. Did he mention the name McIntyre by any chance?'

'As in the chap who builds earthworks with all his bulldozers?'

'The same spelling.' Campion could not resist a smile. 'Only a historian would use the word "earthworks" to describe modern motorway construction, though in terms of leaving a mark on the landscape, it is really quite apt.'

'Well, Duffy never mentioned that name and it's not one I've come across in my work. Should I have?'

Mr Campion blithely ignored the question and changed tack. 'Did Duffy ask about anything else connected to the year 1932?'

'Not that year precisely, but on the subject in general he was very interested in the Battle of Cable Street in 1936. Are you familiar . . .?'

'Of course. That was Mosley and his BUF Blackshirts attempting to intimidate the East End with a show of strength by marching through what was then a predominantly Jewish area. Naturally, local Jewish groups, trades unionists, communists and assorted anti-fascists turned out to stop them. Thousands of police were put on the streets to control the situation, but things soon got out of hand and riotous assembly ensued. A lot of people were injured in the fighting, but I don't think anyone was killed, thankfully. It was quite a sensation back then, and all over the newsreels.'

Professor Danvers put on the expression he normally reserved for tutorials when making a serious point to his students. 'There are those, still today, who call the Battle of Cable Street the defeat of British fascism, but recent research suggests that membership of the BUF actually increased after those disgraceful scenes in the East End.'

'That is a sad and sobering thought,' said Campion, 'and you say Duffy was interested in the BUF march and the rioting?'

'In an odd sort of way, yes. His main interest was the Imperial Fascist League in 1932; he didn't seem terribly concerned with the British Union of Fascists, except for Cable Street, and even then it was a question of geography rather than personnel or politics.'

'Geography?'

'Duffy was fascinated about where the march took place and asked me if I knew the exact route and if I had a map of Whitechapel and Stepney.'

'And had you?'

'The next best thing,' Danvers said confidently. 'I had an old book of street maps.'

'Not a *Bartholomew's Pocket Atlas*, by any chance?'

'Yes, exactly that. I even loaned him my personal copy which I used for my research; not that I'll see that again.'

'I can personally promise that you will, once the police investigation is complete,' said Campion, making no attempt to reach for the book nestling in his jacket pocket.

'Do you mean that the street atlas is connected to Duffy's death?'

'I have no idea, but I have the feeling that the names in his notebook certainly are. Hopefully I will have a clearer picture when I get to see it. You are sure he didn't ask you to check any other names – or a set of initials, perhaps?'

'Initials?'

'Specifically N.H.'

Danvers shook his head.

'Or did he mention the Silver Vaults at all?'

'Not that I recall. He was only fixated on Walter Lillman and Mary Gould.'

'And he never indicated why those two names?'

'Only that those two had appeared in the press report of a court case back in 1932, a court case which, he said, mentioned you by name – and hence your inclusion on Duffy's list. Surely you must remember something like that?'

Mr Campion removed his spectacles and pinched the bridge of his nose between finger and thumb, then shook his head as if to clear it and replaced his tortoiseshell frames before speaking. 'But of course I do; I was there. I was a witness for the prosecution.'

Campion did not see any need to bore Sabin Danvers with the unhappy background to Cassandra Drinkwater's family circumstances, but did feel he owed the historian some form of explanation. There was also the consideration, at the back of his mind, that he might have to call on the professor's expertise again, and so a little elucidation now might be a good investment for the future.

The story he told Danvers was one of a decent young chap (he liked the idea of remembering how much younger he had been in 1932, and mentioned it frequently in the telling) doing a favour for an elderly widow fallen on hard times. With his faithful companion Mr Lugg, he of the distinctive moniker, he had undertaken to establish the provenance of a silver tankard, an heirloom of the impoverished widow. Having consulted his 1878 first edition of Wilfred Cripps's definitive work *Old English Plate, Ecclesiastical, Decorative and Domestic: Its Makers and Marks* (which he just happened to have handy), Campion had decided that there were questions he needed to ask an expert on the hallmarks stamped on the tankard in question.

Such questions, he realized, could only be answered by an expert, and fortunately an entire hive of experts plied their trade almost on his doorstep in the Silver Vaults off Chancery Lane.

The London Silver Vaults had begun life as an enormous subterranean safe-deposit box for the wealthy and, occasionally, the eccentric. Indeed, it had started life in 1885 as the Chancery Lane Safe Deposit, and Campion had loved – and re-told many times – the story of one vault which had been secured by one unusual Victorian depositor, who paid more than £100 in rent before his death, upon which the vault was opened to find that his treasured deposit was a single farthing coin.

Now the vaults were a positive *souk*, a shining bazaar dedicated to the purchase of silverware of all shapes and sizes, offered by dealers who came from all corners of Europe but spoke a single language: silver.

It seemed the logical place to go or, as the distinctive Mr Lugg put it: 'Stands to reason. Silver tankard with a dodgy 'istory; might as well go to the 'orse's mouth.'

TWELVE

Street-fighters

Mr Campion's Memory 3: London, 1932

The actual horse from whose mouth we demanded wisdom was stabled in a small glass box of an office-cum-shop near the centre of the trading hall at the heart of the Silver Vaults. To approach it involved passage along a narrow street of other glass-fronted shops, all displaying bespoke silverware of every conceivable shape, size and utility, ranging from goblets to cauldrons, plates to coffee pots, salts and peppers in myriad designs, even models, fortunately scaled down, of biplanes and naval sailing ships.

It was near to closing time for the vaults, so I headed straight for Nathan Hirsch's personal emporium, with Lugg trailing behind at a leisurely pace, his eyes widening into saucers at the sight of all the shining, silvery loot on display, tantalizingly out of reach in secure glass cases. Among the dealers, the security guards and the uniformed messenger boys carrying oddly shaped packages wrapped in muslin and tied up with string, Lugg could not have looked more suspicious if he had been wearing mask, a striped jumper and had a sack marked SWAG slung over his shoulder. He was probably sizing up the opportunities for a quick bit of smash-and-grab which, given all the shiny stuff on show must have been very tempting, but I had spotted him noticing all the security men strategically placed between him and the exit, and he knew that he would never make it out to the street.

From the central glass cubicle which served as his place of business, the immaculately suited man I had arranged to see bustled from behind his desk without touching or disturbing the dozens of silver plates, goblets, trophies, vases, and various artefacts balancing on thin glass shelves, which seemed magically and invisibly attached to the glass walls.

'My dear Rudolph, how good—' he started before I rudely cut him off with a curt flap of a hand.

'It's Albert these days, Nathan, if you don't mind.'

'So, it's not family business then?' said Mr Hirsch, who was never slow on the uptake.

'Well, not my family. I am seeking your expert opinion on an item. By the way, this devious fellow is Lugg; he's with me. Lugg, this is Nathan Hirsch, silversmith extraordinaire and valuer of family heirlooms. He expects you to behave yourself and is too polite, though I am not, to point out that every item in this office is inventoried, was counted as soon as you entered the building and will be counted once you leave.'

'Mr Lugg,' said Nathan, bowing slightly, 'you are most welcome; please do not take Albert too seriously.'

'I never do,' growled Lugg, admiring his profile in a silver dinner plate engraved with the crest of a member of the House of Lords.

'As the man who knows everything worth knowing about silver, I require your learned opinion on this,' I said, unwrapping the tankard and offering it to Nathan. A jeweller's loupe eyepiece appeared in his hand, as if out of thin air, to aid his careful examination.

It was not a long examination.

'You want to know how much it's worth, I suppose,' he said casually, 'and you will be disappointed.'

'I know the price of silver has been dropping of late with the depression and all that, so I am braced for disappointment, though the owner may not be so phlegmatic. But really, I wanted to know anything you could tell me about it.'

Hirsch screwed the loupe to his right eye and surveyed the rim and then the base of the tankard, both aspects prompting sighs of exasperation.

'There are faint, very crude scratches on the base, which look like the initials E.G., so clearly it doesn't belong to you, unless E.G. is another one of your highly improbable pseudonyms.'

'I prefer to call them *noms de guerre*,' I teased him, 'and whilst I have been accosted in the street by shouts of "Tootles Ash", and may have signed a hotel register or two as "J. Mornington Dodds", I have never used the initials E.G., and can tell you with certainty that they, and the tankard, once belonged to a man called Edward Gidney, who is no longer with us. How about the hallmarks?'

Nathan twisted the tankard under the overhead light and peered closer. 'Well, there's no maker's mark, which would have been useful, though it might suggest whoever made this made them in quantity. The other marks are there: the lion's head, sometimes called the leopard's head but it really is a lion, indicates that it is from London, and the lion *passant* assay mark says it is sterling silver. The date letter is a Gothic "P", which is 1850, and the duty mark, which is rather unclear, almost fudged, is the head of Queen Victoria, which would fit.'

'I sense hesitation in your adjudication, old friend, and experts who hesitate always start the butterflies in my tummy fluttering.'

Nathan turned his head, aiming the loupe straight at me. 'It's a fake, of course. The design is very late Victorian or Edwardian – just look at that curved handle. The early Victorians wanted something more solid, a chunkier handle, to aid their quaffing.'

'Edwardian would fit the picture I've been painted,' I suggested, 'but the hallmarks don't tie in. Is that what you're telling me?'

Hirsch removed his eyepiece and handed back the tankard. 'Edwardian it may well be, and my guess would be that it came from India and had the marks punched to make it appear older, and thus more valuable than it is.' He beamed at me, rather patronizingly, I thought. 'I'm surprised at you, Albert. From the heft, the weight of it alone, you of all people should have known it wasn't sterling silver.'

'I noticed that straight off,' said Lugg smugly.

When Lugg and I emerged on to Chancery Lane, it was into a wispy London fog which diffused the streetlights more effectively than the dark of approaching night. I predicted a longish wait for a taxi, as any available cabbies would be on the look-out for a decent fare courtesy of the legal eagles heading home from Lincoln's Inn to their comfortable wives in the suburbs.

I sent Lugg round the corner to the tube station to buy an evening paper, with strict instructions not to make a detour into the Cittie of York for refreshment, while I kept an eye out for a roving black cab. Nathan, who had stayed behind to lock up his emporium, had given me a bright red silk bag with a white rope drawstring in which to carry the Gidney tankard, as its newspaper wrappings were undignified, reminded him of a neglected fish-and-chip supper and not the sort of thing to be seen leaving the vaults with. Personally, I would have said that a rough bundle of newsprint was less conspicuous than the silk purse which now dangled from my wrist, but the night was dark and foggy and the chances of being seen by anyone I knew were slim as visibility was now down to not much more than a yard.

It was only when I was lighting a cigarette that I noticed the daubs of paint on the stones either side of the entrance to the vaults, and only when the doors opened to allow Nathan to exit and light spilled out from the interior that I made them out clearly.

The paint was yellow and still wet, small droplets dribbling down the brickwork from the foot-long capital letters P and J.

'Still lurking, Albert?' Nathan said as he stepped out towards me.

'I think somebody is,' I said, pointing to the painted letters.

I did not have to explain their significance to Nathan; the look on his face told me that.

P.J. – 'Perish Judah'– the hateful slogan doing the rounds among the no-neck brigade who thought their lives could be improved by use of the jackboot and the fist.

'That paint is fresh, Nathan,' I said. 'Perhaps you should go back inside and telephone the police.'

His disdain poured out. 'I will not hide from cowardly scum who dare not show their faces.'

'Then at least share a cab with me.'

Nathan stepped down on to the pavement and buttoned his overcoat. 'I was born in this city and I will walk its streets.'

Even as he said it, the cowardly scum in question charged out of the fog and attacked us and Nathan was right, they did not show their faces.

There were four of them, though in the gloom and the initial confusion I was convinced they were in platoon strength. Their target was clearly Nathan, and I was unceremoniously shoulder-charged out of the way so they could get at him. They moved as wraiths in the fog, dressed in dark clothing with their heads covered by balaclavas – the sort knitted as comforts for the troops in the trenches – and most of their faces masked by black scarves so that only their eyes showed. Their weapons seemed to be wooden, Indian clubs or pins from a pub skittle alley, wielded like police truncheons, which indicated that their intention was to hurt rather than kill, though I rationalized that only later.

In the heat of the moment, I had no time to think anything other than four-on-to-one, and the one being a friend, was an unacceptable situation, and so, being at heart a fool rather than a careful angel, I rushed into the scrum around Nathan, who had been quickly felled by a blow to the head. The four black shadows bent over him were so intent on administering a beating whilst hissing 'Jew, Jew' that they had probably forgotten about me, or instead were so arrogant that they could not envisage anyone interfering in their unholy enterprise.

I grabbed the nearest thug by the left shoulder with the intention of pulling him up and away from his victim, and instantly realized that he had far more experience of street-fighting than did I. He allowed himself to be pulled up, then he swivelled and used his right shoulder and arm to power the club he held into my midriff. Winded, I found myself on the pavement at eye-level with poor Nathan, as my assailant returned to join his companions in the beating, like four vultures feasting on carrion.

In that position there was little I could do, but seeing, less than a yard away through a forest of legs, the punishment being meted out to their victim, I had to do something. I was at ground level and their legs were the nearest target on offer.

Still struggling for breath, I turned crab-like on my back and shoulder and kicked out. I had once seen an exhibition of *savate*, the French art of boxing with the feet, which had been a demonstration sport at the 1924 Olympics in Paris. I am sure my lashing out of a long leg and a sturdily shod foot would not have won me points for execution from a referee, not even the approval of the street-fighting gangs of north Paris where the 'sport' originated, but I had surprise on my side and I swept the legs from under the nearest assailant.

He went down in a heap next to the howling Nathan and, as he hit the pavement, I scrambled to my feet, just in time to take a blow on the shoulder from the club swung by his compatriot.

In the melee I had lost my spectacles, and that seemed as good an excuse as any to lash out wildly, which I did, totally forgetting that the pretty silk bag containing the tankard was still looped around my wrist. It was immensely satisfying when the bag and the tankard struck the head of the dark shadow just as they were aiming a second strike, and I was sure I heard a bell-like *dong*, albeit muffled by the bag, as contact was made.

The high-pitched howl of pain produced by my makeshift flail as one black-clad figure reeled away was satisfying but short-lived, as the thug I had kicked over had now recovered enough to have grabbed me around the knees, and both of us rolled in an unseemly bundle into the body of Nathan Hirsch, who lay frighteningly inert, his face pressed into a paving slab. The blows continued to rain down like drumbeats, and all I could do was try and shield Nathan from the worst of them in the hope that our attackers, who were still chanting 'Jew! Jew!', would tire.

Then, when it did not seem possible, things got even darker, almost as if a blanket of black cloud had passed over our little ruckus. The clubbing stopped suddenly and the pressure on my legs eased. There was an agonizing grunt from somewhere – I was pretty sure not me – then the distinctive sound of a bone cracking followed by a wooden club falling to the pavement and rolling away. When I heard footsteps disappearing into the fog, I raised my head.

Looming over me like an angry colossus was Lugg, his fists up in a boxer's stance, one of his outsize boots pressing down on the back of the neck of one black-clad figure prone on the ground, whilst another sat slumped against the wall of the Silver Vaults, his balaclava'd head drooping to one side, looking like a puppet with its strings cut.

I gently rolled Nathan over, and to my relief found he was still breathing, before I staggered to my feet.

'You took your time,' I told Lugg.

He patted the evening newspaper which was sticking out of his jacket pocket. 'I was doin' the crossword when I heard the kerfuffle – that's five down by the way: disorganized street brawl, eight letters.'

'Nine, actually,' I corrected him, 'and try not to look so smug when the police arrive.'

'I don't mind this one,' he indicated his prone prisoner who was cringing under the pressure of his boot, 'but I won't take credit for that one with the broken jaw.' He pointed to the figure still spark-out by the wall.

'Why not? I thought you were the proud one-punch man.'

'I don't hit women I ain't been introduced to,' he said with a hangdog expression. Then added, 'Not usually.'

'Quite a story,' said Professor Danvers. 'This Lugg chap sounds a useful man to have in your corner.'

Mr Campion smiled. 'Indeed, although that day, I seemed to

be always in Lugg's corner. Still, I was very pleased that he showed up, even if it was a minute after the nick of time.'

'A really nasty experience. What happened next?'

'An ambulance arrived to take Nathan to hospital. He was badly battered and had a broken rib or two which put him off his feet for a while, but he recovered and, I'm happy to say, in spirit as well as body. Took his family and emigrated to Israel in the Fifties. I had quite a few bumps and bruises and bits of me black and blue for a month after, but the lasting damage was to a perfectly good pair of trousers which had been ripped at the knee in what Lugg called the kerfuffle.'

'I presume the police were called.'

'They were, and they arrived, to use the favourite phrase of a writer friend, with commendable promptitude. They almost arrested Lugg when they took the balaclava off the unconscious thug and found it was a woman.'

'Mary Gould,' said Danvers, 'and the man was Walter Lillman.'

'Indeed. You say Duffy got their names from a press report of their trial?'

'Actually their magistrates' hearing; showed me a photostat of a press cutting. It did not mention your friend Hirsch by name, just described him as a City silversmith, and it didn't mention you or your Mr Lugg at all.'

'He must have got access to the proceedings of the trial, which came later. I was told he was a good investigative journalist and that would be where he found our names, because both Lugg and I appeared prepared to act as witnesses. I remember Lugg being incredibly nervous, but then courtrooms had that effect on him, and I am probably guilty of not taking the case more seriously, or rather not remembering it.'

'It was forty years ago; you can forgive yourself the odd memory lapse. Take a leaf from the Romans, who believed only a man with a clear conscience has a bad memory.'

'You are paraphrasing Quintilian, I believe, and whilst I appreciate the sentiment, I am not sure I fully accept it. Still, it shows your time at Oxford wasn't wasted.'

Danvers grinned sheepishly. 'I have testimonials from several tutors who would disagree. But go on, what was the outcome of the trial?'

'It was fairly unspectacular; a bit of a damp squib, really. There was some argument I vaguely recall about suggesting it was a robbery gone wrong, but that was never going to stand up, so after a bit of legal chit-chat between our friends in the white wigs, the defendants pleaded guilty to assault and affray, with causing grievous bodily harm thrown in there somewhere. Nathan Hirsch wanted to put the whole thing behind him, and no big thing was made of the anti-Jewish aspect. He did not want them to become martyrs and inspire other half-wits; in fact, I don't think their membership of the Fascist League ever came up, but then my memory may be failing me again on that.'

'A sign of your clear conscience.'

'I would like to think so. Anyway, Gould and Lillman both got prison sentences; two or three years each, possibly. Duffy's notebook may tell us more.'

'I would be very grateful if you would share its contents with me,' said the professor, 'or rather any snippets which refer to the IFL or Mosley's Union of Fascists in the Thirties. It would all be grist to my academic mill.'

'Perhaps Duffy found the answers the police and the court could not.' Campion sat up straight in his chair, adjusted his spectacles more firmly on his nose and waited for Danvers to take his cue.

'Answers to what?'

'Gould and Lillman never admitted to having any associates in the attack – they always claimed they acted alone and, because they pleaded guilty, they were probably not pressed too hard on the matter. But there were definitely *four* attackers that night, one of whom I clouted with the tankard. I remember that distinctly, and so does Mr Lugg, and his memory is not troubled by any sort of conscience. We, or mostly Lugg, detained two of them, but two ran off into the fog.'

'And the police never found them?'

'They did not, but perhaps David Duffy did.'

THIRTEEN
The Duffy List

On or off duty, it was unusual for a policeman of Charlie Luke's seniority and importance to be seen in a public house as basic, not to say scruffy, as the Platelayers' Arms. It was a pub which even the most imaginative brewery public relations man would have described as past its best, though no one was quite sure when its heyday of splendour had actually been. It was one of those early Victorian beer-houses within scent and sound, though not sight, of the Thames near London Bridge, effectively camouflaged by post-war buildings which overshadowed the maze of back streets which had once housed its regular customers. Any wandering tourist aiming hopefully for the Tower would either miss it completely or, more likely, take one look at its faded paintwork, grimed windows and sign advertising a brewery which no longer existed except in the memory of Londoners of a certain age, and hurry on by.

Which was their loss in the opinion of Commander Luke, for the snug, inter-connected bars of the Platelayers' were still home to that endangered population of genuine London characters, not music hall 'cockney' comedians, but men and women who worked with their hands, had slept in an underground station during an air raid and regarded anything west of Oxford Circus as 'foreign', anything north of Walthamstow as 'countryside' and everything south of the river as unmentionable.

Although he knew, professionally, that a good proportion of the pub's clientele could never reasonably be described as angels with dirty faces, it was in the main an honest pub where one could leave a jacket over the back of a chair whilst playing a game of darts and come back to find your wallet still in the inside pocket. Luke, in his days as a beat copper, had experienced many a pub where not only would the wallet have disappeared, but also the jacket and even the chair.

Over the years, many years now, he and Mr Campion had
used the Platelayers' as a bolthole for clandestine meetings, as
the pub was well off any beaten track and they were unlikely
to be disturbed by anyone who knew them. And if they were
identified, so what? As a policeman, Luke had, within reason,
every right to go where and when he pleased if a warrant was
not required, and Albert Campion had long held, and taken pride
in, a reputation for frequenting places and mixing with people
whom others of his class and upbringing would politely baulk
at. He regarded his natural talent for cheerfully rubbing shoulders
with thieves and thief-takers as his most endearing feature,
whereas for Charlie Luke it was usually an uncomfortable occupational hazard. He was therefore appreciative of the unwritten
house rule of the Platelayers', which decreed that anyone of a
nefarious frame of mind or actively involved in any wrongdoing
would discreetly leave the pub when Luke entered, whether he
was on duty or off.

It was the convention at their meetings that the social element
should always outweigh the business agenda, and on no account
would official documents be produced by either party and no
written minutes would ever be taken. On that score, Campion
had always said there should be no concern as, when present,
which he often was, Lugg would automatically assume the role
of secretary, his penmanship being so poor that no record of the
meeting would ever stand up in court.

The one and only inviable rule was that whichever of them
was asking a favour of the other should buy the first round. Mr
Campion had a full pint of bitter waiting on the table to greet
Luke's arrival; Lugg was on his third.

'Been here long?' Luke asked, nodding a greeting and
acknowledging the waiting drink.

'A minute or two,' muttered Lugg sheepishly.

'Thank you for sparing the time, Charles,' said Campion. 'Once
again I feel guilty about dragging you away from your duties.'

'No, you don't, Albert, I know you far too well. I am, as usual,
at your beck and call.'

'I would genuinely feel guilty if I was diverting you from your
social life, though. How is Hattie, by the way?'

'On the edge of becoming a teenager,' Luke admitted with a

stage weariness which could not mask his obvious pride in his daughter. 'She runs rings round my old ma, but she loves it really.'

Luke's marriage had been seen as unwise by some and tragically sad by all when his wife died in childbirth, leaving a daughter to be natured and nurtured by Luke's mother, who seemed to have ingested some of Hattie's youthful energy and was now enjoying a new lease of life.

'Any movement on the Kathleen front?' Campion asked lightly.

About ten years after the death of his wife, Luke had admitted in strict confidence that he had finally plucked up the courage to see another woman. That the policeman, who was thought to have nerves of steel, would admit to nervousness under any circumstances had come as a surprise to his friends, but when it emerged that the Kathleen in question was a detective inspector in the Metropolitan Police, they realized that discretion was called for.

'We see each other as often as we can, and she gets on really well with Hattie,' said Luke, 'but if we go the extra mile and marry, then Kathleen will have to request a transfer or turn in her warrant card and her career with it.'

Lugg concentrated on the contents of his glass, which appeared to be evaporating. 'You want to make your move there, Charlie, before the flash boys in the Flying Squad spot her.'

'Ignore him, Charles,' rasped Campion. 'He's behind on his daily quota of uncouthness. Did you manage to dig up anything following my humble entreaty?'

'I have, but I have to ask if it has anything to do with your recent visit to Bedford, where my colleagues are involved in an ongoing investigation into a violent death.'

'I will not lie and am not being evasive, Charles, but the answer to that is: it may. Quite why a forty-year-old court case was of interest to our late journalist friend, however, is still a mystery.'

'A court case which involved you two? I'd have paid good money to be in the public gallery.'

'Couldn't have been that good,' slurped Lugg, glass-to-mouth. ''E couldn't even remember it.' He tapped a finger to the side of his head. 'Probably losing it, I reckon. The old memory bank's 'ad one too many withdrawals.'

'Had I been called to the witness stand, I am sure I would have made an impassioned plea for the prosecution, resulting in a sentence of transportation for the accused, though it seems unfair to lumber Australia with thugs like that. Perhaps Antarctica might have been an option.'

'But you were not called, Albert, and despite that, somehow justice seems to have been done and Mr and Mrs Lillman got sent down to Wormwood Scrubs and Holloway respectively.'

'Oo?' Lugg was quickest off the mark, so surprised he lowered his glass to the table.

'Walter Lillman and Mary Gould as was, they got hitched in 1936 right after they got out of jail. They got two and a half years apiece, but true love knows no bounds, apparently.'

Luke sat back on his chair, a pub-worn wooden affair which creaked under his weight, and waited for the question he guessed was forming behind Campion's glasses.

'How could you possibly know that, Charles? Two minor hooligans convicted of affray and assault forty years ago – how can they still be on your radar?'

'It took a bit of digging, I'll admit, and I had bit of help.'

'Girlfriend come in handy, did she?' smirked Lugg, but the smirk was wiped from his face by a glare from Campion.

'Let me guess, Charles. Walter and Mary were persons of interest to the police *after* they were released from prison and their marriage became part of their record. Was it a case of prison merely punishing and not reforming?'

'You can say that again. Within months of getting out, Walter and Mary had joined the British Union of Fascists – Mosley's mob – and even had an honour guard of Blackshirts at their wedding. They were involved in the Cable Street riot and several other unsavoury incidents, and were arrested numerous times, once by Essex police in 1938 after staging a protest at Dovercourt, up near Harwich, where children from the first *Kindertransport* had been lodged. They were both nasty pieces of work and probably deserved each other. Walter was interned along with a crowd of other Blackshirts during the war, but even that didn't cool him down. Soon as peace broke out, he was on the streets distributing disgusting little pamphlets proving how the communists and the Jews had combined to win the war.'

'That curious old alliance again . . .' breathed Mr Campion.

'He was never among the high-ups in the BUF, only ever a foot soldier, and prone to going off on personal vendettas, which usually got him into trouble with the magistrates. Walter did three short spells inside at His Majesty's pleasure for general affray, and the last time he graced a police notebook was in 1962, when we thought Mosley was making a bit of a comeback, or certainly Walter did. Yearning for the good old days, he picked up a brick and chucked it through the window of a Jewish grocer's in Stepney.'

'So it was back in the jug again for him?' Lugg had clearly been paying attention.

'No, as it turned out. He was spotted in the act by a bobby on foot patrol who gave chase. Walter legged it fast as he could and went straight under the wheels of a number twenty-five bus.'

'Poor devil,' Lugg murmured. 'The bus driver, I mean, not him.'

Campion and Luke exchanged knowing, not unsympathetic, glances.

'And Mary Gould, the widow Lillman?'

'Maybe she saw the light, I don't know, but she seems to have kept her nose clean since the war,' continued Luke. 'Wouldn't swear to her being a model citizen, but she hasn't come to our attention, so maybe she's settled for a quiet life.'

'No children from the marriage? No younger generation of storm troopers?'

'None, though Kath – the person who did the research for me – did turn up that she had a younger brother, Henry, who was a bit of a *cause célèbre* in his own right.'

'He shared his sister's politics?'

'And then some. He joined the army in '38 and was shipped over to France when the war started. He was in trouble right away, spreading dissention in the ranks about how we were fighting on the wrong side. Lost a couple of stripes because of that.'

'Another flamin' corporal stirring things up,' Lugg interjected. 'They should have put him up against a wall.'

'Next best thing happened,' said Luke. 'Before the shooting war started proper, Henry Gould upped sticks and deserted towards the nearest German outpost, with a white flag tied to his rifle and holding a German phrase book open at the page on how to surrender to the enemy. A roving patrol of Belgians challenged him and he must have thought it was the right time to change sides. He fired on them; they returned fire. They were much better at it than him.'

'Good for them.' Lugg nodded approval as he collected empty glasses and heaved himself towards the bar. 'Saved us a job and a bullet or two.'

'Is there any indication that brother Henry was involved with the Imperial Fascist League, as his sister was, back in 1932?'

'You're thinking he might be one of the brawlers who attacked Nathan Hirsch? I couldn't say, but if he was one of that gang it explains why Mary never gave up his name.'

'True, sibling loyalty coupled with political fanaticism would be a powerful combination, and I do think it a distinct possibility that Henry was among our attackers at the Silver Vaults. If it had been anyone other than her brother, she might well have given him up and earned herself a few Brownie points from the court.'

'That still leaves you with one that got away.'

'Yes, it does, doesn't it.'

Helping nephew Christopher in the matter of Lachlan McIntyre, Mr Campion felt, was turning into something of a pub crawl; to which Lugg had responded by asking rhetorically exactly what the problem with that was.

Most of Campion's reservations centred on the fact that he had now fully remembered an incident from forty years before, which he was ashamed to have forgotten, and along the way had learned much about a dark side of British politics, which he wished he could forget, yet little – in fact, nothing – seemed to connect with Sir Lachlan McIntyre or the late and little-lamented journalist David Duffy. He could only hope that Ron Lay-Flurrie, another newshound, might have sniffed out something significant in Duffy's notebook, but in order to hear his report, Lay-Flurrie had insisted on a meeting on licensed premises one minute after opening time at 11 a.m.

The timing and location of the proposed rendezvous were both interesting. It would be rare that, at 11.01 in the morning, even the most dedicated Fleet Street imbiber would be knocking on the door of the nearest pub; rare but not unknown. As the Old Bell Tavern was the final watering-hole on Fleet Street at the St Paul's end, it was likely to be the last choice of the thirsty journalist, and so Lay-Flurrie's meeting with Campion had a good chance of remaining private, or as private as anything could be in that street of sharp eyes and flapping ears.

Mr Campion knew the pub, reputed to have been the lodgings of the seventeenth-century stonemasons who had rebuilt St Paul's Cathedral for Christopher Wren, and appreciated the several shady seating nooks and crannies it offered, from which the main door could be discreetly observed.

He had arrived to find the place totally empty, apart from a bored barman running a damp cloth up and down wooden beer pumps. It was a task he seemed reluctant to abandon in order to serve Mr Campion with a tonic water spiced with a dash of Angostura bitters, but he did apologize for the fact that 'the ice hasn't come up yet'.

Campion told him not to worry, though he had shown no inclination to do so, and took his drink to a small round table in a shady corner. He had only just made himself comfortable when the door opened and Ron Lay-Flurrie bustled in, giving Campion the impression that *bustling* was the journalist's natural form of forward motion. Lay-Flurrie was clearly a regular customer, as the barman had started to pour him a bottled Guinness even as the street door swung closed behind him. The correct money was slapped on the bar, his drink collected and placed on Campion's table, all in a blur.

'I'll make this quick,' he said, fumbling for a cigarette. 'Got to be back in the office by twelve, there's more trouble brewing in Northern Ireland which you'll see on the front pages tonight and tomorrow.'

'And my problems don't amount to a hill of beans, as they say, though I've never quite understood the value of beans.'

'Don't worry about it, I'll get a story out of it.'

Mr Campion was sure he would and the prospect did not elate him.

'Duffy was certainly on to something,' said Lay-Flurrie, lighting up and exhaling smoke in one smooth movement, 'and it involved you forty years ago in an altercation with some British fascists and then a court case.'

'I am curious to know how Duffy associated me with the incident because, as it turned out, I was never actually called as a witness. I made statements to the police, of course, but I can't believe my small part in the affair made even the local press.'

Lay-Flurrie dug into his coat pocket and produced his own notebook, flipping over pages with the hand holding his cigarette and then having to gently blow fallen ash from the pages and then off the tabletop.

'You'd be surprised. Duffy dug up a paragraph from something called *The Passing Show.*'

'I remember that!' Campion exclaimed with glee. 'It was a popular magazine, always had a colour cover even back then; cost tuppence, I think. Did I rate a mention?'

'A short one, in the gossip column.' He took a gulp of Guinness and began to read from his notes. '*A recent unsavoury assault on a leading London silversmith in broad daylight was thwarted by the intervention of a passing pedestrian of note, Mr Albert Campion, the estranged younger brother of Herbert, Viscount K., and his manservant.* That's it, short and sweet.'

'And in the tradition of great British journalism, only about half right. Interesting that it glosses over the vile motive for the assault, which was openly anti-Semitic. Perhaps that was too unsavoury for the gossip columnists of the day.'

Lay-Flurrie leaned forward over the table, a gleam in his eye. 'But the "estranged brother of a viscount" bit was irresistible and still is today. That's why I think there's a story in here. You never took up the title, did you? Why didn't you?'

Campion took a sip of his drink, replaced the glass carefully on the table and, his face serious and blank, stared hard at the journalist. 'If you get a story out of this, it will be about David Duffy and why he was killed. It's his story, not mine, and if you try to put me at the centre of things, then our relationship must end here and now. I am sure there are other outlets in Fleet Street which might be interested.'

Lay-Flurrie ground out his cigarette in the table's ashtray and reached slowly for another, strenuously avoiding eye contact with Mr Campion as he lit up.

'We'll play it your way then,' he said at last through a sigh of grey smoke.

Campion inclined his head in acknowledgement, but decided not to trust the journalist as far as he could throw him. 'Did DCI Castor let you see Duffy's notebooks?'

'Reluctantly, but the girl trying to transcribe his shorthand didn't know T-line, only Pitman's.'

'And you do?'

'I've clocked one hundred and fifty words a minute, was one of the first to qualify when it came in; didn't want my reporters writing rude things about me I couldn't read. I think Castor was grateful for my help in clearing a few things up.'

'Did you find anything to help me in my quest?'

'I'm still not sure what your quest is, Mr Campion, but if you mean finding out who was behind Duffy's death, then we're on the same page for now.'

Lay-Flurrie balanced his cigarette in the ashtray, consulted his notebook then scooped up the cigarette before Campion or, just as unlikely, a passing seagull could snaffle it. The cigarette safely back between his lips, his eyes narrowed against a curl of smoke, he began to read.

'I copied this list just as it appeared in Duffy's own handwriting, not shorthand, though in different pens, which suggests to me the names were added at different times. They read, in order: Walter Lillman and Mary Gould, then in brackets just the initials N.H. Then comes A. Campion and M. Lugg. Then a space and then Henry Gould and L. McIntyre.'

'Was that my sole claim to fame?'

'No, there's a telephone number listed next to the initials A.C., and it's your Piccadilly flat. I checked. Did Duffy ever ring you?'

'No, we never spoke or met. Anything else of interest?'

'A lot of stuff about British fascists in the Thirties and references to that Professor Danvers I put you on to; also copious notes on the Battle of Cable Street as they called it, in '36. In fact, Duffy seemed fascinated with Stepney back then, though we're supposed to call it Tower Hamlets these days. There were a few addresses listed around the Commercial Road at that time, but no indication what they had to do with anything, and most will probably have disappeared thanks to either the Luftwaffe or the Greater London Council.'

'And about the names on the list?'

'There was a line under Henry Gould and a date, 1940. Then another line under Walter Lillman and another date, 1962 this time, plus the word Stepney again.'

'That all makes sense, actually.'

Lay-Flurrie tapped his cigarette on the edge of the ashtray. 'But I can't work out who N.H. was.'

'I can help you there,' said Campion. 'It stands for Nathan Hirsch, the "leading London silversmith" mentioned in that press cutting and a friend of mine. I was able, more by luck than judgement, to interpose myself between him and a vicious attack by British fascists.'

'Why would Duffy be interested in that?'

'I honestly do not know. It was forty years ago, but Walter Lillman and Mary Gould were two of the attackers and they ended up in court and then prison. Two were never identified or caught.'

'Mary Gould.' Lay-Flurrie looked up sharply from his note-book. 'Any relation to the Henry Gould also in Duffy's notes?'

'Brother and sister, though Henry died, somewhat ingloriously, in the war, in 1940 as Duffy noted.'

'Could he have been one of the attackers?'

'It is certainly possible, probably likely, but Gould and Lillman never gave up their accomplices.'

'And from the way Duffy drew a line under his name, it looks like Walter Lillman snuffed it in 1962.'

'I'm not sure "snuffed" is the accurate term for someone who went under a bus, but the sentiment is right.'

'That's a bit harsh, Mr Campion. I'm rather surprised at you.'

'Don't be. I am far too old to waste sympathy on the likes of Walter Lillman, who, I understand, retained his obnoxious world view right to the end.'

Lay-Flurrie's eyebrows rose and he let the moment hang. He ground out his cigarette before saying what Campion had been expecting. 'From the way Duffy listed the names, then, he was connecting Gould and Lillman to the attack on this Nathan Hirsch to you and M. Lugg – who's he, by the way?'

'A person of little consequence, mistakenly referred to as my manservant, though never by me.'

'So can we assume he was also connecting the next two names to the same incident, Henry Gould and L. McIntyre?'

'There's a good case for assuming that about Henry Gould,' Campion said carefully, 'but L. McIntyre, if you are thinking what I think you are thinking, then I simply don't see the possibility.'

'That Sir Lachlan McIntyre, captain of industry and man in line for a life peerage, might have been the fourth of your attackers?'

'I thought the prospect of a peerage was supposed to be secret.'

The journalist shrugged. 'This is Fleet Street.'

'Well, Fleet Street should know that Lachlan McIntyre was a young orphan fresh out of Glasgow in 1932, and highly unlikely to be a member of the Imperial Fascist League. If he had been, Professor Danvers would surely have noticed. Did Duffy note anything which might suggest that?'

'Not specifically.' Lay-Flurrie flipped a page of his shorthand notes which, upside down, looked like hieroglyphics to Campion. 'But among the phone numbers listed was McIntyre's, as well as that of your nephew, Christopher.'

'No surprise there. He had met with Christopher as McIntyre's PR man and was negotiating a face-to-face interview. Was there any indication of what he might have asked Sir Lachlan at that meeting?'

'Not really. The last page only had one thing on it, a name written in T-line: Mary Gould. It might have been a reminder to himself to ask Sir Lachlan about her, but that's pure guesswork. At the very least, though, it suggests she was significant in Duffy's research.'

'My understanding is that that interview did not go well, and McIntyre stood up and walked out rather angrily.'

'Was he angry enough to lure him out into the sticks and shoot him?'

'Unlikely. I think he's the sort who, if scorned by a journalist, would reach for his lawyer rather than his shotgun, but the police are satisfied that he had a watertight alibi for the night of the shooting.'

'Still, isn't it possible that the name Mary Gould could have touched a nerve, been a trigger, so to speak?'

'More guesswork, I think.' Campion noted the journalist checking his watch, and the fact that he was not reaching for his cigarettes indicated the meeting was coming to a close.

'But worth asking him?'

'Now I'm guessing that you mean me asking him.'

'It would come better from you. Journalists are not McIntyre's favourite people at the moment.'

'You may be right. Was there anything else I should be aware of in Duffy's notes?'

'A couple of addresses jotted down randomly. No names with them, just addresses, one in Stepney, one in Dagenham.' Lay-Flurrie produced a ballpoint pen from his top pocket, the end of its plastic tube crushed and scarred where it had been chewed. 'I'll write them out for you. Do you want the phone numbers as well?'

'I know how to get hold of Christopher and Sir Lachlan, and I do try and remember my own number.'

'What about the other one?'

'What other one?'

'Just a number, no name, but Duffy had underlined it twice. It has an 0708 code, which is Romford. Does that mean anything to you?'

'Not a thing.'

'Why don't you ring it and see if it's a clue?'

'We could certainly do with one,' admitted Mr Campion.

FOURTEEN

Armamentarium

'I'm sorry but you can't come in. I don't allow strange men into the house when I'm alone. My husband is away chasing wild geese in Bedfordshire.'

'Then I will have to use force and hold you hostage, fair lady, until you have made a pot of tea and toasted a brace of crumpets.'

'What a cheek! I've a good mind to whistle up one of my many lovers from the ground staff to see you off the premises.'

'You know how to whistle, sweetheart?' Mr Campion did his Humphrey Bogart impersonation, a party piece which usually made his wife dissolve into fits of giggles. 'You just put your lips together and—'

'Enough!' his wife commanded. 'Have you finished running errands for Christopher?'

'For the moment, my dear, but I am on the road again tomorrow. Now, if we have given your lovers time to escape through the bathroom window, which I believe is the traditional route, may I come in?'

Mr Campion had driven home to Norfolk that afternoon, ostensibly to clear his head and marshal his thoughts, not that the long drive would help in that respect. He was well past the age when driving in the countryside had moved from pleasure to chore, unlike those carefree pre-war days – pre-amnesia days – when he and Lugg zipped about in the Bentley chasing, as Amanda would have it, a dubious silver tankard and a boy who had run away with the gypsies. At least his memory wasn't disappearing completely. With a little prompting he had recalled the escapade of the Gidney tankard and the eventual confrontation with Lancelot Drinkwater and, shamefully late in the day, the assault on Nathan Hirsch, though what it all had to do with Sir Lachlan McIntyre and David Duffy was still unclear.

An evening at home with Amanda would help him to order his thoughts or, blissfully and without guilt, legitimately forget the whole affair.

His wife was used to being a sounding board whenever Campion was confused or concerned, though never just a kindly pair of receptive ears. If he had a problem and was willing to talk about it – though there had been a few occasions when he had, on his honour, not been able to discuss certain matters – then she would try and offer a solution. It had become a family saying within the Campion household that a problem shared may not be a problem halved, but now at least two people lost sleep over it.

Over dinner, he recounted the progress of his investigation, confident that he had skilfully glossed over his flickering memory when it came to remembering events of forty years before, but posing the important question of why David Duffy had been interested in those events in the first place. There was no possibility, however, that Amanda would fail to detect the weakness in his story.

'There was a time when Albert Campion would have immediately picked up on the initials N.H. standing for Nathan Hirsch.'

'It was forty years ago, darling, before you took charge of me.'

'And I am sure that back in 1932 you were engaged in street brawls with fascists on a regular basis, and one in particular, where you single-handedly rescued an old friend and prevented Lugg being beaten to a pulp, was hardly worth remembering.'

Mr Campion had the good grace to blush slightly. 'The incident might not have transpired *exactly* as I may have described it . . .'

'I could always ask Lugg for his version.'

'There's no need for that. Once prompted, Lugg remembered the incident quite clearly; I was simply slow on the uptake. I must be getting old. Forgetfulness increases with age, does it not?'

'You are getting old, you silly old owl, but not that old. When you forget to put your trousers on in the morning, then I'll call in the chaps with the electric shock machine.'

'Would that help?'

'Probably not, but it might be amusing.'

'There's a cruel side to you I never knew about.'

'Yes, you did; it's just another thing which slipped your memory, along with my birthday and our last two wedding anniversaries.' Amanda kept a deadpan countenance for a good ten seconds before she burst out laughing. 'Darling – your face! I was joking, but now I am not. Tell me honestly, was this lapse connected to your real bout of amnesia?'

'That was years later, at the start of the war, and I recovered completely.'

'You were bonked on the head and woke up to find yourself married to me.' Amanda smiled sweetly.

'And that's what I call a complete recovery. I don't know what it was which caused my blind spot. Perhaps it was finding myself listed in the notebook of a journalist I had neither met nor offended.'

'Your problem, Albert Campion,' declaimed his wife earnestly, 'is that you have always sought the good opinion of others. When a muck-raking journalist makes a note of your name without an obvious cause, it throws you off balance.'

'We don't *know* that Duffy was muck-raking,' said Campion, although he admitted it sounded weak.

'He was an investigative journalist investigating a millionaire businessman who has been involved in some dubious government contracts in the past and is now up for a peerage. There was bound to be muck to be raked, and not only from his snooty wife's horses.'

'Snooty?'

'Well, difficult, then; unsociable. A woman with a chip – no, a bag of chips – on her shoulder.'

'She does a lot of work for charity,' said Campion, 'you told me that yourself.'

'She has raised cash for Cranfield, that's true, but on the committees that she sits on she's known as "Lady M." but that's "M." as in Macbeth not McIntyre.'

'From what I saw in their house, they have an impressive armoury of rifles, but I didn't see before me any daggers dripping with blood. They are an odd couple, though. They seem to enjoy living an isolated life next to a field full of machinery in a desolated village now inhabited only by their workers – or should that be retainers?'

'They do not have a reputation for entertaining, that's for sure,' said Amanda. 'Perhaps they put a premium on their privacy, which would explain Lachlan's explosion when Duffy asked him personal questions.'

'You could be right,' agreed her husband. 'I wonder if those names on Duffy's list triggered the reaction.'

Amanda fluttered her eyelashes, looking up wide-eyed from under her fringe. 'There was a time when mention of the name Albert Campion could produce a very passionate reaction.'

'I didn't mean me. When we met he was neither shocked nor violent – and certainly not passionate! I was thinking of Lillman and Gould, both the Goulds; and there was a place, Stepney, which keeps cropping up. I wonder if any of those have a special meaning for him. I have set Christopher and Lugg various tasks to help clarify the situation.'

'But you know you will have to confront him yourself, if only for your own peace of mind, which is a polite way of saying the curiosity will drive you crazy if you don't.'

'As ever, you are right, my dear, which is why I have arranged to meet Sir Lachlan tomorrow, beard him in his den and ask him.'

'Are you tackling him in his *armamentarium*?'

'I expect so.'

'Well, for goodness' sake, make sure none of those rifles are loaded.'

Mr Campion had always been slightly embarrassed to admit that guns could be something to be admired, although only antique ones and then only from a safe distance. Perhaps it was a masculine failing to admire the ingenuity, craftsmanship and, yes, exquisite artistry which had, over the centuries, been devoted to making something so deadly so beautiful.

Firearms had fascinated far greater minds than his, as he had learned from a very privileged viewing of Leonardo's design drawing for multi-barrelled 'organ guns' in the Royal Library at Windsor, and he was made aware of their part in London's history when, as a youth, he had seen Samuel Whitbread's collection of muskets with which he had promised to arm all his Chiswell Street brewery workers, had the French Revolution dared to cross the Channel.

He had been drawn to, even charmed, by a seventeenth-century German wheel-lock rifle with an inlaid silver cheek-plate decorated with a scene showing Pyramus and Thisbe, and a double-barrelled sporting gun, its stock intricately decorated in gold and silver, which had been given by Louis XIV to Charles XI of Sweden. In his opinion, the gold damascening had only been surpassed and enhanced with mother-of-pearl inlay when depicting a hunting scene on a pair of English snaphance pistols, which had once been the property of Tsar Michael Romanov and were now grudgingly displayed in the Kremlin.

Even when at their most brutal and severe – perhaps because their business was brutal and severe – flintlock duelling pistols could always captivate because of the stories they might have told. Campion remembered having once handled a pair of Scottish all-steel 'fishtail' pistols, made by Murdoch of Doune near Stirling in 1770, and had been amused to learn that they had proved militarily useless but had become a vital fashion accessory for the well-dressed fan of the romances of Sir Walter Scott. Far less aesthetically pleasing, and probably quite deadly, he had been gratified to discover that a pair of ugly, 'saw-handle' pistols with octagonal barrels, ordered from Mortimer of London ('Gunmakers to His Majesty') by a distant ancestor, had only been delivered long after duelling fell out of favour in England.

Mr Campion's first thought on a close view of Sir Lachlan's armoury was that the iron grilles, padlocked and chained, which imprisoned it were entirely appropriate. There were six hunting rifles mounted horizontally on wooden pegs, one above the other, each of them as coldly impersonal and deadly as the next. Below them, barrels facing in the opposite direction, were hung three shotguns. These were more interesting, historically and aesthetic-ally, as they were genuine antiques and had opted for smooth curves, polished wood and gold inlay, rather than stark, stream-lined functionality. They were also, Campion liked to think, less dangerous than their high-powered rifle cousins, though he would be hard pushed to find a pheasant or a partridge to agree with him.

Pride of place, racked above the other two, was an immacu-lately fine example of the work of Messrs Holland and Holland of 98 New Bond Street, London – the address engraved along the barrel – which, Campion estimated, with a mental sigh of resignation, was at least ten years older than he was.

'Do you shoot?' McIntyre asked, startling Campion out of his reverie.

'As little as possible,' said Campion, recovering. 'Never really had the stomach for it, nor the eyesight to be sure of a clean kill.'

'You can get sights made with your prescription lenses these days, you know.'

'Then I really would be dangerous.' Campion grinned and

pointed at the shotguns in the lower half of the gun cage. 'Not that I couldn't cause a fair bit of damage blasting away with one of those if they still worked.'

Sir Lachlan softened both his stance and his voice. Having first greeted Mr Campion with poorly concealed irritation, he sensed a genuine interest in his prized possessions by the visitor.

'Oh, I think they still work,' he said, not realizing that Campion's curiosity was more inspired by forensics than aesthetics. 'The problem is getting the ammunition. That Holland and Holland you're drooling over was made in 1885, and the company will still make shells for you, but I don't bother. Like looking at them and handling them, but if I'm stalking deer, I need a good modern rifle.'

Campion's eyes flitted around the room, noting the various antlered heads whose glassy eyes seemed to indicate agreement. 'So they would be covered by the latest Antique Firearms Act?'

'I believe so. The rifles are all licensed and we get visits from the police to check up on them.' McIntyre made a derisory snorting noise. 'Used to think of those inspections as a bit of an imposition, but with the recent hoo-hah, it was quite useful to have the local firearms officer back me up and say no ammunition had been used and no rifle fired in the last two months since his regular visit.'

'You have no other . . . exhibits . . . around the place?'

'Spivey, who looks after my wife's horses, has a .410 rook gun out in the stables,' Sir Lachlan answered casually, as if discussing the weather and failing to note the change in Campion's expression, 'to keep the vermin down – where there are horses bedded down, there are usually rats. He sometimes gets lucky with rabbit or a pheasant if they wander within fifteen yards of him.'

'Spivey has a shotgun licence?' Campion's tone was sharper than he had intended.

'Well, no. Technically it's my gun, but I am not interested in potting birds or rodents and it would be useless against decent game, probably downright cruel. I want clean kills, not to inflict injury.' Now his expression changed, his eyes narrowing. 'What made you ask such a thing?'

'I wondered if Mr Spivey, who seemed a perfectly polite and

competent chap when I met him, would be allowed to hold a permit, given his criminal convictions.'

'How did you know about that?' McIntyre spoke with a grimace and Campion was relieved to be standing between him and the display of rifles.

'It was a guess, until you just confirmed it. Your chaps in the depot, the only other residents of Markley Desolation, all have a jailbird hue about them, so I assumed Spivey might be from a similar background. I cast no aspersions; it is noble of you to give reformed offenders a second chance, as long as they are reformed.'

'I do not seek your approval, Campion. I gave those men a second chance when few others would have. As a result, I have created a hard-working and extremely loyal workforce.'

Loyal, or perhaps 'beholden', thought Campion, even possibly 'indentured', given the provision of company accommodation, but he said nothing as he had no desire to antagonize the millionaire.

'I am not interested in how you manage your employees,' he said, 'unless David Duffy was.'

Sir Lachlan arched a lip at the very mention of the journalist's name, determined not to use it himself. 'That man wasn't really interested in the working of my business in the slightest. He only asked damned impertinent personal questions, which is why I wouldn't give him the time of day. Put a flea in his ear, as a matter of fact.'

'So I understand, and I am rather surprised Duffy did not mention the fact in his notebook; it might have made a good headline: Captain of Industry defenestrates a member of Her Majesty's Press.'

Now McIntyre's lip curled into a twisted grin. 'If there had been a window handy, by God I would have chucked him through it. He wormed his way past my public relations man, who isn't the sharpest knife in the kitchen drawer . . . Oh, he's your nephew, isn't he? No offence, Campion.'

'None taken,' murmured Mr Campion complicitly.

'I thought he wanted to talk about my business empire – and don't look surprised I call it my empire, because that's what my wife and I have built up, and we're proud of it. But all *that worm* wanted to ask about was my personal life and my misspent youth.'

'Was it misspent?'

'Wasn't yours? If it was, I don't expect you to tell me about it. My business may be public property, but my private life is mine and only mine. I certainly wasn't going to answer that grubby lowlife's impertinent questions about bloody Stepney before the war.'

'Stepney?' Campion tried to sound interested but unexcited. 'Now Stepney did figure in Duffy's notebook.'

'God knows why he was interested; I've been trying to forget the damn place for thirty years. Did you know the old Stepney, Campion? I wouldn't have thought it was the sort of place somebody like you would be seen dead in.'

'You might be surprised at the places I've been and the things I've seen. They surprise me at times.' Campion beamed what Amanda called his second-best inane grin. 'And I have been to Stepney, as anyone with an interest in English battlefields really has to.'

'Battlefields?'

'Well, perhaps not technically battlefields; one was a siege and the other a riot – Sidney Street and Cable Street.'

If Campion was testing McIntyre, it was a remarkably easy exam, as any Londoner of his generation would be well aware of the story of the siege of Sidney Street in 1911 and the gunfight between the police and the army and a pair of Latvian Bolsheviks, made famous by the presence, duly photographed, on the firing line of the then Home Secretary, a certain Winston Churchill. He was far more interested in Sir Lachlan's reaction to the mention of Cable Street, and the running battle which took place there in October 1936 involving the police – the British Union of Fascists organizing a demonstration in a predominantly Jewish neighbourhood and the local residents and anti-fascist groups determined to stop them. It had certainly been a subject of considerable interest to the late David Duffy.

'I don't think either are places of pilgrimage; certainly not to me. I was glad to get out of Stepney. The slum clearances before the war caused almost as much damage as the Luftwaffe did during it.'

'It was once known as the capital of the East End,' said Campion lightly.

'Well, it certainly didn't feel like a Paris or a Rome, though even they have areas where tourists are not encouraged. Stepney was a place to leave, not visit.'

'But you lived there, at the time of Cable Street.' McIntyre scowled and Campion immediately confessed. 'It is part of your public relations biography on which Christopher briefed me.'

Sir Lachlan seemed less than pleased with the admission. 'Yes, in a gruesome house in Bignold Court which, mercifully, is now long gone, with an aunt of mine who took me in and battered the Scots accent out of me. She'd lived in London since she was a girl and always said that on the docks, they don't trust the Jocks, so I had to try and blend in.'

'I did notice the absence of the Highland lilt I was half expecting.'

'I was never a Highlander, and during the war anyone with a thick Glaswegian accent was only good for the lower ranks of the army or as an engineer's mate on a merchant ship.'

'You stayed on the docks during the war? That was pretty dangerous, wasn't it, being a juicy target for the Luftwaffe? All they had to do was follow the river to find a target, easy enough on a moonlit night.'

'That's why I joined the fire service. Being a dock worker was a reserved occupation so I couldn't join up, but that way I could do my bit. I saw much of Stepney burn and, honestly, didn't shed many tears.'

'You must have felt for your neighbours,' Campion said cautiously. 'All that community spirit – "The East End Can Take It" was the slogan, wasn't it?'

'Perhaps it could, but I could not take the East End.' As McIntyre spoke, his nostrils flared as if detecting a foul smell. 'We moved out as soon as we could and never looked back.'

'But if I may return to Duffy's notebook,' Campion weighed his words carefully, 'he seemed to be interested in certain addresses in Stepney and some people who may have lived there when you did.'

'That was thirty years ago, Campion, and I thought I'd heard the last of Duffy's prying questions.'

Campion risked provoking Sir Lachlan's wrath and pressed on. 'Can I take you back even further, to 1932: does the name Mary Gould mean anything to you?'

'Not a thing, as I told the police.'

'Mary Lillman, perhaps? Or Walter Lillman?'

'Less than nothing.'

'Are you sure? Duffy had an address for them on Bromley Street, and an old street atlas which showed it to be just round the corner from Bignold Court, so you could have been neighbours.'

'Did you not hear me? Those people mean nothing to me.' McIntyre bristled, then his gaze switched to the large rectangular window which looked out over the garden and paddock. 'But if you don't believe me, ask my wife.'

If Sir Lachlan had needed assistance with his irritating visitor, then his wife certainly seemed to be providing it by riding at some speed to his rescue towards the house, hunched low over the neck of the big chestnut which Campion remembered was called Buckland.

He had followed McIntyre on to the slim terrace looking out over the garden, as the horse and its rider approached the paddock fence with such velocity that Campion was sure the intention was to jump it. There was definitely something of the avenging fury about Lady M., as he now thought of her, for she seemed to be auditioning as one of the Four Horsewomen, but there was to be no apocalypse. She reined in her mount and brought Buckland to a snorting, steaming halt by the fence opposite the hideous ornate fountain in the middle of the garden, just as Campion and her husband reached it.

She slapped the neck of the horse and whispered sweet nothings, or lethal commands, in its ear before deigning to acknowledge the two men.

'Darling, Mr Campion wants to know something,' said McIntyre, making no attempt to move closer, a decision which Mr Campion, remaining at his side, was sure was a wise one.

'I'm sure he does,' shouted back the horsewoman, who made no attempt to dismount but made a show of rubbing Buckland's withers and then wiping her hands on the hem of her light brown tweed hacking jacket.

'Don't do that,' wailed Sir Lachlan. 'Let Spivey rub him down; you'll have to get that jacket dry-cleaned.' Then, out of the corner of his mouth, he whispered to Campion in man-to-man confidentiality, 'Cost me a fortune from Laura Ashley, that did.'

It was, thought Campion, the rich man's prerogative to worry about the cost of his wife's fashionable riding coat rather than that of the horse, its feed, stabling and grooming.

'Carl will cool him down.' Carl Spivey was indeed approaching, right on cue, from the stable block. 'What is it Mr Campion wanted to know?'

'A little bit of history,' Campion said, pre-empting Sir Lachlan, 'about when you lived in Stepney before the war.'

Whether her grip tightened involuntarily on the reins or her knees dug into his flanks, Buckland startled and his front legs rose up. It was a movement not violent enough to unseat, or even disturb, this rider, and reminded Campion of one of the famous Lipizzaners practising a dance move in the Spanish Riding School in Vienna. It did cause Spivey to increase his bow-legged gait and close the distance between them and, by the time Buckland had all four hooves back on the ground, Spivey was fondling his nose, making calming cooing noises into his flared nostrils.

'That is a place and a time I would rather forget and certainly have no wish to remember, apart from the early days of marriage to Lachlan, of course,' said the dutiful wife, aiming her words at her husband before turning to glare at Campion. 'As you can see, we have moved on since then.'

Even though he was well out of range of flashing hooves and snapping teeth, Mr Campion felt distinctly uncomfortable as the woman literally talked down to him from astride the horse. It was almost as if he were a small boy being admonished by a strict, and very tall, headmaster, or in this case, headmistress.

'It's a small thing, Lady McIntyre, and I have asked your husband, but if you could cast your mind back to your first days of wedded bliss in Bignold Court in Stepney, can you recall someone, a neighbour perhaps, called Mary Gould? Her married name was Lillman if that helps.'

Lady McIntyre raised her eyes to the sky and reached a hand behind her head to pull her long blonde ponytail around, laying it over her right shoulder and breast. Once it hung there down the front of her coat, she clutched it with a fist and repeatedly pulled down as though wringing water from it.

'Does my husband remember that name?'

'He said he did not.'

'Then it means absolutely nothing to me. Take us in, Carl, if you would.'

Campion was in no doubt that he had been dismissed, but he stayed where he was and watched as the diminutive Spivey took Buckland's reins and led horse and rider towards the stable block. He could tell that the woman was now using both hands to pull and squeeze her long braid of hair, and wondered if the affectation had anything to do with her apparent aversion to wearing a riding helmet.

One thing he knew for sure; that she had lied to him.

Just as her husband had.

The thought and the image of Lady McIntyre looking down at him from her horse haunted Campion for most of the drive to London, but at Bottle Street he did not mention his creeping unease, rather he insisted on debriefing Christopher and Lugg.

'I tracked down Sabin Danvers as you requested.' Christopher had the PR man's knack of making a simple phone call sound like a quest to find a Yeti. 'He did some checking and discovered that Henry Gould was indeed a member of the Imperial Fascists at the same time as his sister and Walter Lillman. Does that mean he was one of your friend Nathan's attackers?'

'Not conclusively,' Campion had said, 'but very probably. Thank you, that was useful.' He turned to Lugg, who was busy levering the top off a pint bottle of brown ale. 'And how about your expedition to the East End?'

The fat man carefully poured beer into a glass until the foaming head was to his required depth and drank deeply before answering.

'I've a pocket full of bus and tube tickets for which I will require reimbursement, not to mention a couple of receipts from licensed Hackney carriages,' he announced with gravitas.

'Oh, please,' scoffed Campion. 'I know you get your taxi receipts knocked up by the score in that dodgy printworks over Southwark Bridge. Now, get on with it.'

'So I goes out to Stepney to find half of it's not there any more, certainly not this Bignold Court you're so interested in so, against my better judgement o'course, I asked around in a couple of the pubs off the Commercial Road. I fink it was the Lord Nelson, but I may be wrong, where I struck gold. Just about all the reg'lars in the public bar 'ad 'eard of Walter Lillman an' his wife Mary and all agreed they were a pair of nutters, always on about Jews and communists and stirring it up, which the locals didn't like 'cos it attracted the attention of the coppers.'

'What about Lachlan McIntyre?'

Lugg shook his massive head. 'Nothing doin' apart from one old boy, used to be an ARP warden, who thought he remembered a young Jock called Leckie who was a fireman and had a reputation for being the first into a burning house during the Blitz. Said he should have got a medal, though he didn't know what happened to him.'

'That sounds like a dead end,' said Campion, 'which is a pity.'

'Hey! I ain't finished,' Lugg complained, attempting to look hurt. 'Being one who always follows orders—'

'The script says *pause for laughter* at this point. Sorry, do continue.'

'—so I followed up the gossip on this Mary Gould. Word was her and her husband got moved out during the war and got resettled up in Dagenham on the Becontree council estate. One of the locals even had a bit of an address for her, for forwarding the post; mostly bills and summonses, from what I heard.

'Anyway, your good soldier here slogs over to Dagenham and the estate and finds the right banjo. That's what they call a cul-de-sac, pardon my French, on the Becontree, 'cos of the shape the houses are laid out. I finds the right house, but there's nobody home, leastways nobody called Mary Gould.

'According to the neighbours, after her husband died – and Walter was not much missed, by all accounts – the widow Lillman came into a load of money and she moved up in the world. No more dodging the rent man for Mary; she bought herself a house in a posh bit of Romford. Don't know where, though.'

'Romford?' Campion clapped his hands together. 'There was a Romford phone number in Duffy's notebook. We can trace an address from that.'

'I thought only policemen could do that,' said Lugg lugubri-
ously, 'and pretty senior policemen as well. Know any?'

FIFTEEN
The Fire Pirate

Even before he rang the doorbell, Mr Campion knew things
were not going to go to plan. He had told Christopher to
be prepared to put his foot in the door, which would probably be slammed in their faces, but Christopher was sulking
following the ridiculous argument they had had on the drive into
Romford.

As they passed the famous Ind Coope brewery, Christopher,
as driver and self-appointed tour guide, announced the event just
in case his uncle had failed to notice the large, imposing building
with its explanatory signage. The problem was he pronounced it
'*Eye*-nd Coope' and Mr Campion could not help correcting him.

'I think you'll find it's Ind as in "in" not as in "mind" or
"blind".'

'Are you sure? I did some research on them with a view to
pitching for their public relations account. All the larger breweries
are now looking for PR men since that Campaign for Real Ale
ginger group was set up. All the beer drinkers I talked to called
it "Eye-nd" Coope.'

'Well, you can always ask Lugg, who is the authority on such
matters, but I prefer to believe the very nice chap I met a couple
of years ago who introduced himself as George *Ind* and said "as
in the brewery".'

'He was the owner?'

'Not at all, said he no longer had anything to do with the
family business as he would have been quite useless at it, but
he had inherited a barrel-full of shares and lived quite comfortably off the income. Never had to have a proper job, so devoted
his life to birdwatching. That's where I met him, on a ramble
through some woods up near Pontisbright. A charming fellow,

and one of the happiest and most contented chaps I've ever come across.'

Christopher, now convinced he had failed to land the brewery's public relations contract because he had pronounced its name incorrectly, drove in silence until they reached the address kindly provided through yet another favour from Charles Luke and Scotland Yard.

'Perhaps you should have brought Lugg,' he said when Campion, finger poised over doorbell, suggested he should have his foot ready as a doorstop if needed.

'Don't be silly. I have probably changed beyond all recognition in forty years, but Lugg's dimensions have not. I doubt I could pick her out in a line-up, but I bet she remembers that looming figure from outside the Silver Vaults who socked her in the jaw. Probably still has nightmares about it. I have nightmares about Lugg and he never laid a glove on me.'

The doorbell pressed, they heard the tinkling echo of a chime which reminded Campion of an ice-cream van disappearing around a corner. The house it guarded was a respectable-enough post-war semi in an avenue of identical ones, and distinguished from its neighbours only by an unkempt front garden and the fact that the window frames were in need of a coat of paint. It had, like every other dwelling, chintz curtains ideal for twitching and there was no sign of a car parked in the road nearby, so when the curtains failed to twitch, Campion feared no one was home.

Then came a scuffling sound followed by the click of a Yale lock, and the door was partly opened by a small, dark-haired woman wearing an ankle-length housecoat and pink fluffy slippers. She wore National Health spectacles, behind which her eyes were narrow slits against the smoke curling up from a cigarette dangling from a slash of bright red lipstick. Unconsciously Campion could not help comparing the woman to his own Amanda, something he did whenever a new female from the same generation came into his orbit. He knew the woman must be of a similar age but, even being charitable, she looked ten years older, her lips and cheeks puckered and creased by a lifetime of smoking.

Mr Campion removed his fedora as he asked, 'Mrs Lillman?'

'Yus?' Her voice confirmed the smoking theory.

'I wondered if you could spare my colleague and me a few minutes of your time?'

Christopher smiled his best public relations smile to prove, if the woman needed convincing, that he was an unthreatening, innocent participant. If she noticed him at all, she did not seem threatened, but she did tip her head on one side to examine Campion more carefully.

'I ain't buying nothin' and I got squat to sell if you're totting.'

Campion resisted the urge to smile, partly at Christopher's bemused expression and partly at his own thought that you might take the girl out of the East End, but you'll never get the East End out of the girl. 'I assure you, we are not rag-and-bone men,' he said, mainly for Christopher's benefit, 'and we have absolutely nothing to sell. We just want a word, that's all.'

'What abaht?' the woman said suspiciously. 'I don't give 'ouse room to religions of any stripe nor anyone wanting my vote, an' I 'aven't let a rent man across the threshold in years.'

As if that settled the matter, she began to close the door. Seeing that Christopher's foot was not forthcoming as a blocking device, Campion placed a palm on the door and gently pushed back.

'It's about an incident in London some time ago, forty years ago in fact, which involved you and your late husband,' Campion said slowly and carefully, 'and possibly your brother Henry.'

'He's dead too, long gone.' The woman said it without a trace of emotion, then she opened the door wider and looked her visitors up and down from head to toe. 'You ain't police.'

'We're in public relations,' said Christopher, and Mr Campion winced, but snapped himself to full attentiveness at the woman's response.

'You'll be after a story, then. Well, I don't come cheap these days.'

Christopher's mouth fell open and he could manage only a shocked stare, whilst Campion leaned forward until his face was only inches from the woman's, partly to distract her from his nephew's dumb show, but also to get a closer look at her – and allow her a closer look at him.

'We are indeed after a story, Mrs Lillman,' he said eagerly, 'and of course we are willing to pay the market price and cover any out-of-pocket expenses. May we come in? Business such as ours is best not discussed in the street.'

Mrs Lillman studied Campion's face before answering, though Mr Campion could not tell if there had been any spark of recognition behind those health service glasses. For his part he was sure, despite the ravages of time, bad diet and cigarettes, that this was the woman Lugg had laid low outside the Silver Vaults on a foggy night in 1932. Immediately he felt a sharp stab of guilt that for forty years he had retained no memory of this woman whom he had helped send to prison. Perhaps if he had confronted her across a courtroom from the witness box, he would have retained a more lasting impression. The question now before him was had she remembered him?

The woman considered Campion's offer for perhaps ten seconds of silence, then allowed the door to swing fully open.

'You'd best come in then, but I'm on the evening shift down the Golden Lion and I'll have to get ready for that, so you take me as you find me.'

Now that we have found you, we will, Campion thought as he followed her into the house and the front sitting room, where he guessed no piece of furniture was more than five years old and the tiled fireplace now housed a quite ghastly three-bar electric fire, nestling among plastic logs and imitation flames. There were no books visible anywhere, something Campion always checked for when entering a room for the first time, but one of the largest colour televisions he had ever seen. Parked strategically in front of it was a pair of chrome-and-faux-fur recliner chairs, complete with matching footstools. When waved to a seat, both he and Christopher opted to perch on the very edge of a floral two-seater sofa, which on first contact clearly offered less lumbar support than a plastic bag of cold porridge.

'So what's your offer?' said the woman, ignoring her guests and striding to the fireplace, where she retrieved a packet of cigarettes and a box of matches from the mantelpiece.

Only when he had firmly planted his feet and was sure he was not going to sink back and be swallowed by the fabric of the sofa did Campion answer.

'My offer is for Mary Gould and it relates to a little piece of history we share,' he said as a judge might pass sentence or a vicar announce the text he had taken for his sermon.

Whilst he had suspected the woman was not a regular church-goer, her reaction still startled him as she leaned over him and blew a stream of smoke directly into his face.

'Should I know you?' she snapped and then, more aggressively, 'What's your name?'

Unnerved, Christopher stuttered 'C . . . c . . . Campion.'

'Which one of youse?'

'Both of us, actually,' said Mr Campion, 'but I am the senior one.'

'That's bleedin' obvious, but it means nothing to me. Now, what're you after?'

Campion studied the woman's face and could detect no sign that she had recognized him or his name.

'I'm interested in your life in Stepney, before the war, and whether you knew a man called McIntyre back then.'

Mrs Lillman put her fists on her hips and leaned back, so that her next stream of smoke from the cigarette now clenched between her yellowing teeth went harmlessly over Campion's head. 'I guessed as much.' As she spoke, her hands still on her hips, the cigarette danced across her mouth, spilling ash and sparks down the front of her housecoat. 'So what's your offer?'

'I'm sorry,' said Christopher, bemused. 'Offer?'

'For my story. How much?'

'I take it you've already had an offer,' said Mr Campion smoothly. 'May I be so bold as to ask whether it came from Mr David Duffy?'

Now the senior Campion had her full attention.

'That may be so, but it would be my business.'

'I'm afraid any agreement you had with Mr Duffy may now be null and void.'

She snatched the cigarette from her mouth and pointed its glowing end at Campion. 'What yer mean by that?' she rasped.

'You don't know, do you? David Duffy is no longer in the market for your story. I'm afraid I am your best and only customer now.'

Mrs Lillman jabbed the air with her cigarette, as if stabbing an invisible wasp. 'You stay put; I'll be back.'

She left the room in a pall of smoke and a rustle of nylon, closing the door firmly behind her.

'Where's she gone?' whispered Christopher.

Mr Campion, his ears pricked for the sound of a telephone he had noticed in the hall, answered in a similarly conspiratorial manner. 'I think she's ringing her public relations consultant.'

When the lady of the house returned, she had a face worthy of a professional funeral mourner, which Campion thought was perfectly apposite. She fumbled a packet of cigarettes out of a pocket in her housecoat, thought the better of it, and thrust them back out of temptation's way.

'Mr Duffy not available?' Campion asked innocently.

'No,' said Mrs Lillman slowly, shaking her head.

'Let me guess. Your call was answered by a police operator who was intercepting all calls to his number.'

The woman nodded silently.

'You didn't know he was dead, did you?'

'How?'

'There is no easy way to say it, but he was murdered; shot near the home of Sir Lachlan McIntyre.'

The most surprising thing about Mary Lillman's reaction was that she did not seem at all surprised. 'I warned him he was playing with fire, and it sounds like he got well and truly burned.' Then the woman surprised both Campions by issuing a high-pitched laugh that could so easily have become a *glissando* into a scream. 'Hah! I told him not to light a fire under a man who made a fortune out of putting them out.'

Christopher looked to his uncle, his face a picture of pained bewilderment. 'What's she talking about?' he whispered out of the corner of his mouth.

Mr Campion tapped him reassuringly on the knee but did not take his eyes off the woman.

'She's talking about Lachlan McIntyre, sometimes known as Leckie when he lived in Stepney during the war – where he was a fireman during the Blitz, and a brave one according to gossip Lugg picked up. Supposed to be the first into a burning building. Tell us about him, Mary.'

'What's in it for me if I does?'

'What did Duffy offer you?'

'Five hundred pounds for the story if it made the papers.'

'What story?' hissed Christopher.

Campion ignored him. 'I can offer you something much more valuable.'

'What's that then when it's at home?'

'That you won't end up dead in a ditch like Mr Duffy.'

Mary Lillman considered the older of her visitors, looked askance at the younger one and then reached for her cigarettes, drawing one from the packet and lighting it with slow, deliberate movements. She picked up a small brass ashtray from the mantelpiece and balanced it in her lap as she sat in one of the recliners facing the television, deliberately ignoring her guests. She spoke, and smoked, without once looking at them.

'Duffy tracked me down – Gawd knows how – and wanted to know about Leckie and how he made his money in Stepney during the war. He'd already been snooping around the area and some flapping gums had given him bits and pieces, but none would go on the record as he called it. The East End trusts newspapermen less than they do coppers.'

She stared at her image in the dead television screen and had to be prompted by Mr Campion.

'I thought Lachlan McIntyre made his fortune in construction equipment *after* the war.'

'That's when he made his millions, right enough, but he made his seed-corn in Stepney. That's what allowed him to move onwards and upwards.'

'He worked the docks, didn't he?' said Campion. 'That always was a lucrative trade.'

'If by that you mean he was on the fiddle, then yes, sure he was. We all were.' The woman's voice hardened but she remained fixated on her image reflected in the television. When she spoke it was almost as if she was mouthing the words of her holographic self. 'Everyone who worked the docks lived above the shop, as they used to say. Anything that wasn't tied down got pinched. The shipowners allowed for it, called it "natural wastage" and the local coppers would turn a blind eye if it meant their missus got a bag of sugar and their kids got fed the odd tin of ham.'

She gave a little snort and smiled at her reflection, as if thanking it for prompting a memory. 'There was a Dutch ship in 1940, diverted up the Thames because the Germans had invaded Holland. It was carrying a load of coffee beans from Java. They was easy pickings, trouble is we didn't know what to do with all them beans an' none of us drank coffee anyway, so we had to take them up West and flog 'em to the posh hotels. But that was small stuff. Leckie wasn't above a bit of pilferage, but he also had another scheme on the go, which was far more profitable once the bombing started.'

'That would be when Lachlan was a firefighter,' gushed Christopher, delighted that he had remembered the potted biography he had written for the press.

Mr Campion, leaning forward with his hands on his knees, raised the forefinger of his left hand, a signal to his nephew to let Mrs Lillman tell the story.

'Firefighter? Fire pirate is more like it,' she said, almost spitting venom at the Mary Lillman mirrored in the twenty-six-inch screen. 'Oh, he was always the first to rush into a burning building, that's for sure. Even got a medal for it, but it wasn't the going *in* that was important, though that took guts, there's no denying that. But it was what he came *out* with that made him do it.'

'You mean survivors?' Christopher was clearly perplexed, but secretly happy that Mrs Lillman was looking at herself and not at him. 'The people he rescued?'

'I think,' said Campion quietly, 'that he emerged from the bombed-out houses with more than that.'

Christopher turned a face contorted in confusion towards his uncle in a plea for clarification, and Mr Campion mouthed the word *Pirate*.

'I take it,' he said aloud, 'that Leckie, as you called him, was not averse to a bit of speculative looting whilst going about the noble business of fighting fires in wartime. Is that what you are suggesting?'

'Nothing speculative abaht it,' said the woman through gritted teeth. 'He didn't go charging into every house, only the ones where he knew there was something worth taking and that he could carry without being spotted.'

'Jewellery, cash, silver perhaps?'

'Anything that could be stuffed into a gas-mask bag. We girls always got in trouble for using them as handbags, but no copper or warden would ever question what a fireman had in his.' Her voice drifted away and her reflection in the television screen became an even more ghostly echo. 'There was gold as well. Not just rings and brooches, but sovereigns and even small ingots; there were loads of them squirrelled away. They all had them.'

Campion again leaned forward and found himself addressing the television set.

'They?'

'The Jews, of course.'

'Jews? I . . . I . . . don't understand . . .' Christopher mumbled.

Be thankful for that, Mr Campion thought, but when he spoke his voice was hard-edged.

'Let me be clear, Mrs Lillman, you are telling us that Jewish homes in Stepney were looted after they were bombed in the Blitz?'

Mary Lillman made a noise in her throat which might have been a vocal shrug or a strangled laugh. 'After? It was mostly done during, while the Blitz was on; fewer witnesses that way with the bombs falling. Leckie would run into a burning house to look for survivors or them too daft to get to the shelters. Often he found some and then he really was a hero, but there were certain houses where he knew there were no people but he still came out with something worthwhile.'

'So he targeted the homes of Jewish residents deliberately?'

'They were the only ones that had anything worth taking; everybody else was church-mouse poor. They knew which were the Jewish houses; all they had to do was wait for the bombs to come close and the fires to start. You didn't usually have to wait long, living that close to the docks.'

'You say "they" knew which house to target,' said Campion deliberately. 'Did Leckie have a partner?'

'Oh, yes.'

'Was it Mr Lillman?'

'Walter? Oh no, my husband had been interred by then, along with Sir Oswald and the big shots in the BUF – not that Walter was a big shot, but he got rounded up with the rest of them. Quite proud of that he was. Made him feel important.'

'So who was Lachlan's partner in crime?'

Mrs Lillman finally turned to face the Campions. 'That cunning little minx, Miss Nose-in-the-Air Southall, as I called her.'

Clearly the name failed to register with either of her visitors and she responded with a snort of exasperation.

'Lucy Southall as was, Leckie's wife as is. That stuck-up bitch, Lady Lucy McIntyre.'

Mr Campion felt Christopher quivering through the soft cushions of the sofa, but whether it was the shock of what he had just heard or the urge to interject he did not know, but he felt he needed to avert an outburst.

'You told David Duffy all this?' Campion kept his voice low and level, in his own interpretation of a caring doctor's most soothing bedside manner.

'He knew, or had guessed a lot of it,' said his patient. 'He just wanted an eyewitness who was prepared to talk.'

'And you knew the McIntyres well back then, didn't you?'

The woman nodded.

'And now? Are you still in touch?'

Mary Lillman bristled. 'Ain't seen 'im since they moved out of Stepney towards the end of the war.'

'And her?'

Now she shrugged and answered too quickly for Campion's liking. 'Not seen Lucy for nigh on ten years.'

'That would be about the time your husband Walter died, wouldn't it?'

'Around then, yes,' she said cautiously.

'And before the war you were all quite close. You, Walter, Lucy Southall, Leckie and your brother, Henry?'

'Depends. We was neighbours in Stepney, but we didn't live in each other's pockets.'

'But you were, shall we say, politically active?'

'You mean Cable Street? Yeah, we were there, and we were fighting on the right side before you ask.'

'I am sure you thought you were,' said Campion, controlling himself, 'but I was thinking of earlier than 1936. Say 1932, when you were members of the Imperial Fascist League.'

'Duffy found that out as well, thought he could hold it over us, but I wasn't ashamed. Not then, not now. We were defending our country; we weren't doing anything wrong.'

'We must agree to disagree on that, as did the magistrates when they jailed you and Walter for assault on a respected London silversmith.'

For the first time Mary Lillman looked surprised; not worried, but mildly intrigued. 'You've done your homework, I'll say that for you, but Duffy got there before you.'

'I've seen his notes,' said Campion. 'It seems there were four of you involved in the assault on a gentleman called Nathan Hirsch, outside the Silver Vaults.'

The woman screwed up her face, pursed her lips, and blew a dismissive 'raspberry'. 'That weren't no gentleman, that was a Jew.'

Now it was Christopher who noticed that his uncle's left knee was quivering with contained rage, but Mr Campion did nothing more explosive than remove his spectacles and polish their lenses on the white handkerchief he had magicked from the breast pocket of his jacket.

'You and Walter were arrested, I believe, but your two colleagues got away. I'm guessing your late brother Henry was one of them.'

'It can't do him any harm now to say it was, but Duffy wasn't interested in Henry, he just wanted dirt on Leckie.'

'Was McIntyre the fourth member of your gang for the attack on Mr Hirsch?'

'Nah, we didn't meet Leckie until '36, at Cable Street, like I said. That's the story Duffy wanted and I was going to give it to him.'

'Not exactly give,' Christopher interjected. 'Don't you mean sell?'

'So where's the crime in that?' Mrs Lillman snapped, with enough venom to make the younger Campion shrink back into the folds of the sofa. 'I'd be doing no more than telling the truth.'

'Selling the truth would be more accurate,' said a tight-lipped Campion as he replaced his spectacles and pushed them on to the bridge of his nose with his forefinger, 'but I suppose the labourer is worthy of his, or her, hire. Mr Duffy may be out of the picture, but I can make sure you get the £500 he promised you.'

'You can?'

'If you are prepared to tell your story – all of it, leaving nothing out – to an associate of mine who will call on you at your convenience with a tape recorder.'

'I could do that.' She raised a preening hand to pat her hair. 'It'd be like bein' on the telly.'

As Christopher unlocked the car door and opened it for his uncle, he said, 'She didn't recognize you at all, did she? Or the name Campion, not even when you mentioned the incident with Nathan Hirsch.'

'I cannot honestly say I recognized her,' said Mr Campion, slotting his legs into the passenger seat footwell of the Scimitar, 'though I do not count that as a loss. It was a long time ago and we had the briefest of meetings before dear old Lugg punched her lights out, bless him. She's aged, of course, and not well, whereas I am still in the full flush of youth.'

Christopher leaned over the steering wheel as he started the car and turned his face to check whether Uncle Albert was joking.

'I have a very flattering bathroom mirror,' said Campion, 'plus a postgraduate degree in self-deception. Now please navigate a course for Markley Desolation.'

'The McIntyre place?' Christopher glanced at his wristwatch. 'We won't catch Sir Lachlan – he's out this evening talking to a Rotary Club in Northampton. I wrote his speech for him.'

'That is of no consequence; in fact, it may be an advantage. I have no wish to confront Sir Lachlan just yet.'

'Confront?'

'I would be interested to discover how he reacted to being blackmailed.'

Christopher's foot slipped from the clutch pedal, causing the car to hiccup forward. 'Blackmail? David Duffy was blackmailing him?'

'Not Duffy, but I am sure the odious Mary Lillman was. Her husband, whom I suspect was never a high earner, died ten years ago. Unless he had remarkable life insurance, how was his widow able to move from a council house in Dagenham to a private semi-detached in leafy Romford? On what? Her wages as a part-time barmaid? I suspect she might have had her claws into the

McIntyres for some years. By the by, did you say McIntyre was in Northampton this evening?'

'Yes, why?'

'Oh nothing, really, it's just that the business with the silver tankard all those years ago, that ended in Northampton. Nothing to do with Lachlan McIntyre, of course, it just triggered a memory.'

'You never did tell me what happened after the fracas with Nathan Hirsch.'

'Then I will tell you as you drive to pass the time, as the radio will only offer depressing news or ridiculous music. It's not a very edifying story, though, and nowhere near as scandalous as Mary Lillman's.'

'Are you really going to send someone with a tape recorder to take down all the gory details?'

'Of course,' said Mr Campion, 'and it will almost certainly be one of Charles Luke's female detective officers, in the sincere hope that Mrs Lillman will incriminate herself.'

'Are you going to warn her about that?'

'No,' said Campion firmly, 'I don't think I am.'

SIXTEEN

The Silver Man

Mr Campion's Memory 4: Kent, 1932

It was several days after the brawl outside the Silver Vaults before I was able to pursue my quest for the Gidney tankard. Not that it was really a quest; after all, I was not searching for it, it was in my possession. In fact, as a rather officious desk sergeant at the police station where our assailants were being booked pointed out, I had on my own admission used the tankard to belt one of them around the head. That had not, as Lugg rather unhelpfully remarked, stopped them escaping into the fog, whereas the two he had tackled were safely in custody being examined by a police surgeon for, respectively, a suspected broken rib (due to being sat upon as a means of restraint) and possible concussion (due to being punched).

Nathan Hirsch had come off worst of all with several broken bones, numerous bumps, and multiple bruises the colour of a seriously depressed painter's palette. I had been correct in my assumption that the weapons employed had been Indian clubs, as two had been recovered from the pavement outside the vaults, dropped by the thugs Lugg had incapacitated. Sadly, the two who had fled the scene had retained their weapons, which would have carried their fingerprints.

Lugg and I gave fulsome statements to the investigating officers, with me helping him out with the long words, and the next day visited Nathan in the hospital to which he had been rushed, to find him in the capable hands of doctors, nurses, and something like a dozen female relatives who all professed to know the best course of treatment needed. Once reassured that Nathan would make a full recovery, I was happy to leave him in so many capable hands, and indeed had more sympathy for the plight of the poor doctors looking after him under such strict family supervision.

We filled the Bentley with petrol and, because I had granted Lugg the right to drive, this also involved stocking up with 'iron rations', as he called them, for the journey. These consisted mainly of a pile of sandwiches he had made from potted meat and flabby sliced white bread, a recent abomination which most decent bakers insisted was a passing fad. To keep him going between fistfuls of limp sandwich, he had bought half a dozen of the new Mars bars, which I feared he might have become addicted to, whilst I kept a reserve of cigarettes – Du Maurier cork-tips, which Lugg turned his nose up at, saying they were bad for his wind.

For most of the journey along the A2 into Kent, the sound of Lugg chewing competed successfully with the hum of the Bentley's engine but, as we approached Faversham, he began to use his jaws to reminisce about his boyhood days hop-picking in the fields owned by the town's brewery. He had come from a part of London where the only possibility of a summer holiday for a family was a week or two living in stables or under canvas, stripping the fragrant hop flowers from the parallel lines of tall bines. The pickers would spend a day in the fields and then be fed and watered by the hop farmer, even paid for their labour and sometimes treated, after dark, to a silent film projected on a white sheet nailed to a nearby barn. It had been, Lugg said, a formative and invigorating experience, which had given him, very much the urban urchin, an appreciation of nature, fresh air and the countryside, and the gratitude he felt for not having to live there.

As we approached Canterbury, I tried to interest him in the ecclesiastical history of that 'cruel see' and the importance of north-east Kent as a whole in the story of England, as it was the place where invaders such as Romans, Angles, Saxons, Jutes, Friesians and then Christian missionaries had all landed. Yet before I could get into my stride, Lugg pointed a wilting potted-meat sandwich to a road sign directing us towards Sturry, a mere three miles hence.

I had never visited Sturry, but I knew of its existence, due to two totally unconnected facts which had somehow lodged themselves on the back shelves of the dusty library of my brain. Firstly, the local Sturry doctor and his pharmacist daughter were making a name for themselves in local archaeology, helping to piece together life in post-Roman Kent, shedding light on what my schoolmasters always called the Dark Ages; and secondly, I had read somewhere that the village retained exactly the same parish boundary as had been recorded in the Domesday Book.

Dredging up neither of these titbits would help us locate the gypsy camp we hoped to find, but thankfully neither were necessary because the encampment, in fields on the outskirts of the village, was impossible to miss.

The Sturry camp had more of an air of permanent settlement than the one at Butcombe. At least a fifth bigger, the camp had a settled, lived-in feel, the traditional Vardos, interspersed with a few modern caravans, parked in two parallel lines, creating the impression of a high street. All motorized transport was parked neatly next to the van it towed, adding to the impression, at least through my rose-tinted spectacles, that this was a proven community with established, self-imposed rules about off-street parking; surely an indicator of English civilization.

At the far end of the 'street', the ponies which pulled the

traditional Vardos had been turned loose in a neighbouring field, under the supervision of half a dozen raggedy children, who appeared to be organizing their own version of a gymkhana, which had none of the pomp but all of the chaos of any run by a county pony club, and probably more violence and rule-bending, with several of the older children in charge of side bets.

Lugg parked the Bentley a good fifty yards away from the nearest caravan, having turned it back towards the Canterbury road on the very sensible premise that it was always wise to be pointed towards an exit should a fast escape be required.

I insisted that our approach should be one of non-aggressive infiltration, at which Lugg scoffed, although long words were never his *forte*. He did play his part, though, despite looking like an off-duty undertaker, his bowler jammed firmly in place so that it could deflect shrapnel, as he held the Butcombe tankard to his chest as though presenting a sacrifice to a demanding god. He had administered a severe polishing that morning, so that 'it buffed up *luvverly*', and seemed rather proud that the shiny mug immediately attracted the eyes of the women and children buzzing around the horseshoe-ends of the multi-coloured wagons.

We strode slowly but purposefully down the middle of the street formed by the two lines of caravans. Every silent human eye was focused on Lugg's shiny prize, whilst all the camp's dogs – thankfully tied to the wheels of most of the wagons – were far from silent in their growling and slobbering appreciation of Lugg's meaty ankles and calves.

I rather relished the spectacle we were making of ourselves, and played to the gallery by tipping my hat to the determinedly uncurious mothers and grandmothers, and waving to the less in-hibited children who waved in greeting or, in one case, shook a fist.

We saw no males in the camp – I assumed they were all out working on the local fields – and no one questioned our presence until, roughly halfway along the street, we were brought up short by a deep-throated challenge from the steps of one of the traditional wooden Vardos. The voice came from an old woman smoking a clay pipe, as if posing for a Hogarth print, most of her face concealed by a large tartan headscarf knotted under a bony chin.

'You'll be wanting the Silver Man, then.'

It was a statement not a question, and declaimed in a voice which brooked no argument. Here was a woman whose bark and bite were almost certainly worse than that of the suspiciously well-nourished bull terrier lying dormant at the foot of the steps she was sitting on, thankfully restrained there by a length of clothes line. Well, I assumed it was tied up and not simply secured by the woman having planted a worn Victorian button boot on the rope attached to the dog's collar. Perhaps it needed no more than the presence of the woman to ensure the good behaviour of the hound, for she certainly exuded a powerful personality and clearly issued commands psychically.

I doffed my hat to her with my best flourish, though neither the woman nor the dog seemed impressed.

'Yes indeed, madam,' I said, 'we are here to see Lancelot.'

The woman – I dislike the term 'crone' but I admit it sprang to mind – did not react to the name. She removed the pipe from her mouth and pointed with the stem down the line of vans.

'His Vardo's the green 'un on the sinister, second from the end. His chimney's going so he's in.'

I gave my fedora an extra tip in appreciation of her use of 'sinister' and we turned smartly on our heels and made our way over to the left side of the street, Lugg conveying the tankard in front of him as if he were a boat boy carrying the incense in a church service, though a less innocent junior acolyte or assistant to a thurifer it was hard to imagine.

The Silver Man was indeed 'in' and, responding to a knock on the green door of his wagon, seemed surprised but not alarmed to see us.

'I half-expected the long arm of the law, but perhaps not so soon,' he said as he leaned out over the top half of the split door.

He was a small, thin man who spoke in a thin, reedy voice. He wore a collarless shirt two sizes too big for him, the voluminous sleeves of which were kept under control by wide leather armbands, and he blinked rapidly at us from behind spectacles with lenses as thick as Kilner jar bottoms. I knew he was a dozen years older than I, but the few sparse wisps of white hair which decorated his bald head nudged him from middle-age to old man.

'My name is Campion,' I said, 'and this is my associate, Mr Lugg. Neither of us are with the police. We have come from Little Butcombe bearing gifts, or rather returning them. Assuming of course, that you are Lancelot Drinkwater.'

'I was,' he said with a tinge of sadness, his eyes on the tankard grasped between Lugg's paws, 'but in this life I am known as Lance.'

'That's a pity,' I said rather too flippantly. 'It's a splendid name and I could never understand why Lancelot Brown, the famous landscaper, preferred to be known as Capability, though I suppose it is a decent enough nickname. Yours, I believe, is the Silver Man.'

A sliver of a smile creased his thin lips. 'It is, and the Silver Man does not do business in the open air, so you had better come in.' He stared hard at Lugg. 'You might have to breathe in.'

Lugg grunted and eyed up the narrow door leading into a presumably slim interior, and did indeed attempt to pull in his stomach as we squeezed up the steps. Inside the van, Lancelot himself moved with a natural stoop which I automatically adopted, being taller than our host, and we shuffled our way along carefully until a blanketed surface, clearly a bed, offered us a place to sit, our host choosing a three-legged stool, the three of us, our knees almost touching, giving a fair imitation of a tin of sardines. It was difficult to relax, not that there was the space to do so, because every spare inch of the Vardo's interior walls sported narrow wooden shelves loaded with small items of silverware, including beakers, ashtrays, cruets, thimbles, Vesta cases, visiting card holders and decanter labels. A sudden movement – the very act of Lugg attempting to stand up – might rock the boat and bring the whole lot crashing down around us.

I could tell Lugg was concentrating hard and doing a mental stock-take rather than pondering on how the Vardo could move under horsepower without dislodging the glittering display.

'I am proud of my Silver Man title,' said Lancelot. 'I have some expertise in the subject, and that has proved useful to my travelling family. Gypsies have always put their faith, and wealth, in silver, and they look on me as a sort of bank manager.'

'Not worried about a bank robbery, then?' asked Lugg, his eyes taking in the array of silver baubles which glinted in the light from the van's single oil lamp.

The Silver Man dismissed the question smoothly. 'Did you notice how many dogs you passed since you left your car?'

'Nine,' responded Lugg immediately.

'Very observant,' conceded Lancelot, then waved a hand in the general direction of the silverware surrounding us. 'But my little collection here is not our bank vault; these are mere trinkets. The really valuable pieces are well hidden, and the dogs would find a robber long before he located them, but you don't look like robbers, and you say you are not police, so what are you?'

'We come out of curiosity,' I said enigmatically.

'My mother sent you.'

Clearly, I had not been enigmatic enough.

'Lady Drinkwater does not know – specifically – that we are here. She merely asked me to investigate the provenance of the tankard my friend is nursing, clearly depressed by the fact that it is empty.'

'She knows well enough what it is. It belonged to her husband the Galloping Major Gidney, until he pawned it.'

'Your stepfather.'

'No, my mother's second husband.' The Silver Man spoke severely and sucked in his cheeks, as though the subject had a sour taste for him. 'He was in no part a father to me. He was a bully and a despot, as well as a shyster and a wastrel. When I heard of his death, I positively rejoiced.'

He was not acting, but speaking directly from an ice-cold heart.

'And you thought your mother would appreciate the return of his tankard via Shadrach Lee? How did it come into your possession?'

Lugg lifted the tankard off his lap almost as an offering, but the Silver Man refused to look at it, concentrating on a pair of silver sugar nips balanced precariously on the shelf above Lugg's head.

'A member of my new family, my travelling family, spotted it in a pawnshop in Northampton last year and thought it might be a good investment,' he said dreamily. 'He brought it to me for appraisal and I recognized it and took it off his hands.'

'Little Butcombe is not far from Northampton, and where you joined that new family, isn't it? There's an annual encampment there; have you ever been back?'

'We make our home wherever we are welcome. Little Butcombe has always made us welcome.'

'I meant Butcombe Manor rather than the village.'

'That has not been my home for many years. It was not much of a home when I lived there. I have no reason to go back there.'

Rather than look at us, Lancelot's eyes flicked along a shelf lined with silver pieces, which probably twinkled like a string of Christmas tree lights as they reflected the orange glow of the oil lamp when dusk fell.

I had no idea if Lancelot was thinking that, but I knew he was lying.

'I think you have been back to the hall.'

My dramatic accusation was received in distinctly undramatic fashion, with a barely perceptible twitch of the shoulders and an instant confession.

'Very well, then, I did go back to the hall when we camped in Butcombe, but just the once. When I saw the state of the place and realized the financial straits my mother was in, I thought she could sell the tankard for a few pounds.'

'A few pounds more than it is actually worth, I think.' I fired my second barrel, which had as little impact as my first.

'I don't know what you mean.'

'I think you do, and I am pretty sure you went back to Butcombe Manor to burgle it.'

'What is left there to steal?' sneered the Silver Man.

'Not a lot,' muttered Lugg, who always felt the need to express a professional opinion when burglary was mentioned.

'Some tools, perhaps? From the cellar. Some specialist tools?'

Lancelot's face froze, apart from his eyes, which blinked rapidly behind those thick lenses. 'If I said "Titivillus" to you, would it mean anything?'

'Don't to me,' said Lugg, so I turned to him, allowing Lancelot to squirm.

'I didn't think it would. Titivillus was the original printer's devil, a demon who introduced mistakes into the works of scribes and, later, printers. Our friend Lancelot here will know exactly what I'm talking about.'

Lancelot was determined to avoid admitting anything, having turned his face away to survey his shelves of silvery ornaments.

'The printing press at Butcombe Manor, now confined to the cellar: that was a passion of yours, was it not?' And to make sure I got his attention, I added, 'A passion you shared with your father.'

'With my *real* father, yes.'

'You or he, perhaps together, designed that interesting typeface which you called, amusingly, Badinage, and you employed it to print the Butcombe Manor stationery. I think you helped yourself to a supply of it when you broke in through the cellar skylight, and you gave a sheet to your delivery man, Shadrach Lee. But I am really interested in what else you took from the cellar. Let me guess; you picked up some tools and helped yourself from the hellbox.'

'Wot the 'ell is an 'ellbox?' spluttered the fat man.

'It's the box where a printer, or his assistant or apprentice, throws broken or used lead type from whence it can be repaired or melted down and recast as new type.'

'And what's that got to do with the price of fish?'

I indicated that Lancelot might wish to field my colleague's rather ungainly question, but he retained a sullen silence.

'If our resident printer's devil refuses to comment, allow me to speculate,' I said, taking a childish pleasure in the fact that I could show off to Lugg and intimidate Lancelot simultaneously. 'A printer used to working with lead type and capable of designing a unique typeface to produce impressive headed notepaper, would almost certainly be skilled enough to fashion characters such as a leopard's head, a lion rampant, a profile of Queen Victoria and a gothic capital letter "P". These individual lead characters, which I think are known as "sorts", could be used not on a printing press, but as metal punches, and with a few skilled hammer blows, one could add hallmarks to turn a cheap, low-quality piece of imported silverware into something far more valuable, at least to the untrained eye.'

Lugg examined the tankard on his lap and allowed himself a soft, low whistle, though I suspect not in appreciation of my exposition but in admiration for the criminality I was suggesting. 'You mean to say you can fake these 'ere official marks?' He spoke to me, but he looked straight at Lancelot.

'Given a skill with hot-metal-press typefaces, some specialist tools and a source of heat, which would not be difficult to find in a gypsy encampment with horses and horseshoes and therefore a blacksmith, I would think it relatively easy to produce a die punch.'

'And that's not exactly legal, is it?' Lugg addressed Lancelot with the air of a barrister who had just discovered the meaning of 'rhetorical'.

'In Shakespeare's day, forging essay marks was punishable by the pillory and the loss of an ear. Later, as we became more civilized, counterfeiting carried the death penalty, and in 1844 it became an offence to make or even possess a forged die, due to the popularity of faking early Georgian silver. I suspect, my dear Mr Silver Man, that you are rather skilled at making die punches, given your long interest in metal type, and this tankard here is probably not Exhibit A, but merely the latest item off your production line.'

'You can't prove a thing,' said the Silver Man, looking me in the eye for the first time, even though we had been no more than a foot and a half apart since entering the confines of his Vardo.

'The police could easily get a search warrant,' I said. I had no idea if this was true, but I enjoyed the way Lugg squirmed when he heard the words 'police' and 'warrant'.

Lancelot was decidedly unimpressed. 'Do you think this camp would still be here by the time a warrant was served?'

'Probably not,' I admitted. 'I feel you are a valued member of this community—'

'Family.'

'Very well, family; a family which no doubt appreciates how you have increased the value of some of their silver, for I suspect this tankard was not your first attempt at altering history. By the way, as a piece of friendly advice, your duty stamp with Queen Victoria's head is a little smudgy. My expert picked up on that immediately.'

'Who is your expert?'

'An old friend from the Silver Vaults, Nathan Hirsch.'

Lancelot, for the first time, seemed impressed. 'He knows his silver,' he said with deliberation, 'but he, like you, cannot prove wrongdoing on my part.'

'I do not have to prove anything, I was merely asked to

investigate the provenance of this tankard, which left Butcombe Manor for a Northampton pawn shop, was legally – as far as I know – acquired, and then returned to Lady Drinkwater as a family heirloom by a somewhat unusual delivery method, but with no associated demand for recompense. Any, shall we say "cosmetic" alterations that may have happened to it are surely irrelevant, unless someone tries to profit from them.'

Lancelot removed his spectacles and pinched the bridge of his nose with a forefinger and thumb. He was buying himself thinking time; I knew the manoeuvre well. 'Am I being scolded?' he asked after replacing his glasses.

'You probably are. Treat this as a fair warning to think carefully before decorating any more pieces of silver, and we will leave you with your new family and return the tankard to your old one. Do you have a message for your mother?'

The Silver Man gaped at us as if we had just landed from another planet. 'No.' Then he looked at the tankard still nestling in Lugg's paw. 'She will know what to do with it.'

'So the prodigal son ain't going home to the fatted calf then?' Lugg ruminated as we strolled back to the Bentley, at least two dozen pairs of human and canine eyes tracking our departure. We had given the residents no reason to suspect us of anything nefarious. Clearly we were not policemen (the dogs would have howled continuously); we had arrived bearing a single silver trophy and were leaving with the same, Lugg holding it in plain sight. The Silver Man would probably explain away our visit as a pair of innocents seeking an evaluation, for which, being city-dwellers and therefore slow on the uptake, he was able to charge an outrageous fee.

'I never expected him to,' I said, 'and especially not after the number of references he made to his new family here. Not that Butcombe Manor would have much in the way of fatted calves to offer these days.'

'He'd be lucky to get a pennyworth of chips there,' said Lugg, practical as ever, 'and be charged extra for the salt and vinegar. You might say Lady Drinkwater hasn't got a pot to . . .'

'Lugg, desist!' I commanded. 'You know I hate vulgarity, unless it can be employed to usefully embarrass the pompous.'

'I was going to say,' Legg stuck out his bottom lip and tried to look hurt, 'that she hasn't got a pot to put in her display case, but now she will have. A treasured memento, a present from her wayward son. If we're taking it back to her, that is.'

'We are.'

'But we're not returning her son?'

'We were never asked to, only to follow the trail left by the tankard.'

'Without so much as the offer of petrol money,' grumbled the big man.

'My dear old fruit, if you ever attempt to read a popular novel these days, you will know we live in a golden age of private detectives who solve crime and help out damsels in distress. Charging a fee or demanding a *per diem* would be positively uncouth.'

'Not to me, but then I was born vulgar,' said Lugg as he clambered into the Bentley's passenger seat.

Whereas others achieve vulgarity and some have it thrust upon them, I mused as I climbed behind the wheel and started the engine.

'So you were showing off your fancy detective skills back there?'

'What do you mean?'

'All that stuff about him breaking into the cellar at Butcombe and raiding that 'ellbox for bits and pieces to make a die punch to fake those hallmarks. 'Ow did you detect all that?'

'I did what all great detectives in books do.' I laughed. 'I guessed.'

SEVENTEEN

Inside Story

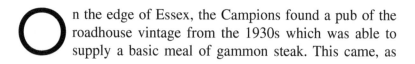

On the edge of Essex, the Campions found a pub of the roadhouse vintage from the 1930s which was able to supply a basic meal of gammon steak. This came, as did everything else on the menu, with chips and, to add colour and a touch of the exotic, a tinned pineapple ring.

Although he was driving, and therefore restricted himself to lime and soda, Christopher demanded a wine list, and when it became clear that the pub offered only one wine, a Portuguese rosé in a bottle designed as a lampstand, he apologized profusely to his uncle. Mr Campion said no apology was necessary, and that he would take half of lager in lieu and, before Christopher could complain about the food, he quoted the old soldier's maxim that one should never go into battle on an empty stomach.

'Are we going into battle?' asked his startled nephew.

'It's a distinct possibility,' said Mr Campion.

It was dark by the time they had crossed Bedfordshire, following signs 'to the M1' and, had it not been for those highway reminders flashing by, pondered Campion, the unwary traveller coming from the east might have missed Markley Desolation completely. Unless, that is, they realized that the cone of yellow-tinged light in the distance, visible from more than a mile away, marked the spot.

The road from Cranfield allowed, through the trees, a view of the glowing dome over Markley formed by the lights of the McIntyre Tyres compound. From the motorway the illuminated scene was the most garish of all possible adverts for Sir Lachlan's eponymous business. Floodlights atop the wire-mesh fence were mere sprinkles compared to the spotlights aimed up from the ground at the huge, elevated advertising hoarding. The intention had been Hollywood, but the effect was that of a prisoner-of-war Stalag, and it no doubt served as an aid to navigation to any night flights to or from the British Airports Authority's outpost at Stansted Mountfitchet. At ground level, or at least car level, that unearthly radiance in the night sky reminded Mr Campion of seeing the silhouette of London burning in the Blitz – and now he was aware that one evil act of war was providing cover for an invidious spate of thievery.

As they passed the lay-by and telephone box where David Duffy had been assassinated – waiting for a call, perhaps? – Mr Campion told Christopher to turn off the Scimitar's headlights. There was enough ambient light from the glow over the McIntyre empire to drive the final stretch into what used to be the village without danger, on the assumption they would not meet a large earth-moving vehicle coming the other way.

'Go slowly and as quietly as possible,' instructed Campion. 'I want us to glide by Cruachan and park up somewhere beyond the cottages, preferably without being seen.'

'We could park in the compound,' said Christopher. 'Who would notice a car among all that machinery?'

'Do you have access?'

'If the lights are on, there'll be one of McIntyre's men on duty as nightwatchman, probably waiting on the return of something that's been hired out. The big stuff often travels at night when the roads are quieter.'

'Any idea who will be on duty tonight?'

'No, but they all know me by sight, it shouldn't be a problem.'

'But it's not likely to be Carl Spivey?'

'Not at all,' said Christopher confidently, 'he works for Lady M. in the stables at the house. He doesn't venture into the compound, preferring his horsepower to have four legs rather than four wheels or caterpillar tracks.'

Christopher glided the car along the unkept road that had once been Markley's high street and automatically ducked his head as they passed Cruachan, where porch lights illuminated every awful angle of its design. His uncle was more concerned with the left side of the road, taking a great interest in the curtained windows of the first cottage and the light behind them.

'He's home,' he said, but so quietly Christopher did not hear him. He was leaning forward, peering through the windscreen into the compound's illuminated perimeter, flicking the Scimitar's lights back on as he pulled up to the gateway.

A shadowy figure stepped into the beams, holding a hand to his eyes to shield them.

'It's Old Nick, he'll let us in.'

'Tell him we'd like a word,' said Campion, as Christopher wound down his window and asked if the kettle was on, the all-purpose passwords needed to gain access to almost any installation in Britain.

Christopher parked beyond the watchman's hut, between bulldozer and a large cement mixer mounted on a flatbed truck, and the Campions joined 'Old Nick' in the site office which, judging by the boiling kettle and an invitation to 'guess that tune' from a Radio 2 announcer, courtesy of a bright red transistor set, served as a snug sanctuary for whoever drew nightwatch duty.

'We've not had much chance to talk, Mr Campion,' said Andrews, pulling a pair of dusty mugs from an enamel washing-up bowl.

'Is there any reason we should have?'

Andrews busied himself with the kettle and spooned tea from a tin caddy, which proclaimed it was a souvenir from the Queen's coronation, into a brown teapot of a similar vintage. 'I was warned you might be sniffing around asking questions about that dead journalist young Mr Christopher brought here.'

'And I was warned not to play cards with you.'

'I've warned myself not to play with me!' As Andrews brayed loudly, his hands holding kettle and teapot shaking dangerously, Campion realized he was in the presence of one of those men who always laughed at their own jokes, but fortunately did not make many.

Mr Campion offered him no more than a faint smile. 'Was it Sir Lachlan who warned you about me?'

'Aye, it was, but it wasn't a warning like he was marking your card, just a friendly tip-off.' Andrews paused and looked surprised, in the best tradition of a music hall comic turn. 'Marking your card, there I go again! Sure you don't fancy a quick hand?'

Once again the ridiculously loud, braying laugh, which Mr Campion decided suggested the sound a donkey in a bear-trap might make.

'My mother told me never to play Old Nick at any game of chance, and that I should never think of asking for his help or advice.'

Andrews nodded politely at the mention of his nickname, then screwed up his face as a cheeky schoolboy might when asking an impertinent question. 'Was your mother a religious woman?'

'Yes, when she was alive,' said Campion, straight-faced, 'but as for now I could not say and, actually, I am ignoring her very sensible advice.'

Andrews, clearly confused, composed himself for another bout of braying laughter but restrained himself.

'I don't follow.'

'I appear to be supping with the Devil,' smiled Campion, raising his chipped and stained mug towards the teapot's spout, 'and asking Old Nick for advice.'

'Me? How can I help you? I only met that Duffy chap when young Christopher here brought him to the yard for a look-round. I told the coppers that. Sir Lachlan said I had to cooperate with them.' Then, as if quoting, 'Cooperate fully.'

'Which probably went against all your natural instincts.'

'What d'you mean by that?'

'Would I be more than a mile off if I were to suggest you have helped the police with their enquiries in the past, perhaps on a, shall we say, personal level?'

'You talking about my record? I ain't ashamed.' This 'Old Nick' was as defiant as his namesake. 'I done my time, paid my dues and been out for these past ten years. Who's been saying different?'

Mr Campion sensed Christopher bristle at his side but retained his composure, making great play of savouring his tea, even though it tasted quite as vile as it looked.

'No one has said anything, Mr Andrews, at least nothing untoward about your good self. I am simply asking you to indulge an old man's insatiable curiosity, which was sparked when I caught sight of the tattoos on the arms of yourself and your workmates. They struck me, and I mean no disrespect, as examples of prison art rather than having been done by a professional tattoo artist.'

'Well then, it's a fair cop! Is that what you wanted me to say?' Old Nick's laugh boomed out again, but there was a nervous tremor to it.

'I am not asking you to justify yourself, far from it. You do not have to justify anything to me, only to your employer' – Campion held up a hand to halt any interruption – 'and Sir Lachlan assures me he has total faith in you and your colleagues. My interest in your past is somewhat more esoteric.'

'I don't know what that means.'

'It means I am being nosey, that's all, and I'm asking you to humour me. I am not asking you to incriminate yourself and I am not suggesting you have done anything wrong.' Mr Campion

put his head on one side and opted for what he felt was his
'friendly uncle' expression.

'What d'you want to know?'

'When you were . . . inside . . . and I do not require details,
was it with your colleagues Andy Todd and . . .'

'Frank Green,' supplied Christopher, hovering behind his uncle.

'No, Frank and Andy both did their time in different nicks
after my stretch.'

'What about Carl Spivey?'

'Oh, yeah, I knew Carl inside. You might say I kept an eye
out for him.'

'Really? How?' Campion pressed gently.

'He was pretty small, and one of the youngest inmates, so he
got picked on, and he was inside for something daft like doping
a horse. He kept up with the gee-gees, though, and often gave
us some good tips. We made a few bob, thanks to Carl.'

'Whilst in prison?' spluttered Christopher, much to Campion's
annoyance, especially when it prompted another explosive laugh
from Old Nick.

'There were always screws willing to put bets on for us,' said
Andrews, 'for a share of the winnings, naturally.'

'So you knew Spivey back then – ten years ago or more,' said
Campion, before Christopher could summon up more righteous
indignation. 'What about Walter Lillman? Ever come across him?'

'Lillman? Lillman? Should it ring a bell?' Andrews spoke
lightly, innocently, but as he did he held up his cup to obscure
much of his face; a gesture which did not go unnoticed.

'Probably not,' replied Campion equally blithely, 'it would
have been too much of a coincidence to discover you were a
would-be Nazi too.'

Old Nick laughed, but this time it was a nervous giggle, not
a thunderous roar. 'Don't taint me with that brush. I never did
politics, in prison or out, and I never had time for Little Hermann.'

'Little Hermann?'

'Lillman, that's what we called him, after Hermann Göring.
Couldn't stand the feller meself, but poor Carl couldn't get away
from him 'cos they shared a cell for six months.'

Then Andrews let loose his raucous laugh.

'How was that amusing?' asked Campion seriously.

'Because Carl fancied his chances with Lillman's missus; always said he'd look her up once he got out. As it happened, Little Hermann was released before him and then went and got himself run over by a bus. Carl was over the moon at that, thinking he had better odds with the merry widow, but nothing ever came of it.'

'Had Spivey ever seen Mary Lillman?' Campion asked, determined not to sound judgemental.

'Oh yes, on prison visits. She came several times, used to try and bring Little Hermann some books, but never got them past the screws. They weren't dirty books, mind you, they was all political stuff – and pretty ripe politics at that.'

'I can imagine the content,' Campion sighed, 'though you say it never appealed to you?'

Andrews squirmed at the question. 'Can't say they were completely wrong about some things, but I wasn't one for putting on uniforms and *Sieg-Heil*-ing anybody. I have a brother buried somewhere in Italy fighting people like that.'

'Was Spivey of a like mind?'

'I don't think Carl ever gave politics a second thought, but he wasn't after the widow Lillman's political views.'

'So he saw her after he got out and after Walter had died?'

'He was off to Dagenham like a rat up a drainpipe, the minute he got out.' Old Nick's grating laugh could no longer be contained. 'Not that he got his shoes under her bed, but they kept in touch and he did get a job out of it.'

'His job here, at McIntyre Tyres?'

'Technically, he works at Cruachan with the horses. He was an ex-jockey, for Gawd's sake, and the engines he knew about ran on hay and oats, not petrol!'

Mr Campion willed Old Nick not to guffaw again, but to no avail.

'He had no skill with machinery, and would be about as much use as a chocolate teapot round here.'

'But you – and I would guess Frank Green and Andy Todd – had mechanical know-how?'

'Too right we did. The jobs here were perfect for us, so we've made sure we've kept our noses clean.'

'May I ask how you got the job?'

'Same way Carl did, in a way, thanks to a prison visitor.'

'Mary Lillman?'

'No, not her; her best mate who came with her to see Little Hermann one time. She came back after Carl was released, said he'd been singing my praises and thought her husband could use a man like me.'

When asked, Andrews explained the nightly routine at the compound. Whoever was on duty would make a final internal tour of the perimeter fence to check for breaches and intruders, and whilst potential interlopers were most likely to be badgers or muntjac deer, they had on one occasion discovered a trio of young rascals playing hide-and-seek among the towers of spare tyres and parked vehicles. They were duly ejected with clipped ears and a severe lecture about sticking to their Dinky toy collections in future.

Once that final patrol was completed without incident and no returning machines were expected, the duty watchman would lock the gates after turning off the compound's lights, usually at nine o'clock, including the spotlights illuminating the giant advertising – not because they might distract low-flying aircraft, but to save on the McIntyre electricity bill. Nobody minded, said Andrews, threatening to snort another surge of laughter, as thanks to the miners' union, people were getting used to power cuts these days.

Mr Campion suggested that he and Christopher should accompany Old Nick on his rounds and they duly followed, some yards behind, as he paced down the lines of silent, but somehow still menacing, rows of machines. No bulldozers seemed to have been stolen and no backhoe diggers had been taken for joyrides. In the north-eastern corner of the compound, where rubber towers of large tyres lined the fence, Andrews dutifully gave each tower a kick round about the third tyre.

The tyres, designed to fit large lorries and earth-moving equipment, were huge and so solid that a kick even in a steel-capped boot from a mere mortal would have little impact. Andrews, though, was satisfied by the dull thudding sound as he lashed out at each pile, explaining that it disturbed the rats, at which Christopher took an involuntary step backwards.

Mr Campion was not deterred and squeezed between two tyre towers, the smell of dirt and rubber assaulting his nostrils, in order to get a view through the fence over the paddock at the rear of Cruachan. There were lights on in the house, but Campion strained his eyes beyond the house and the stable block and the distant trees to see if there was direct sight-line to the Cranfield road and the lay-by where Duffy had been killed. He could not detect one, though he admitted to himself that his ancient eyesight would not be an acceptable witness in any court of law.

He let Old Nick get ahead of them and pulled Christopher close, keeping his voice low. 'I'm going to disappear for a while. I want you to keep Old Nick in the watchman's hut until I return, but let him turn off the lights as per normal. On no account – and this is important – allow him to use the telephone in there.'

'How do I do that?' whispered Christopher.

'You're in public relations; you'll think of something. Wait, I just have. Do you have any cash on you?'

Christopher did a quick mental calculation. 'Eight or nine quid, I think.'

'That'll do. Get him to teach you how to play three-card brag.'

Before he left the compound, Campion borrowed a hefty metal torch from the watchman's hut, claiming that he did not want to trip in a pothole as he walked around to the lay-by on the Cranfield road 'to get the lie of the land at night'. His rather vague excuse was noted with a grunt of acknowledgement by Old Nick, who was already shuffling a dog-eared pack of cards, and who clearly had no interest in an elderly gentleman's eccentricities, but offered the comfort that at least it wasn't raining.

Campion caught Christopher's eye then stared at the white Bakelite telephone dotted with black, oily fingerprints. Christopher nodded briefly, indicating that he had remembered his instructions, and then returned his somewhat worried gaze to Old Nick's hands and the speed with which they were manipulating the cards.

Mr Campion consulted his wristwatch, noted it was a few minutes before nine, and left to walk down the road until the lights around the compound went off, at which point he turned on his heels and retraced his last few steps until he was opposite the cottage where Carl Spivey lived. He had no need of the torch he carried, as McIntyre's electricity-saving regime had not plunged the surrounding countryside into darkness, far from it. Headlights from the constant flow of traffic whining past on the elevated motorway, which provided quite a definite full stop to the extent of Markley Desolation, gave off enough ambient light to rival the wattage of a rising harvest moon. A moonrise, however, never produced the constant angry-wasp whine of engines straining to break the speed limit in the motorists' false confidence that, because it was dark, they could get away with it. And it seemed that many did.

There was light behind the curtains of the front room of Spivey's cottage, which did not appear to have a name. If it had a postal address Mr Campion assumed it would be Number 1, The Only Street, Markley Desolation, though as there were only four domestic dwellings, plus the compound and Cruachan in the place, he doubted that a postman, should one ever come calling, would have much of a problem with deliveries.

He used the borrowed torch to rap on the front door, gauging its weight as he hefted it, for although he did not think he would need a weapon, it was comforting to know he had one and that, should anything untoward happen, he could look Amanda in the eye and say he had not gone into the unknown unarmed.

Carl Spivey opened the door and presented the least threatening depiction Campion could possibly imagine as he looked down on him from his height advantage. Clearly, he had caught the ex-jockey in a state of relaxation. He was wearing a thick wool cardigan over a greyish-white vest, with yellow braces holding up brown corduroy trousers, and was shoeless, the nail of a big toe poking through a hole in his left sock. There was a distinct aroma of whisky coming off him.

'Oh, it's you. I thought it must be Old Nick on the borrow as usual,' he said. 'You lost?'

'No, Mr Spivey, I am exactly where I want to be, or I will be when you invite me in.'

'Why should I do that?'

'Because I need to ask you some questions and as you can see, I am a polite, elderly gentleman with, I like to think, impeccable manners, visiting you in your own home. The alternative, later tonight or very early tomorrow morning, could be a visit from a pair of much younger, larger, and probably uncouth constables, charged with escorting you to the police station in Bedford. The choice is yours.'

The small man tensed his wiry body and Campion could swear he heard the cogs of a brain grinding as the former jockey looked him up and down as perhaps he would have examined a horse, while judging its chances of winning a race at the quoted odds.

'Suppose it's nice to have a choice for once,' he said, opening the door.

Mr Campion stepped into the house, directly into a front room unchanged since Markley had been desolated for the second time by the construction of the M1. The wallpaper, carpets and furnishings seemed to have sprung from the pages of a Fifties mail-order catalogue, with the exception of a pair of easy chairs, which were in fact deckchairs, the faded stencilling down one side of the wooden frame claiming that they had once been the property of the town council of a sedate seaside resort on the south coast.

Between the two sagging deckchairs was a nest of three small coffee tables, on which sat an ancient radio in fake walnut, which a family might once have gathered around to hear news of the Abdication. The room reeked of dust, with faint notes of spilled whisky and something animal, which Campion's nose could not instantly identify but which he guessed might be horse sweat.

'It's not much, is it?' said Spivey, and Mr Campion felt slightly ashamed that he had given away his thoughts so easily. 'But I don't need much.'

'Just as well. I take it McIntyre doesn't pay much – if anything at all.'

'I won't hear a bad word about the McIntyres. They've given me a job, a job with horses, and a roof over my head and the wages are fair and regular. It's just I don't spend on creature comforts. I put my money to work.'

'Not on the gee-gees I hope,' said Campion, knowing that he was sounding pompous. 'Those creature comforts can be an expensive luxury, as I am sure you of all people would know.'

'I don't go near a racetrack these days; too many bad memories. Most everything I earn goes towards my pension.' Spivey caught Campion's surprised expression. 'Got to think of when I'll be too old to handle anything bigger than a donkey on Brighton beach.'

'Wise man,' said Campion, who remembered an incident when he had feared for his life under the flashing hooves of an angry horse. 'I can understand your loyalty to your employers, but I need to ask you about that.'

'You'd better sit down, then.'

'I don't think I will, if you don't mind,' said Campion, resting a hand on the creaking frame of the nearest deckchair. 'If I got down into one of those things, I doubt I could get my old bones upright again without the aid of one of Sir Lachlan's cranes.'

'Well, I don't suppose this was going to be a comfortable conversation anyway, so you'd better get started.'

'Very well, let me ask you about your relationship with Mary Lillman.'

'Mary Lillman?' The small man was genuinely puzzled. 'Haven't seen her for years, not since . . .'

'You got out of prison.'

'That's not a secret.'

'Where you shared a cell with her husband, Walter Lillman.'

'*That's* not common knowledge.' Spivey's brain cogs were now whirring at high speed.

'After your release you, shall we say, pursued her, once she was a widow?'

'Your kind might put it like that. I'd say I fancied my chances, but Mary was havin' none of it. She'd done all right out of Walter's accident, gone up in the world and got out of Dagenham. Must have been an insurance policy or something, 'cos I never got the impression Walter was a good earner. Inside he was always moaning that every penny he had went to the cause.'

Mr Campion took a deep breath to steady his voice. 'That cause being a political one, an anti-Semitic one?'

'If that means blaming the Jews for everything under the sun, yes. Walter was nuts on the subject, completely bonkers; in fact, that's why he'd had his collar felt, after a bout of what he called "Yid-bashing". The man couldn't talk about anything else and was always playing the hard man, though he wasn't anything of the sort. He was one of those who was a tough guy in a crowd but on his own you could knock him down with a feather.'

'And I suppose you felt sorry for his widow,' Campion offered.

'Not for long. She was quick to ditch her widow's weeds, but she said she'd had enough of men to last a lifetime, so I got the brush-off in no uncertain terms. Still, she did me a big favour.'

'She introduced you to Lucy McIntyre.'

Spivey nodded. 'Her and Mary went back a long way – before the war, she said – when they were young 'uns. Lady M. used to come with her when she visited Walter; it was like they'd been in the same gang at one time, which is funny come to think of it now, because you wouldn't have thought they had much in common, the McIntyres having all that money and the big house and horses.'

'Which was why you were offered your job, wasn't it?'

'For which I was grateful, still am.'

'How exactly did that happen?' Campion noted Spivey's confusion. 'I'm just curious, that's all.'

'After I got out, I turned up at Mary's new house in Romford and Lady Lucy was there – just visiting, I suppose. Said she needed someone to look after her horses, and Mary reminded her I used to be in the business. Simple as that. When Sir Lachlan was looking for men to work here in Markley, I recommended Old Nick, and then she picked up Andy and Frank Green on her other prison visits.'

'Didn't it ever strike you as odd that someone like Lucy McIntyre would become a prison visitor?'

'Never thought about it.' Spivey shrugged his shoulders. 'She always said it was good for her image. A bit of positive public relations on her part, she called it.'

'Yes, well,' said Campion, 'you can never have too much of that, can you?'

EIGHTEEN
Game Worth the Candle

A telephone bell rang loudly and harshly in the small room.

Mr Campion's first reaction was one of annoyance with himself as he had not located an instrument on entering and failed to do so now. His second reaction was of frustrated anger aimed at his absent nephew. Had he not made it clear that Christopher should keep Old Nick away from the telephone? But very quickly he realized that he was blameless, and so was Christopher.

As the telephone clanged again, Spivey scuttled over to the deckchair he had been relaxing in and pulled it away to reveal the black telephone which had, along with a half-bottle of whisky, been hidden under the sagging striped fabric of the chair. Campion forgave himself for not having noticed the black wire snaking across the floor from the skirting board, and then forgave his nephew when Spivey, sinking down on his haunches, picked up the receiver and answered the call.

'Hullo? Yes, missus, o'course I can. Let me get me boots on and I'll be over to see to Buckland.'

He replaced the receiver and rose slowly up to his full height, which was still some way short of Campion's, though there was no doubt that in his mind he was squaring up to his uninvited visitor.

'I take it that was Lady McIntyre,' said Campion.

'I've got to go to work.'

'At this hour?'

'When the boss rings, I go to work. Buckland needs to be bedded down after her ride.'

'In danger of repeating myself, I have to say: at this hour?'

'She likes riding at night,' Spivey answered, implying it was the most natural thing in the world. 'I've got to go.'

'A quick question,' said Campion, holding up a forefinger. 'Did you ever see Mary Lillman here in Markley, at Cruachan?'

Spivey shook his head whilst remembering. 'No, can't say she ever came here that I know of, and I'd no reason to keep in touch after she'd given me the brush-off.'

'Did you not think that odd, given that Lady McIntyre and Mary Lillman were such old friends?'

'Not my area of expertise, Mr Campion.' Spivey spoke the phrase as if he had learned it for an exam. 'Women, I mean. Horses, now, that's who I get on with, not women. Horses usually do what's best for them; women never do what you tell them.'

'My wife would love to debate your logic, Mr Spivey, but that must be at some future date. You have to go to work – in the stables at Cruachan, I presume?'

'Of course.'

'Then I'll walk over there with you. You don't mind, do you?'

'I'm going to the stables,' Spivey said slowly, 'not the house.'

'Sir Lachlan told me you keep a gun in the stables; he called it a rook gun.'

'I use it to keep the rats down, mebbe get the occasional rabbit for the pot. Ain't much good for anything bigger.'

'I'd like to be sure of that,' said Mr Campion. 'Shall we go?'

Spivey sat in a deckchair and pulled on Wellington boots, apparently noticing the hole in his sock for the first time, then put on a faded leather jacket and a flat cap before holding the front door open for Mr Campion. He had the air not of someone being polite, but of a homeowner making sure a visitor was not leaving with the silver spoons, which amused Campion who had seen little of value in the house other than the remains of the whisky.

Whatever Carl Spivey spent his money on, it was not his creature comforts. Perhaps he really was saving every penny for his retirement; perhaps his time in prison had conditioned him to a Spartan lifestyle. The little man with the gait of a sailor on a rolling deck was difficult to gauge, and Campion speculated briefly that his life might have been so much different had the widowed Mary Lillman not rejected his advances so firmly. But then, Mary Lillman seemed to have done very well for herself, whereas Spivey had become a middle-aged stable boy, and both their fortunes were connected to the McIntyres.

Campion used the torch, the beam pointed at his feet, to avoid the cracks and holes in the road caused by the traffic of heavy machinery as they walked in silence, though it was far from a silent night thanks to the constant hum of cars zipping along the motorway in the distance behind them.

When they were almost opposite Cruachan, Campion waved the torch beam ahead of them towards the roundabout and the turnings to Cranfield and Bedford.

'Any idea why David Duffy parked his car in that lay-by round the corner?' he asked.

'So that's what all this is about.' Spivey stopped in his tracks and glared at Campion, who resisted the urge to turn his torch vertical to light the smaller man's face as if he was telling a ghost story around a campfire.

'I am afraid it is,' he said gently. 'I wish it were otherwise, but a man has been murdered.'

'I've told you, and Gawd knows I've told the cops, I never knew the bloke, so how do I know why he parked where he did? Mebbe he needed the phone box there, had to phone somebody. Well, if he did, it certainly wasn't me.'

'Perhaps he was *waiting* for a call, not making one.'

'Well, it wasn't from me. How many times do I have to say I didn't know him from Adam, so why would I . . .' Spivey's mouth clamped shut as if spring-loaded, then his eyes widened. 'That's why you want to see my rook gun, isn't it?'

Campion remained impassive.

'Don't know how much good that'll do you, whatever it is you're after. The police never bothered with it, didn't even ask to see it.'

'Which is precisely why I thought I ought to,' said Mr Campion.

Spivey said nothing, but led the way up the drive of Cruachan, following a paved path to the right of the brick-and-glass monstrosity. With the footing in front of him now firmer, Mr Campion turned off the torch; it was unnecessary in the lee of Cruachan, which reared up on his left, light spilling from its multiple windows. To Campion, it was a scene which made him think of what the view from the iceberg must have been as the *Titanic* nudged by.

The stable block was a long, low, flat-roofed building of brick and black timber, its interior lit by a series of protected bulkhead lights along its walls. To one side were four stalls, each separated by metal railings, the heads of a pair of incumbent horses poking inquisitively out of two of them. A third horse stood outside the furthest empty stall in the body of the stable, secured casually to a tie-ring, its nostrils flaring and its chest pumping slowly as it waited patiently to be unsaddled and rugged up for the rest of the night. It had clearly been ridden through mud.

There was no sign of its rider.

Everything that a well-equipped stable could possibly require for the comfort and pampering of its equine residents lined the walls. Bales of sweet-smelling hay were stacked neatly, and already stuffed hay nets dangled from hooks. Outdoor horse rugs were hanging like curtains on a rail above a large wooden blanket box, its lid secured with a hefty hasp and a large, shiny padlock. To either side of the box were neatly ranked mucking-out tools – a wheelbarrow, shovels, forks and long-handled brooms – and strategically placed sand buckets and a bright red fire extinguisher.

At the far end, beyond the horse waiting patiently to be cosseted, was the tack area. There were riding saddles on racks with bridles and bits hanging beside them, and a unit of shelving displaying an assortment of riding hats, leather straps and other unidentifiable but no doubt vital equestrian items, along with a long oak valet box which reminded Campion of the portable kits carried by professional shoe-shiners on Oxford Street, or under-butlers in the grander country houses of his youth. Truly, everything the well-groomed horse could want for, with a willing manservant to tender to his, or her, every whim.

From the open doors to the paddock, the fruity tang of manure wafted in on the night air. Carl Spivey made no move to close the doors, presumably on the assumption that Buckland, for Campion was sure it was he, had enjoyed sufficient exercise that evening and was unlikely to be tempted to bolt and run.

In the company of the horses, Spivey was clearly in his element and visibly relaxed as he went about his work. He no longer stabbed suspicious glances at Mr Campion; indeed, he seemed to have forgotten his presence completely as he dedicated all his attention to Buckland. With soothing neck strokes and comforting whispers into the beast's ear, he ran up the stirrups, undid the girth and removed the saddle and the soft pad cushioning it, which Campion knew was called a numnah, a word once heard, rarely forgotten. Ever since he had first encountered it, its child-like resonance had appealed to him.

'Does Lady McIntyre often go riding in the dark?' asked Campion.

'Two or three times a week,' said Spivey, almost with a touch of pride.

'Isn't it dangerous?'

'Not if you know what you're doing, and Buckland does.' He gave the horse a resounding slap on the neck but the horse did not seem to mind. 'Horses have eyes that are more sensitive to weak light, so they're pretty good at night, plus Buckland knows the paddock and Daffodil Wood better than any gamekeeper. He could find his way back here blindfolded.'

Mr Campion did his best to look impressed. 'And she just parks him here and wanders off for a gin and tonic or a cup of cocoa or whatever, leaving you to put the nag to bed?'

Now Spivey turned and looked at Campion with a mixture of surprise and indignation. 'That's my job, ain't it? Grateful to have it an' you don't keep a dog and bark yerself.'

Standing behind Spivey, and well out of range of Buckland's hindquarters, Campion observed the middle-aged stable lad at work as he opened the valet box and revealed a comprehensive grooming kit, including dandy brushes, bristle and goat hair body brushes, curry combs and a selection of dangerous-looking hoof picks.

'It's too cold to wash you down tonight, boy,' Spivey addressed the horse, 'so a quick brush and we'll get your rug and make you comfy.'

Buckland gave a soft whinny of agreement, or perhaps he was issuing instructions to his faithful servant. Spivey certainly seemed to enjoy the role of horse butler, as he applied a pair of dandy brushes – one on each outstretched hand – with enthusiasm, along the flanks and down the legs of the animal which towered over him.

'Give us a hand with the jute,' he said over his shoulder as he pulled his hands out of the leather grips of the brushes.

'I beg your pardon?'

'Buckland's jute rug – it's in the blanket box. It's toasty and it's supposed to help him groom his own coat, but it weighs a ton.'

Spivey indicated the large wooden container, producing a bunch of keys and unlocking the padlock which secured the lid.

The folded jute rug, a thick grey blanket padded with straw, was the top item in the box, and so bulky and heavy it seemed impossible that there was room for anything else. Campion began to lift it out and, when Spivey joined in to take the strain, he was surprised at the smaller man's strength.

'Nothing better for drying off a sweaty horse, and the texture is good for his skin. It's like he grooms himself.'

Campion could only admire the speed and skill with which the diminutive bow-legged man flapped the heavy rug over the horse, with no more effort than shaking a duster out of a window, then manoeuvred what must have been a thousand pounds of horseflesh into its stall. Once there, the docile Buckland was rewarded with a full hay net and feed bucket, and Campion half-expected Spivey to read him a bedside story, but a steady stream of whispered sweet nothings seemed to suffice.

Only when Spivey had backed out of the stall and closed the gate did Mr Campion raise the subject really on his mind.

'That's your rook gun in there, isn't it?' Campion said, indicating the large blanket box with its lid gaping open.

'That's where we keep it, all proper, out of sight and under lock and key.'

Beneath the bulk of the jute rug and a tangle of straps and ropes, Campion had seen the unmistakeable outline of a rifle wrapped in hessian sacking secured with string, lying diagonally across the bottom of the box. Nestled in a corner was a dirty, squashed cardboard cube containing .410 shotgun shells.

'May I?'

'Help yourself,' said Spivey, 'it's what you came for.'

Campion bent over the box and reached in to remove the weapon, judging its weight to be about five pounds and its length something short of four feet. The string ties holding the hessian covering were simple shoelace bow knots which came away easily, allowing him to unfold the piece of hessian and allow it to float down back into the box.

'Before you ask, there'll be my fingerprints all over it.' Spivey spoke with the resigned air of one expecting to be accused of something.

'And now mine.'

The gun was a bolt-action Webley & Scott shotgun, probably of venerable age but seemingly well cared for, its wooden stock unpitted and highly polished. Mr Campion's hands caressed its smooth contours and his fingertips closed on the knurled knob of the looped bolt ejector lever. From ancient army training days, he pointed the barrel of the gun into the blanket box, just as a soldier coming off guard duty would unload his rifle into a sand box for the sake of safety in case a rogue bullet was still 'up the spout'. The chances of that in this case he knew were slim, as it was a single-shot weapon, but old habits militarily installed died hard.

He worked the bolt and peered into an empty breech, then raised the mechanism to his face and sniffed loudly, but registered only the faintest whiff of cordite and gun oil. It confirmed something he had always suspected; that as an olfactory detective he was sadly lacking, as he had no idea how long it had been since the gun was fired.

Carl Spivey did however have the skill of reading Campion's mind. 'I used it to blast a rat that had its little red eyes on a bag of Buckland's oats.'

'Can you remember when that was?'

'Day before yesterday.'

'Would you swear to that?'

'If I had to,' said Spivey, his tone suddenly less confident.

Mr Campion sighed then leaned into the box again to retrieve the sheet of hessian and, as he did so, his hand brushed against the cardboard box of cartridges. 'Do you keep a count of the shells you use?'

'Not really. I use 'em when I have to, and when the box is empty, Sir Lachlan orders some more.'

'Does Sir Lachlan ever use this gun?'

'I've never seen him with it. He's got enough of his own to pick from.'

'He certainly has quite an armoury,' Campion said, his head still inside the blanket box, 'all bigger and more lethal than this little rook gun, and this ammunition would be no good for any of his blunderbusses, would it?'

With the shotgun in his left hand, held away from his body, Campion's right hand grasped the box of cartridges and popped the lid open to reveal the half-dozen shells rolling around inside. This told him nothing of interest but, as his fingers trailed over the box, he lifted it out as he straightened up and showed it to Spivey.

'That's odd.'

'What is?'

'I thought at first it was glue, or mud, or something more . . . biological . . . but look, down the side; the cardboard has been splashed by wax – candle wax.'

Spivey screwed up his eyes to focus on the cardboard cube and the coin-sized spots of grey wax which had dripped and solidified down one side. He looked at Campion blankly and shook his head. Mr Campion returned his stare.

'I am not *au fait* with the current discussions about health and safety in the workplace, but to my rather simple mind, it seems rather risky for someone to be using a lighted candle when examining shotgun shells stuffed with gunpowder. Indeed, using a candle at all in a building which houses so much hay and straw and yet seems to have perfectly functioning electric lights would seem unwise.'

'I ain't never brought a lit candle in here,' said Spivey. 'Don't even allow smoking. The horses don't like it.'

'I have seen how you treat Buckland and I am convinced you would not allow anything to upset the livestock. Has anyone removed the cartridges from here?'

'Why would they? They wouldn't fit any of the rifles in the house, and those antique shotguns Sir Lachlan collects will all take twelve-bore shells if they still work.'

'Good point, now hold this, would you?'

Campion handed over the shotgun, hoping that Spivey took it as a sign of trust, although he had reassured himself that the breech was open and the gun was unloaded. Then, holding the box of cartridges in his left hand and his borrowed torch in his right, and having jammed his fedora tightly on his head, he pushed his midriff into the edge of the blanket box and bent his long thin frame into an acute angle so that the top half of his body disappeared into its depths.

Numerous scents – horse, hay, old sacks, dust and saddle soap – assailed his nostrils, causing him to hold his breath. He carefully replaced the cartridge box where he had found it, though not before scanning the inside of the blanket box with his torch. There were small pimples of wax in one corner, confirming his suspicion that a lit candle had indeed been used *in situ*.

He gathered up the hessian which had wrapped the gun and brought it out, straightening up with only, he noted proudly, the slightest twinge to the muscles in his back, and tossed it towards Spivey. 'You'd better wrap it up again. It seems to be in good working order. Is it?'

'Oh, aye, it's a good little gun as long as you get close enough to what you're trying to hit.'

'Twenty-five yards to be sure; more than fifty and even a good shot could miss a barn door.'

The voice, deep but definitely feminine, caused both men to swivel towards the open stable doors where Lucy McIntyre stood, wide-legged and hands on hips. She wore a long, brown, waxed-cotton riding coat over a white polo-neck jumper, skin-tight black trousers and long brown boots. She screwed up her eyes and turned her head as Campion's beam caught her full in the face.

'Apologies, Lady McIntyre,' Campion said, switching off the torch, 'I do hope we have not disturbed you.'

Though that, he thought, would depend on how long you've been standing there.

'Not at all, Mr Campion, I just popped in to say goodnight to Buckland – and to Carl.' She strode forward and patted Buckland heartily on the rump. The horse, its head deep into a feed bag, did not seem to notice.

Lady McIntyre turned smartly on her heels with parade-ground precision and strode for the open door. 'I'll leave you to lock up, Carl,' she said without looking back. 'Why don't you join me for a nightcap, Mr Campion?'

'Why not indeed? I wanted to have a word with you,' Campion

said enthusiastically, despite thinking that he would have much preferred neutral territory.

'Then come along. The French windows are open and I'll put the patio lights on for you.'

Then she was through the doorway and out of sight, leaving a rectangle of dark night, the diminishing clicks of her boot heels and a faint trace of a perfume strong enough to survive the animal muskiness of the stables.

Carl Spivey raised his eyebrows but said nothing, simply produced his bundle of keys and jangled them.

Mr Campion raised his torch in a mock salute, nodded to him and followed the sound of footsteps out into the dark.

Halfway along the patio, the outside lights came on, temporarily blinding him, and he cursed himself for being surprised both by the sudden illumination, even though the woman had warned him in advance, and by the fact that he had missed entirely her arrival in the stables. He must, he decided ruefully – and not for the first time – be getting old. To look less foolish, he turned off his torch and thrust it into a too-small jacket pocket, where it swayed precariously and threatened to fall out as he walked.

The French windows were half-open, and Campion could see down the length of the entrance hall to the front door and, immediately to the right, the door – also open and with the lights on – to Sir Lachlan's study, the room he now automatically thought of as the armoury.

Lucy McIntyre appeared from a door down the hall, holding a small tray on which were balanced two large tumblers containing amber liquid and ice cubes which tinkled as she walked towards her guest.

'Lachlan doesn't drink,' she said as if an explanation was needed, 'so all the booze is stashed in the kitchen. Scotch and soda OK for you?'

'Perfectly acceptable.'

'Good, then please go through and try and make yourself comfortable in one of Lachlan's ghastly egg chairs. He keeps them for business partners he doesn't like; he prefers it if they don't get too comfortable.'

Mr Campion removed his hat and waited politely for his hostess to precede him into the room, where he noted that a Venetian blind now covered the long rectangular windows, denying a view of the ultra-modern interior to any old-fashioned poacher wandering by hoping to view the lord of the manor's trophies.

'I encountered those chairs when I met your husband, and it wasn't a question of getting too comfortable: the problem was getting *out* of one. Far too modern for my old bones, I'm afraid. After you.'

'No, please go ahead. I have to turn the outside lights off.'

As Campion stepped into the study, she moved behind him, the tray of drinks in one hand, and he heard the click of a switch and the patio was plunged into darkness. He heard more clicks as she closed the French window and turned a key to lock it, then she was up close behind him, the tray she was holding nudging him forward until she could put it down on Sir Lachlan's desk. She handed a glass to him, making a 'cheers' motion with her own.

Mr Campion acknowledged the toast and was tempted to raise his glass to the decapitated animals dotted round the wall, their glassy eyes glaring disapprovingly down on him. Instead, he found his own gaze drawn to the iron grilles guarding Sir Lachlan's collection of long guns and he realized that his hostess had spotted him doing so.

She had pinned her long blonde hair into a chignon bun, which did nothing to soften her naturally stern countenance. Campion was once again intrigued by her face, which was both round and, at the jawline, angular at the same time; almost a face sketched by a cubist in a bad mood.

'I never asked what you were doing snooping around my stables,' she said, touching her glass to her lips.

'Actually, I was having a chat with Carl Spivey in his cottage when you rang him, and there seemed far more profitable snooping to be done in the stables, so I took the opportunity to tag along.'

She did not ask the question Campion had anticipated, but indicated that they should sit in the dreaded egg chairs. With some difficulty because of his long legs, Campion followed the advice Amanda had given him and perched uncomfortably on the lip, balancing his fedora on his knees. He noted that Lady

McIntyre was adopting the same posture, even though neither of them were wearing short skirts.

'Was it interesting, your chat with Carl – or profitable?'

Campion sipped his drink and squirmed in the chair, having discovered that the torch in his jacket pocket now had a mind of its own and a vendetta against his kidneys.

'In many ways, yes; certainly more profitable than when I asked your husband more or less the same things when I was last in this room – in this very chair, in fact.'

'My husband was unhelpful?' she asked from behind her glass, her eyes gleaming over the rim.

'I'm afraid so.'

'Intentionally?'

'Almost certainly, although I did not ask the right question. You see, I was working from notes made by the late David Duffy; notes that had included my name on a list which had a connection to the year 1932. That list of names comprised Walter Lillman, Henry Gould, Mary Gould and L. McIntyre, and perhaps I should have made some connections earlier, but it was forty years ago and my memory is not what it was.'

Lady McIntyre took a long drink of whisky. 'Are you saying my husband lied to you and, by implication, the police?'

Campion met her gaze. 'It was my fault entirely. I specifically asked Sir Lachlan if he knew any of those names *in 1932*, and of course he did not, then. It was later – 1936 perhaps, around the time of the Battle of Cable Street? – that you all got together. And, in my stupidity, I was asking the wrong person because in Duffy's notes the L. McIntyre referred to was Lucy, not Lachlan. If only he'd used your maiden name, I might have seen things more clearly, because in 1932 you were Lucy Southall – and that was when we first met, on the steps of the Silver Vaults.'

The woman balanced her glass on one knee and reached up with her left hand to touch the back of her head through the coil of curled hair. 'Your memory seems to have returned,' she said through tight lips, 'but I still have a dent in my skull where you hit me with a cosh to remind me.'

NINETEEN
Tigress by the Tail

'You didn't recognize me when you came to see my husband,' she said, breaking the heavy silence that had descended.

'No, I did not,' said Campion, 'my memory failed me there, but I do remember the incident. It wasn't a cosh, by the way, it was a silver tankard that I had been showing to my friend Nathan Hirsch, the man you and your gang had set upon.'

'The Jew,' she sneered.

Campion snorted in disgust. 'You were masked and I had no idea you were female. Under normal circumstances, recalling the experience, I would be mortified at the thought of hitting a woman, but strangely I feel rather smug about it.'

'Your fat butler back then didn't have any problem punching a woman.'

'Ah, yes, your good friend Mary Lillman, née Gould. The gentleman in question, who is even fatter now but still not a butler, did feel terribly bad about that . . . for almost half an hour . . . and Mary, of course, was subsequently apprehended. Whereas you were not because you ran away and left her.'

'She knew the risks, did her time and kept her mouth shut for the cause.'

'A quite repugnant cause in my not-so-humble opinion, but Mr and Mrs Lillman, as they became, were neither reformed nor disillusioned by their time in prison. In fact, Walter became something of a regular customer. You and they, and Henry Gould, became active in Mosley's mob in Stepney, and that's where you recruited Lachlan to your pathetic little gang.'

The woman showed a cruel smile. 'He didn't take much recruiting; he just fell into my arms. Or, to be accurate, I fell into his, quite literally. You were right, it was during the Whitechapel rally in 1936.'

'Lachlan was marching with your fascist chums?'

'Not at all, he was an innocent abroad, simply an onlooker. He wasn't with us, nor with the Bolshevik Jewish scum who attacked us. It was on Mansell Street, outside Gardner's department store, which always amused me as it specialized in Scottish clothing and Leckie was Scottish rough and true. The police horses charged *us* rather than the communist militia which tried to stop us marching, and I had what you might call an altercation with a mounted constable.'

'I doubt a magistrate would have put it that way,' sniped Campion.

'I was knocked to the ground and Lachlan, seeing all this, was sure I was going to be trampled by the police horse. He rushed in and gathered me up in his arms, taking a few baton blows on my behalf. I was dazed and felt sick and he was really quite handsome, so I put on a bit of a faint and let him take me back to his digs in Stepney. Fortunately his aunt was out, so I was able to show him how grateful I was. He had never been shown a woman's gratitude before.'

'And from that moment he was hooked?'

'Oh, I wouldn't put it like that.' Lucy McIntyre attempted a coy smile.

'I would,' said Campion grimly. 'I think you got your claws into him from the start.'

'He was young and innocent, he needed moulding.'

'Indoctrinating him so he followed the party line?'

'Oh, Leckie was never really interested in politics, just interested in me. I was his first, you see, and he's been ridiculously faithful ever since, which made him very *compliant*.'

Mr Campion shuddered at the word but kept his voice level. 'So you pulled him into the orbit of your little gang in Stepney and, when the war came, business boomed.'

For the first time since they had entered the room, Lucy McIntyre looked worried, but before he could compose a thought, Mr Campion played one of the trump cards in his hand.

'You were wrong about good old Mary Lillman; she didn't keep her mouth shut, did she? Walter Lillman stayed true to the cause and continued to vent his spleen on what he saw as the world conspiracy of Judaism, and was constantly in and out of prison, so I doubt he was a good provider. When he died, I think his widow turned to her old friend and fellow prison visitor for help; financial help in buying a house of her own. Otherwise, she might have been tempted to tell stories about the East End in the Blitz and how a successful British businessman, on his way to making all the right connections, had acquired his seed money. Tell me, did she approach Lachlan direct?'

'He knew nothing about it,' said the woman, shaking her head, 'and he was making so much money then, it was easy enough to shuffle a couple of thousand Mary's way without him noticing.' Campion noticed a smile – no, a smirk – crease her lips. 'Especially as most of his assets are in my name and I help him do his accounts. It was supposed to be a one-off settlement.'

'But that's the problem with blackmail. Once is never enough. Mary came back for more, didn't she?'

'Not directly. It was Duffy who came knocking, snooping around because Lachlan was being touted for a life peerage, but it was clear to me that he was being fed things by Mary.'

'Did you talk to her?'

'No, I haven't spoken to her . . . yet,' she said ominously.

'And Duffy?'

'I never met him.' She said it coolly and precisely, but with the air of someone wanting to add *and you can't prove I did*.

'But you spoke to him?'

'Only on the telephone.'

'The last time being when he rang you from the telephone box round on the Cranfield road. Or did you ring him?'

Lucy McIntyre stared hard at Campion and, although her face remained nerveless, almost blank, her eyes flashed venomously.

Mr Campion realized he might have gone too far, too soon.

And now he could be in danger.

She said nothing and did nothing more menacing than leave her chair with a feline grace that Campion envied and walk slowly and deliberately around Sir Lachlan's large desk to sit down gently in his black leather chairman-of-the-board swivel chair. Leaning back in the chair, only her face and neck were visible over the forest of telephones and office detritus on the desktop. It was her silence which was threatening.

Campion squirmed in his uncomfortable egg chair, feeling at a distinct disadvantage as they stared at each other over ten feet of dead air.

'I take it,' she said at last, 'that you have spoken to Mary.'

'Earlier today, as a matter of fact, and she was very forthcoming about your husband's wartime career in the fire brigade.'

'For a price, I'll bet. How much?'

'Duffy had promised her five hundred.'

'Pah! Mary always did think small.'

'Five hundred pounds for some thirty-year-old memories? I do not think that a derogatory offer. You could buy a Mini or a small Fiat with that.'

'Compared to the damage it could do Lachlan's reputation – and prospects – I think it is. For God's sake, I would have offered her more!'

'You are very protective of Lachlan's reputation.'

'Protective? I built his reputation! Yes, I intend to guard it! I have moulded his image since we got out of Stepney. Leckie needed a firm guiding hand.'

'I have no doubt he got it,' said Campion. 'The knighthood must have been a milestone in your plan, the impending life peerage your crowning glory.'

'It's no more than he deserves. He runs a business which helps build roads and houses and contributes to the economy, creating thousands of jobs. We make a point of employing rehabilitated criminals where we can, not to mention supporting dozens of charities. He is a captain of industry, without a stain on his character.'

'Apart from his activities as a "fire pirate" during the Blitz.' Campion's eyes widened behind his spectacles as he spoke. 'I think you guided his activities at that time and accumulated a start-up nest egg in the vilest of ways.'

'We only stole from Jewish houses because they deserved it! They started the war!'

'If you believe that, then you are both ignorant and disgusting, madam, and I for one will take an un-Christian delight in your fall from grace.'

The woman tapped the fingers of her right hand on the desk as she gathered her thoughts. 'But Mr Duffy is in no position to print scandalous stories about a prominent businessman, and respectable newspapers would be sued for slander if they even considered it without concrete proof.'

'It would be libel,' said Campion, pleased to score a point of order. 'If it is in print, it would be libel. If it is a spoken accusation, it's slander, and I promise I can be very slanderous.'

'We would sue and – win or lose – it would surely be the end of your nephew's career in public relations.'

'That would not be the end of the world for either Christopher or the public relations industry, but even a whiff of scandal would scupper Lachlan's chances of a peerage.'

'You'd see to that, would you? You and your upper-class friends who have always looked down on the likes of us.'

'If you mean by "us" a gang of badly educated, intolerant bullies who preach hatred and spew bile, then yes, I do look down on you, and from the greatest height possible.'

At the back of Campion's mind, a warning bell rang faintly. He was poking a tigress with a sharp stick and a tigress who was younger, more muscular and probably stronger. He was relieved that if the tigress was not in a cage, there was at least a desk between them.

'You have not a shred of proof of anything,' she snarled.

'I have a witness.'

'Mary? She won't talk. She's been bought off once, she can be bought off again.'

'But David Duffy could not be bought off; he had to be silenced.'

'I am sure a worm like him would have plenty of enemies.'

'That's a reasonable assumption, given he was a journalist, but possibly a sweeping judgement. I cannot speak to his qualities as I never met him.'

'Neither did I. You look surprised, Mr Campion, but I assure you David Duffy and I never met face-to-face. You will find no trace of him, not a hair or a fingerprint, anywhere in this house.'

'But you knew what he was doing.'

'Digging dirt is what he was doing! Of course I knew. Lachlan tells me everything, and your idiot nephew had done a background brief on Duffy, which was quite helpful.'

The frown on Campion's forehead cleared and he felt a surge

of energy. 'You are doing exactly what your husband did, being evasive in the literal. When I asked him if he knew Walter Lillman or Henry and Mary Gould in 1932, he said no because that was, in 1932, literally true; it was only later he met them. And now you have just adopted the same tactic. When you say you never met David Duffy *face-to-face*, that is technically probably true, because you came up on him from behind . . .'

Lucy McIntyre powered her way out of her chair; it was the only way Campion could describe it. One moment she was lounging deep in the leather chair, the next she was on her feet, her clenched fists pressing knuckles down on the desktop as if she had been spring-loaded, like an Olympic gymnast jumping to attention. She was clearly bursting to say something, but through an iron will and tightly compressed lips, the tigress remained silent, and Campion could not help but tugging her tail one more time.

'You are not a tall woman,' he said, as if he had only just acknowledged her presence in the room, rather than to deliberately wrongfoot her, although that was the result.

'What the hell are you talking about?' As she spoke, her arms began to tremble as she pressed down through her fists on to the desk, as if trying to slowly punch through it.

'David Duffy was assassinated, and I do not consider that to be too strong a word, by a gunman who approached him from behind and shot him through the rear window of his car. The police theory, which seemed to make perfect sense to me, was that his assassin was very tall and firing slightly downwards. As you stand before me, you are not a tall woman, but on the back of a horse like Buckland, you would be elevated to the required height. As I have learned from Mr Spivey, Buckland is a former Military Police horse, and has been trained not to panic at the sound of gunfire. He is also, thanks to your riding habits, perfectly happy to be out and about after dark, which explains another thing which puzzled the police. How had Duffy's killer got so close to him without him apparently noticing? Another car pulling into that lay-by would have had its headlights on or, if not, there would at least be the sound of an engine. At night, coming out of the woods, crossing the Cranfield road higher up and staying off the tarmac, a rider could approach Duffy's parked car silently and almost invisibly. If poor Duffy had looked in his rear-view mirror and seen a horse approaching out of the night, he probably wouldn't have believed it anyway.'

The tigress exhaled slowly and the tension seemed to slip from her frame. She unclenched her fists, then slotted her hands into the pockets of her open riding jacket and casually slid from behind the desk. Her movements were lithe and sinuous, definitely tigerish, as she crossed the room, walking so close to Campion's chair that he could have reached out and touched her, or stuck out a long leg and tripped her. So close he could detect the scent of horse on her clothing.

'Are you saying I shot that journalist in cold blood?' She threw the words over her shoulder as she reached the iron grille doors of Sir Lachlan's gun cabinet and looked up and down the rack of rifles and shotguns, as if seeing an exhibit in a museum for the first time.

'There are some who would say it is the only way to deal with journalists, but I hope I could not bring myself to be so heartless. You, on the other hand, I think could be.' Campion strained forward on his perch in that ludicrous egg of a chair and the hairs on the back of his neck crackled as if he had touched a live wire as he saw Lucy McIntyre casually pull open the iron grille, reach in and remove one of the rifles from its mounts.

He could not tell which rifle it was – not that it mattered – except that it was not one of the antique shotguns. What did matter was that the woman clearly felt comfortable handling the weapon, which she held with both hands at the slope across her chest, the muzzle pointing to the ceiling at a forty-five-degree angle, blissfully, for the moment, without Campion in its sights.

'Would I have used this, my favourite rifle? The one I always use when Lachlan and I go stalking?' she said calmly, her eyes flicking to the nearest wall-mounted trophies as if seeking validation. 'Because the police certainly do not think so. Their experts do not believe this gun has been fired recently, which it has not, and they could find neither a spent bullet nor an ejected cartridge case to test against it.'

Mr Campion took a deep breath and reassured himself with a silent mantra: *the rifle is not loaded; no one keeps a loaded rifle on display, even in a locked display case.* And then the sickening thought struck him that the woman had pulled the grille door open without needing to unlock it, and she had prepared this little scene in advance by opening and removing the padlock.

Determined not to be intimidated, Campion stood up out of the chair, stretching his long legs and rolling his shoulders as he did so, but controlling his movements so as not to startle the woman who was standing, poker-faced and stiff-backed like a sentry on guard duty. He was not sure that standing facing the woman with the rifle, watched by the dead eyes of a herd of previous victims, was any less intimidating than cowering in that stupid chair where he must have looked like an ungainly baby crocodile struggling out of its birth egg.

'But you did not use that gun, or any of those there in Lachlan's armoury,' said Campion, determined to keep his voice level, 'you used the shotgun Carl Spivey keeps in the stables for shooting rats. I suppose, according to your twisted logic, that's what you were doing. Killing David Duffy was no more than pest control as far as you were concerned.'

Lucy McIntyre's face remained impassive, her body almost frozen. Only her hands moved, and then only slightly, and only the fingers as she flexed them, her left hand supporting the fore-stock of the rifle, the right still around the butt grip where they – uncomfortably for Campion – hovered over the trigger. They were small movements, flutterings only, but packed with menace.

If he had expected her to break down and confess to her crime, Mr Campion would have been disappointed, but he had never really had much hope of that. He was more and more convinced that this bizarre situation would only end one way, and that being violently. They stood some five yards apart – she cradling a rifle, hopefully unloaded, he armed with nothing more dangerous than his fedora, which he held by the brim down at his right hip. He realized it was not only a mismatch in weaponry, for although he had the advantage in height, she was younger by some fourteen years and kept herself in good shape physically, her body toned and her arms and legs muscular, no doubt due to regular horse riding and, if Sir Lachlan and the trophies on the wall were to be believed, her energetic tramping up and down Scottish mountains stalking the indigenous wildlife.

Campion decided to play one more card, to prove to the

woman that the game was up, and in the hope she would accept her fate, though even as he spoke he was frantically trying to remember the distance to the door and gauging his chances of getting there unhurt.

But it was Lucy McIntyre who broke the silence and gave Campion his cue. 'Prove it, if you can, which you can't.'

'I do not have to,' he said, 'the police do; and I think they will, once they know what to look for. They looked at those guns, as you say, and found nothing incriminating, just as they found neither a spent bullet or an ejected cartridge case at the crime scene. That is because the weapon in question normally fires cartridges filled with birdshot, but in this case the cartridge had been opened and hot candle wax dripped into it. Once the wax solidified around the shot, you had in fact created a solid bullet which, when fired, becomes a lethal, high-velocity projectile at close range.'

'Sounds fanciful.' She was dismissive, but at least it was a reaction of sorts.

'I would have said gruesomely ingenious. After impact, the pellets of birdshot would dissipate, the wax would have melted. Perhaps traces can still be found on the body or in the car, though it might take a magnifying glass and a fine-tooth comb. Point is, the police were looking for a spent high-calibre bullet, not .410 shotgun shot glued together with wax. And there was no ejected cartridge case because it is a single-shot gun and you saw no need to reload. Did you have just the one cartridge? You must have been very confident of your marksmanship. Perhaps you prepared spares and disposed of them later, along with the spent casing. I doubt the police will ever find them.'

'So your fanciful theory is just that: a theory that you cannot prove.'

The index finger of her right hand stroked the trigger guard of the rifle she held and, even though it was not pointing at him, Campion felt a twitch of real fear.

'Fingerprints,' he said, with far more conviction then he really felt.

The woman's only reaction was a slight, quizzical tilt of her head.

'I know, I know,' Campion continued, 'your fingerprints on

that rook gun can be easily explained. It is kept in your stables, after all, and you may even have potted a rook or a genuine rat – not the journalistic kind – recently, but on the box of .410 cartridges there is a puddle of candle wax and in that wax is a very clear fingerprint visible to the naked eye, and I'm betting it's yours. You really should have held the candle well away from the box of cartridges. Naked flames and gunpowder are not good companions, especially not in a stable full of hay and straw. For once you were not thinking about your horses, were you?'

'Enough.'

It was not a command; she said the word almost to herself, as if agreeing with a private thought.

For Campion it was a warning, a final warning. His whole body tensed, as if his spine was a rubber band being twisted taut, but his eyes never left the woman's right hand as it moved, not towards the rifle's trigger mechanism as he had dreaded it might, but to the pocket of her riding jacket.

He had just enough time to formulate the reassuring thought that the rifle was not loaded, when it was dashed from his mind, as the hand came out of the pocket grasping something pointed and metallic, something brass.

Campion heard the dread, doom-laden clicking sound of the rifle's bolt being pulled and the breech opened, and he waited no longer. He skimmed his fedora across the room towards Lucy McIntyre, hoping to distract rather than disarm, and ran in long, loping strides towards the door to the hall.

At the door he had the presence of mind to hit the light switch and plunge the study into darkness, just as the first shot rang out.

He would never know whether it was the flinging of his fedora, his successful slapping at the light switch or simply the sight of a tall, thin, white-haired pensioner running for his life in a style that could only be classed as 'gangling' that put Lucy McIntyre off her aim, but the first bullet whizzed past Mr Campion's head as he burst into the hallway and smashed the large left pane of the French windows.

There was no time to congratulate himself on somehow upsetting what should have been a lethally easy shot, even from the hip, as Campion could already hear the *click-clack* sound of the rifle bolt as she reloaded. To his right, down the hall, was the front door of Cruachan, which would almost certainly be locked at this time of night, but now, immediately to his left, was the shattered French window, or at least a large pane of glass in a locked door with a hole big enough to put his head through, though if he did, the jagged teeth of the glass still intact would be the guillotine that negated the need for a second bullet.

The broken window was not simply Campion's nearest exit point from the house, it was his only one. Desperation and instinct overwhelmed rational thought as he reached for the metal torch still bulging from his jacket pocket and, wielding it like a hammer, he attacked the largest shards of remaining glass and barged through, feeling his jacket snag and then rip and then, painfully, a stabbing pain in his upper thigh.

But then he was out on the patio, the night air on his face, trying to remember the layout of the garden and the paddock which stood before him in the dark, where darkness could be his friend. He knew he had to get away from the house in case his homicidal hostess remembered to turn on the patio lights. Two lunging strides and he was on damp, greasy grass and not concrete, and some buried instinct told him to run in a zigzag pattern.

The sound of the second shot spurred him on into a sprint no white-haired gentleman having enjoyed more than his allocated three score and ten years should have to endure. The additional crack of the bullet hitting something solid and sending chips of stone into the air was strangely reassuring, for it meant Campion had narrowly avoided running full pelt into the mock Oriental fountain-cum-birdbath in the centre of the lawn.

It was still too close for comfort, and Campion zigged and zagged to put the wounded statue between himself and the house, in the faint and false hope that lightning, or bullets, rarely strike the exact same place twice.

But there was no third shot and suddenly Campion was at the chest-high wooden fence which bordered the paddock. He did not stop, but flung away the torch, which he could not use for fear of giving away his position, so that both hands were free and he could execute a textbook gate vault, using his stomach on the top fence rail as a pivot and swinging his legs around and over. It was a skill he normally practised on five-bar gates on country walks with Amanda, who often gave him gymnastic marks (low ones) for grace and agility.

There was nothing graceful about this landing, which ended with him on his knees in the damp and muddy grass of the paddock, wincing with a burning pain in his right leg. A tentative investigation with his fingertips revealed a rip in his trousers and came away slick with blood; though, as far as he could tell, no major artery in the leg had been severed and he felt he could still stand on it.

That, however, was not necessarily a sensible option. The closer he was to the ground, the safer he felt.

For the first time, Campion risked a look back towards the house from under the lower rail of the fence. The patio lights had not come on, but there was enough light from the shattered French window to have illuminated a sniper should there have been one, but there was no sign of life at all.

Then Campion heard the sound of a bolt being drawn – the sort of bolt which secures a door or a gate, not the breech of a rifle – and an oblong of light appeared over to the left of the house.

Campion scrambled to his feet and began to run in the opposite direction, silently cursing his old bones for not moving fast enough.

He had instantly chosen not to wait for confirmation that it had been the doors of the stables which had been opened, nor for what was inevitably due to emerge through those doors.

Mr Campion was no longer being chased; he was being hunted.

TWENTY

Cavalry

'What was that?' asked Christopher, glad of any distraction now he was down to his last ten pence piece and still no wiser about the rules of three-card brag.

'Poacher probably,' said Old Nick, shuffling the pack of oil-stained playing cards as he considered a supplementary answer. 'Though it could be Carl taking a pot at a poacher.'

It took Christopher a good twenty seconds to process that thought but, before he could say anything, they heard the dull thud of a second shot.

'Mebbe there were two poachers,' said Andrews casually, 'they sometimes work in pairs.'

'But Spivey is with my uncle.'

'So Carl took him out to poach the poachers. He often goes out and beats the bounds if he thinks there's poaching going on. Nobody but the boss man and his lady are allowed to shoot anything round here.'

'I don't think skulking around in the woods at night is the sort of thing Uncle Albert goes for. He's quite elderly, you know.'

Old Nick tapped his forehead with a nicotine-stained fingertip. 'He might be of pensionable age, but he's still sharp as a tack up top.'

'What makes you say that?'

'He didn't offer to play me at cards. Another hand?'

Christopher moved to the door of the hut, opened it and stuck his head out, but heard nothing further untoward. 'No more cards. I'm going round to Spivey's place, see where Albert is.'

'You don't think Carl's using your uncle for target practice, do you?'

From what Christopher knew of Albert's far from sedentary life, he was tempted to say that he would not have been at all surprised, but he saw no reason to provide the man he regarded as a card sharp with gossip fodder. 'I'd be happier if I knew where he was.'

'Then save your shoe leather. Let me ring him.'

Christopher, deciding that the current situation did not go against his uncle's strict instructions, nodded in enthusiastic agreement as Andrews reached for the telephone and dialled. He moved to stand at old Nick's shoulder and discovered the frustration of only being able to hear one side of the conversation.

'Carl? It's Nick . . . Who else would be ringing this time of night . . .? That Mr Campion. Is the old gent still with you? He said he was . . . Oh, I see . . . Did you? Right . . . And then what . . .? Fair enough. No, just wondering where he was. You didn't hear any shots just now . . .? No, I didn't say they came from your place; they were more over towards the woods or up near the house . . . Well, if you didn't, you didn't. Just asking.'

He slammed the receiver back down on its cradle and scowled up at Christopher hovering over him. 'Carl's playing silly buggers for some reason,' he said, 'and pulling on a bottle if I'm not mistaken. That's not like Carl. Nothing spooks him usually.'

'What about my uncle?'

'Carl took him up to the stables at the big house to see to one of the horses. He left him there with Lady Macbeth.'

Christopher recoiled in mild shock. 'You call her that too?'

'Only behind her back,' said Old Nick thoughtfully. 'Mind you, the very idea of being alone with her in that house is enough to spook anyone.'

He took it from the speed with which Christopher left the hut that the young man agreed with the sentiment.

Campion heard his doom before he dared to look back and see it approaching. Indeed, he imagined he could feel the thud of hooves through the damp ground as he desperately sought to establish the best direction in which to propel his stiff and disobliging legs.

He knew that off to his left would be the McIntyre Tyres compound with its – as far as he was concerned – un-climbable fence, though quite where or how far away, it was impossible to guess, given there were no lights showing. Directly in front of him, across the paddock, was Daffodil Wood, from which he had seen Carl Spivey emerge with Buckland, a reacquaintance with whom he now wished to avoid. Some primal instinct told him that being pursued through a dark wood at night was marginally preferable to being pinned against a wire fence, though both seemed options that an unlucky rabbit would lose heart over.

He chose the wood in the faint hope that it would at least slow down Buckland and his rider, and forced himself into a shambling run towards the blackest part of the nightscape before him. Two thoughts swirled around his brain: if he could pull the darkness of the wood round him like a blanket, he would surely be safe, and running across a field at night was undoubtedly a young man's sport.

Except this was not sport and Daffodil Wood proved not to be the safe refuge he had hoped for.

Campion crashed into wood quite literally, his shoulder colliding with a tree and his feet tripped by an exposed root sending him sprawling in the spiky underbrush. As he pulled himself upright, with the aid of the tree that had rushed out and attacked him, he looked back across the paddock and saw that his pursuer was far too close for comfort.

Lucy McIntyre was riding Buckland bareback with no saddle, controlling him with her knees and heels in his flanks and clutching one handful of hair on his mane. She looked frighteningly proficient, and Buckland, perhaps delighted at another nighttime trot, was responding to her commands, bucking and snorting with enthusiasm. To Campion's despair, she was gripping the rifle diagonally across her chest, but he had no intention of making it easy for her to take aim. His one overwhelming desire was for the wood to swallow him and hope that Buckland's night vision was as bad as his now that he realized, to his horror, that he had lost his glasses and quite possibly had trampled them underfoot when the tree roots had so viciously tripped him.

He blundered blindly, deeper into the wood, brambles clawing at his trousers and thin branches whipping at his face, spurred on by the sound of something much larger than him crashing loudly through the foliage, so loudly that he half expected to feel a hoof planted between his shoulder blades at any moment. At the same time the small part of his brain which remained rational wondered why he was blaming Buckland for his current distressed state. Buckland was not hunting him, his rider was.

Campion was now feeling his way through the wood, the night and the loss of his spectacles having reduced his vision to a minimum. He could, just about, see his hands in front of his badly scratched face and, coupled with the exertion of his run across the paddock and the increasing pain in his leg, his progress was now little more than at walking pace. Every tree he managed to avoid and every clawing thorn he pulled away from he counted as victories.

Without realizing it, he came to a halt, automatically went into a crouch and tried to control his breathing so that he could hear, as well as not be heard.

A horse such as Buckland was a big beast, measuring an impressive number of 'hands', whatever that meant (he had never been sure), and with a rider, even on familiar territory, could not move in total silence. If Campion could not see his pursuers, perhaps he could hear them, but only if he got his breathing – now a roaring thunder in his head – under control.

He heard nothing and risked straightening up, wincing at the pain in his leg as he did so, and found he had to put a hand against a tree bole to steady himself. The silence should have been reassuring, but all it did was provide the opportunity for his bruised and battered body to remind him that he was far too old for such nocturnal exertions.

He took one, then two, tentative steps forward, his hand out in front of him like a blind man feeling his way, and then he heard it: a snort, a distinct animal snort.

Mr Campion had seen nothing, sensed nothing and heard nothing, apart from that snuffled exhalation, and he had no idea from which direction it had come, but he instantly flung himself face-down on the ground, just as the shot rang out and cracked large chips of wood from the tree trunk he had been leaning against.

As he heard, quite clearly, the sound of a rifle bolt being worked, he relied on a long-forgotten memory of the military training he had suffered in his youth, and he began to crawl forward on his stomach.

'That one came from the woods,' spluttered Christopher from the hut doorway. 'I saw the flash; it was bloody close!'

'Keep your hair on,' said Old Nick, concentrating on making a pile of the coins he had won from his visitor, 'it'll be poachers, like I said, but I'll ring the house if you like.'

'Do that. Should we put the compound lights on?'

Andrews began to dial on the telephone. 'If it's young teara-ways out on a jolly, you'd be making us a prime target.'

'Has that happened before?'

'Once or twice. Motorbikers out on a bender come through the wood from Cranfield and take potshots at some of the diggers. Seems to amuse them; that's why we piled the spare tyres down that end. Bulletproof, they are: the bullets just bounce off 'em.'

'I had no idea it was the Wild West out here.'

'It only happened a couple of times.' Old Nick paused, holding the telephone receiver away from his ear. 'That's funny, there's no answer from the boss's house. I'll try Carl again, see if he heard that one.'

'No!' commanded Christopher with an authority which surprised him. 'Phone the police. Now!'

Campion used his elbows to propel himself, his face ploughing through the undergrowth and the accumulated litter of fallen leaves, rotting wood, moss and fungi, having given up any attempt to avoid spiky brambles and stinging nettles, and wincing silently when they struck home. He writhed silently onwards like a snake, and just as blind, with no inkling of which direction he was travelling, except that it had to take him away from Buckland. He listened carefully for the telltale sound of an equine snort, or the thump of a hoof or the crack of a twig, knowing full well that the horse's ears were similarly pricked.

He had lost all sense of time as well as direction, and resisted the urge to bring his wristwatch close to his face, for he was of the generation brought up on war stories of snipers able to spot a luminous watch dial across no man's land, but he estimated that two minutes had passed before he risked raising his head. With small, contained movements, he wiped muck and leaves from around his eyes and tried to focus on the nearest tree to get a crude bearing, then turn his head slowly, trying to distinguish shapes in the shadows.

He thought he saw a flash of something white, possibly the jumper worn by Lucy McIntyre, and immediately dropped flat again and began to crawl in the opposite direction. He covered perhaps twenty yards, confident that he had made no more noise than a light-footed vole or mouse, until he came up against a tree of substantial girth. Slithering around the bole, he put his back and shoulders to the bark and squirmed his way into a sitting position, anxious to get his breathing under control and again straining his ears.

The silence of the night was welcome and also frightening. Campion had no idea where he was, nor where his enemy might be, but then he got help from an unexpected source, Buckland himself.

Somewhere out in the darkness – Campion could not even guess from which direction it came – Buckland gave a brief, high-pitched whinny, cut short by the sound of a slap against solid horseflesh. Whether it had been a hunting cry of victory or a warning to the intended victim, Campion could not tell, nor did he let it trouble him.

That short neigh in the dark was enough to spur him into action. He could see neither horse nor rider, but the fact that he had heard the sound meant they were too close for comfort.

With his hands behind him, clutching the bole of the tree, he clawed himself up until he was standing, thinking that he was now in the classic position of a prisoner at the stake awaiting the order of the firing squad commander. He shook his head to try and clear his watering eyes, took two short breaths and then one very long one, and set off on a loping run.

He took the path of least resistance, which in his case meant keeping going until something tripped him, and miraculously nothing did. Even more wondrously, the exertion seemed to be improving his night vision, as the darkness in front of him turned grey, with the effect of a photographic negative. The future was, quite literally, getting brighter, assuming he had a future.

Yes, it was definitely getting lighter, but dawn, he knew, must still be hours away, and then he realized he had run out from under the canopy of the trees and was standing on the edge of the paddock. With a sinking heart he narrowed his eyes and could, just, make out the outline of Cruachan in the distance and, to the left of it, a smaller shadow displaying a tiny lozenge of orange light, which he assumed came from the doors of the stables.

The realization hit him that all his struggles through Daffodil Wood had been a futile, circular campaign, or – to be more precise – semi-circular, as he had entered the wood from the paddock and ended up back in the paddock, albeit far closer to the McIntyre compound. So close that he could make out the line of the fence which guarded it and the dark shapes of the dormant mechanical beasts behind it.

But it was the thought of a large, powerful, snorting type of beast which scared him into action. Returning to the wood and risking a collision with too, too solid horseflesh did not appeal in the slightest, and running across the open ground of the paddock would present a half-decent target to a more than half-decent shot. At least running directly across the paddock to Cruachan would, and here Campion almost congratulated himself on thinking clearly for the first time since escaping the house, where he had no intention of being trapped again.

Instead, he turned to his right and set off at a lumbering trot towards the compound fence, hoping that his own outline would be lost against the dark horizon of massed machinery and equipment behind it. Never shoot in poor light was the golden rule of stalking, wasn't it? And why should he think of that? Because he was being stalked, that was why.

As he stumbled forward, he could feel twigs and leaves and grass falling from his torn and mud-spattered suit and the cut from the glass in the French window, which he was pleased he could not see, had resulted in a dull pain up to his thigh. As every step became an effort, he bit his lower lip against the pain until he could taste blood, but he took heart from the fact that the fence was definitely getting closer.

Closer, in fact, than his reduced eyesight realized. A tussock of grass tripped him and he automatically put both hands out in front of him as he fell forward, only to wince as his palms smacked into the wire mesh before his face did. He sank to his knees, his chest heaving, relieved that he had achieved his goal; and though climbing it was beyond him, he could at the very least guide himself along the length of the fence – on his knees if need be – until he reached the Markley road.

With a supreme effort he pulled himself to his feet, using the mesh of the fence for handholds, only for the small flame of optimism he had kindled to be snuffed out by the crash of Buckland and his rider emerging from the wood and the thumping of hooves pounding towards him at speed.

The fence he had seen as his salvation now held him prisoner. He could not go over it and he did not have the strength or speed to run along it, certainly not the speed to outpace Buckland. He was trapped, with his back against the fence, and all he could think of was that he was 'hanging on the wire', an image from a war ingrained into his generation.

The horse pulled up ten yards from him, blowing heavily, a

foreleg pawing at the ground. Campion imagined he could feel Buckland's exhaled breath, and perhaps he hoped for a glint of compassion in those fiery eyes, but he knew his fate was in the hands of the animal's rider.

Through blinking, watery eyes he could see that her hands were full of rifle, and she was pointing it directly at him. Somehow he knew she was savouring the moment, but could not think of a single thing to say which might alleviate the situation. He had said too much – played all his trump cards – in their confrontation back in Cruachan and she, who he now thought of as his personal Lady Macbeth, was concentrating on her aim and showing no sign that she wished to explain her actions or offer mercy.

Later, much later, he would like people to believe that Buckland had saved him by springing backwards and jolting his rider off her aim, but in more serious moments he had to concede that it had been Christopher who had charged to his rescue like the cavalry arriving in the nick of time.

The horse, only controlled by his rider's knees as she levelled the rifle, had indeed jumped up and back in some ungainly dressage move gone wrong, but it was not an act of defiance towards his owner, nor out of compassion for Mr Campion's predicament as a sitting duck. Buckland, and Campion for that matter, had been startled by an explosion of light and sound, a loud, deep roar which Campion felt through the soles of his shoes, as clearly Buckland had.

The light came as a flood rather than a lightning strike, illuminating the scene like a stage, and Campion could now see his enemy clearly, her long blonde hair having unwrapped itself and flailing behind her as she struggled to remain seated on the bouncing horse and use the rifle with both hands. Even on such an unstable platform, her concentration held as she took aim and squeezed the trigger.

Mr Campion saw the muzzle flash but did not hear the sound of the shot over the roaring mechanical growl coming from behind him. Neither did he feel the impact of a bullet. Instead, he looked on in horror – fully lit horror – as Lucy McIntyre's body jerked backwards, her white sweater blooming red, and she was pitched off Buckland's bucking rump and thrown to the ground.

The horse reared up on its hind legs, punching the air with its front legs, then bolted for the dark sanctuary of Daffodil Wood at high speed, just as Christopher Campion, at the controls of one of McIntyre's bulldozers, its headlights blazing and its blade raised like a battering ram, smashed through the compound fence and into the paddock, the sound of metal twisting counterpointing the growl of its engine.

Mr Campion had the good grace to raise a limp hand in greeting before he fainted and slid gently down the wire mesh and embraced the damp earth.

'I never seen anything like that before in my life,' said Detective Chief Inspector Castor.

'It does take some believing,' said Mr Campion, 'and I was there, on the spot, when it happened.'

Campion had been revived with the help of an overcoat provided by Christopher to keep his extremities warm and several generous swigs of Lamb's Navy Rum from a half-bottle produced like a conjuror's trick by Old Nick Andrews. The perimeter lights had been turned on and Carl Spivey had been roused from his cottage and charged with finding and recapturing Buckland before the first flashing blue lights had been seen approaching from Bedford.

There had been time for the two Campions, having retreated to Christopher's car, to get their stories straight before the police – and the ambulance subsequently called – arrived.

'Will I be blamed?' Christopher asked, dabbing a handkerchief soaked in rum on to the wound in his uncle's leg.

'For her death?' said Campion between winces. 'I shouldn't think so. You were aiming the bulldozer at the fence, not at her, whilst she, on the other hand, was quite deliberately aiming a rifle at me. When she fired, her shot missed me and ricocheted back off the blade, hitting her. It was a freak accident certainly, but the shot came from her rifle and she fired it. An imaginative coroner might suggest a verdict of suicide by bulldozer, but accidental shooting is far more likely. You may, of course, lose the McIntyre public relations account.'

'Personally, I would not lose sleep over that, but Sir Lachlan is certainly going to need some good public relations now.'

'I sense you are already composing a press release.'

Christopher dismissed the thought. 'Not me, that's for sure. I can't think of any way to make this look good for him, unless he claims he was unaware he'd been married to a madwoman for twenty-five years, but then if Mary Lillman comes out of the cupboard with her stories about his "fire pirate" activities during the war, he's sunk again.'

'So you have no expensive advice for him?'

'Nothing that shouldn't be obvious.'

'I thought obvious was the maxim of the PR man. You borrow a man's watch and then charge him when he asks you the time.'

'Hah-hah-hah.' Christopher did his best sarcastic laugh. 'My honest advice – which will not be asked for – would be for him to sell McIntyre Tyres and that ghastly house and make a size-able donation to charity, then retire to a crofter's hut in Scotland and grow potatoes, or heather, or whatever they can grow up there.'

'That's not bad advice,' admitted Campion.

'But he wouldn't take it.'

'He might, now his Lady Macbeth is no longer around to dictate things. I am sure she controlled him from the get-go in most things. A strange woman: very hard, very severe and sustained by some evil beliefs. She was driven to better herself and did it by using people quite ruthlessly along the way.' He paused thoughtfully. 'Odd that I call her Lady Macbeth, considering she chased me through Daffodil Wood. Perhaps Dunsinane would be a better name, or I suppose Birnam Wood would be more accurate.'

'Good to see your sense of the absurd has survived,' said Christopher, 'considering your own public relations problems.'

Mr Campion strained forward to get a better look at his nephew's face under the car's interior light. 'What do you mean by that?'

Christopher shrugged his shoulders and took a swig from the rapidly declining level of rum in Old Nick's bottle before he answered. 'Well, just looking at you. Your suit is torn to shreds, there are leaves and twigs in your hair, which is not a good look, and your shirt looks and smells as if it has been used to wrap compost. You've lost your hat and your glasses and there's a deep cut on your leg which might turn septic at any moment. You've been tearing about the countryside in the middle of the night, chased by a horse and shot at by a homicidal female. You might even be held responsible for the destruction of property and the misappropriation of a bulldozer, and you'll certainly be spending a considerable amount of time helping the police with their enquiries.'

'And you think I will be in need of some good public relations advice?'

'I certainly do,' Christopher grinned impishly, 'when Amanda hears what you've been up to.'

TWENTY-ONE
Gypsy Punch

Mr Campion's Memory 5

'There's one thing I never told you,' said DCI Castor, leaning over Campion as he lay on the stretcher trolley in the back of the ambulance.

'There are probably several things I should have told you, Chief Inspector,' said Campion quietly.

'I had my eye on Mrs McIntyre from the off.' He tapped the stem of his unlit pipe (the ambulance crew had forcefully prevented him from lighting it) against the side of his forehead to imply shrewdness and brain power. 'Ever since we had that old lag Andrews in for questioning after we found Duffy.'

Campion appeared confused, which given his physical state was not a difficult act to pull off, and fluttered a hand demanding more detail.

'It was something Andrews said almost in passing. Made a bit of a joke of it he did, but then it doesn't take much to set him off. He'd laugh at his own appendicitis, that bloke. I was asking him about the McIntyres and whether they'd ever shown any violent behaviour to them that worked for them. He said no, but

Lady M. had once scared him by asking how long it would take one of their excavators – those motorized digger things – to dig somebody's grave. Old Nick didn't think she was kidding, either, but she never said who she had in mind.'

'I understand Old Nick came good for me in my hour of need.'

'If you mean he was the one who dialled nine-nine-nine, aye, it was. He was looking out for himself, mind you; he doesn't fancy another spell at Her Majesty's pleasure. Neither does that stable chap, Spivey, who rounded up that big horse before it wandered on to the M1. Both of them were only too keen to help once they realized the evil witch was dead.'

'She wasn't a witch, Chief Inspector,' Campion said wearily, 'but she was a fellow traveller with evil when it suited her.'

'You can say that again! If she really did ride up to Duffy's car and do him from behind, well, that's cold and vicious in my book – downright sneaky. When I was younger and boxing for the county, we'd have called that a gypsy punch – back of the neck when you weren't expecting it. Typical woman to be that devious.'

'Now that's just silly, Chief Inspector. I know lots of women who are the polar opposite of devious, whatever that is, and I'm delighted to have been married to one for more than thirty years.'

'Then you're a very lucky man, Mr Campion, to have a wife who's never thought of murdering you.'

'Oh, I wouldn't go that far . . .'

'Albert Campion, I could kill you, putting yourself in harm's way like that! It sounds as if you were being chased by the four horsemen of the apocalypse.'

'Horse*woman* – and there was only one of them.'

'But you knew she was violent, you'd known it for forty years, for goodness' sake, yet you let yourself be alone with her in a room full of guns . . .'

'And her known to be a crack shot,' Christopher pointed out.

'Dearest nephew, that's not helpful.' Mr Campion sighed.

Christopher had driven his uncle home so he could claim a spare pair of spectacles, have a bath and change his clothes, all of which he could have done at the Bottle Street flat, but for the need to give Amanda a full report before she heard of his alarms and excursions from a less diplomatic source.

He had spent what remained of the night in a private room in a hospital in Bedford, with DCI Castor and a rather sleepy off-duty WPC who had been requisitioned to take notes in shorthand. Eventually he was left alone, and managed to sleep through the strident call to arms which signified hospital break-fast time, only to be shaken awake by a very pretty nurse warning that 'Mr Sleepyhead' was now in danger of missing luncheon.

Somewhat reluctantly he brought himself back into the land of the living, if only to rescue the pretty nurse from Christopher's insistence that he help her plump pillows, serve a lunch on a tray, straighten the blankets on the bed and open doors, all of which actions he seemed convinced she could not manage unaided. He was, however, grateful that Christopher had appeared at his bedside, for he brought news as well as transport, and the reassurance that he had personally telephoned Amanda to inform her of her husband's whereabouts.

In the necessary preliminaries of any hospital visit, Christopher established that the senior Campion was not fatally injured and life-assurance policies would remain unclaimed. The deep cut on his leg had been staunched in the ambulance and sewn and bandaged in the hospital. His trousers and shirt, he remarked, were beyond saving, but his body was ready to discharge itself and he actually felt that his unshaven, much scratched face and uncombed hair gave him a certain roguish air.

Once the medical niceties were out of the way, Christopher briefed him on the general situation at Markley with all the subtleties of a smooth PR man, in that he never attempted to downplay his own contribution to Mr Campion's rescue, pointing out that all those hours learning to drive a bulldozer to impress journalists on behalf of McIntyre Consolidated had finally been put to good use.

The word had gone out on the police network, and Sir Lachlan had been located and escorted back to Markley Desolation to formally identify the body of his wife and then report for an interview – likely to be a lengthy one – with DCI Castor that afternoon. By which time, Christopher was sure, he would have assembled a platoon of lawyers rather than a PR team to protect him, although it was still uncertain whether or not he would face any specific charges. It seemed likely, however, that Christopher's professional guardianship of McIntyre's reputation with a view to securing his peerage was now in jeopardy, as the award of a peerage must be in doubt given the events, past and present, which would come to light.

(Silently, Mr Campion agreed, for he intended, at the first opportunity, to place telephone calls to certain dignitaries who had influence over such matters.)

In the meantime, Mr Campion had to make himself available to dictate and sign a formal statement about the events of the night, as the briefing he had given Castor from his hospital bed needed embellishment, though it would have carried more weight legally had it been a death-bed confession, at which point Mr Campion had remarked, 'Sorry to disappoint.'

There was, Christopher had said, a detail which the police had asked him to pass on. In their search of Cruachan, a sharp-eyed constable had noticed a message pad near one of the telephones on Sir Lachlan's desk, on which had been scribbled a number he recognized as that of the telephone box in the lay-by on the Cranfield road. (He shyly admitted to his superior officer that he knew the number as he had used it in his youth to arrange regular trysts with a girl from Cranfield who was not on the phone, but who had a bicycle.) The current police theory, based on this circumstantial evidence, was that David Duffy had called the house, perhaps asking to speak to or see Lucy McIntyre in private. She had stalled him somehow and offered to ring him back, automatically writing down the number. When he gave it to her, he must have added that he was nearby, waiting in the lay-by, and she decided to visit him in person rather than telephone – in effect signing Duffy's death warrant.

Mr Campion had agreed that it was a likely hypothesis, but what he really needed now was to get home, and Christopher could give him 'the important story' on the drive there.

Obviously pleased with himself, Christopher proudly produced Mr Campion's jacket, which he had dried on a radiator overnight then removed the caked mud with a stiff brush. Amazingly, given his exertions, his wallet, a fountain pen and even some loose change were still in place in its pockets.

With the jacket draped over his shoulders, and wearing hospital pyjamas which he promised to have laundered and returned, Mr Campion exited the hospital in a wheelchair propelled by his nephew as far as the car park and, without a shred of embarrassment, climbed into the passenger seat of Christopher's Scimitar, declaring loudly, 'Home, James!' to the small audience of hospital visitors who were arriving bearing floral tributes to sick relatives.

Once they were under way and speeding along the Cambridge road, Christopher asked his uncle what he had meant, back in the hospital, by 'the important story' he was expecting to be revealed en route.

Mr Campion appeared surprised, but then his face relaxed almost immediately. 'I had forgotten for a moment that you are not married, so you must trust me. Before we reach home, you have to tell me *exactly* what you told Amanda on the telephone. It is absolutely vital that we get our stories straight.'

Amanda had waited until after dinner before giving her somewhat explosive verdict on the events at Markley and, having heard and carefully considered reports from both Christopher and her husband, solemnly declared that she was delighted Mr Campion had survived the night, thanks to his nephew's gallant rescue, because she could now murder him at her leisure.

Mr Campion humbly acquiesced to his fate on condition that his wife took not less than twenty years to complete her mission.

'One thing, though,' said Amanda, in a tone which made Mr Campion flash a telepathic warning to Christopher. 'This business with the shotgun shells and the candle wax. Where did you learn how to do something as hideous as that?'

'Good Lord, I've never done such a thing, but I have read about it in police reports, and I suspect the technique has been covered in the more enthusiastic American shooting magazines to which the McIntyres were subscribers.'

'Chief Inspector Castor was most impressed that you'd spotted that,' interjected Christopher with enthusiasm, 'though he said it would have been difficult to prove. When Lady Macbeth went after Uncle Albert, she was using regular rifle bullets . . .'

'I remember them well,' said Mr Campion nonchalantly.

'. . . and if she made more than the one that did for David Duffy, then she must have disposed of them. Mr Castor said it would have been really useful to have found her fingerprints in the wax dribbled over the cartridge box, but there simply weren't any.'

'A great pity,' said Mr Campion innocently, 'that would have clinched it.'

'But you deduced that was how she did it.' Amanda spoke with the steel of a prosecuting barrister supremely confident of his facts.

'Modesty prevents me from claiming it was more than a guess, but it was a good guess and she did not deny it.'

From the look on his wife's face, Mr Campion realized he had perhaps made a tactical error.

'And yet, Albert Campion, and yet . . .' This was Amanda displaying her fierce side. 'You confronted a murderous . . . murderess . . . whilst you were alone with her in a house full of guns. What on earth were you thinking? You knew she was a dangerous woman more than forty years ago.'

'In my defence,' Campion tried a smile, 'my memory did betray me on that one, though there were extenuating circumstances. She was never identified in the attack on my friend Nathan. It was David Duffy who deduced that.'

'That in no way excuses your reckless behaviour.' Amanda had moved from fierce to adamant. 'Putting yourself in harm's way like that – and at your age! You really should know better. As I am sure your mother said on frequent occasions, Albert, I am not angry, just disappointed. *She* would probably have sent you to your room without supper, but I can't do that because it's our room and anyway, you've had your dinner. I would like it noted, however, that I am seriously displeased, and my displeasure will last at least until breakfast.'

'The cooling of your heart is duly minuted and I can only grovel for forgiveness, my dear.'

'That I look forward to, but in the meantime, I am going to bed. I take it Christopher is staying the night as it's far too late to drive back to London, and that way I can hold him responsible for making sure you don't go on another midnight ramble. Now please have the good manners not to giggle like schoolboys until I have dramatically stormed out of the room with great umbrage.'

Both male Campions kept their eyes firmly downwards on the dining-room table as Amanda scraped her chair back, stood and regally flounced out. Only when he heard her steps on the stairs – a sure sign that she was angry, for, like a cat, she could vary the weight of her tread at will – did Mr Campion raise his face.

'Be a good lad,' he said, 'and pour us some brandy. I always need a reviver after a scolding by Amanda.'

Christopher made his way over to the large Regency mahogany console with a marble slab top, on which rested silver trays housing decanters and glasses. 'Is it my fault you're in the dog house?' he asked as he poured generous measures into a pair of balloon glasses.

'No,' said Mr Campion, 'but I am very happy to blame you and, of course, you'll be doing the washing-up. I should have stressed the need to downplay things where Amanda is concerned. She does worry so much about me, which is terribly sweet and makes me a very lucky man.'

'I think she has had rather a lot to put up with,' said Christopher, emboldened by the wine at dinner and now a very fine cognac. 'According to family lore, you were always getting into scrapes.'

Mr Campion studied the contents of his glass. 'Scrapes? You could say that, I suppose, but I was always on the side of the angels, or so I like to think. The family never feared for my safety, only that I might dishonour the family name, which is why I adopted a *nom de guerre*, as indeed you did. That way I could play the games I wanted to.'

'This one was a rather dangerous game though, Uncle dear, and Amanda has every right to be upset. You really were risking it tackling that woman alone when you knew how she'd despatched David Duffy. That was cold, really cold and merciless, sneaking up behind him like that.'

Mr Campion acknowledged the point with his brandy glass.

'DCI Castor thought it had a touch of evil about it as well. He called it a "gypsy punch", which reminded me of Lady Drinkwater and that silver tankard all those years ago and, in a way, it was that tankard which introduced me to Lucy McIntyre. Now that is an example of a real gypsy punch.'

'You mean when you hit her with it, even though you didn't know who she was, or even that she was a woman?'

Mr Campion shook his head. 'I know Lugg would say that if only I had hit her with more force, it might have saved a lot of trouble in future years, but no, I wasn't thinking of that. I was thinking of what happened when we took the tankard home.'

Northamptonshire, 1932

I could tell Lugg was ruminating as we headed out of London aiming for Husbands Butcombe once again. His whole demeanour – lips pursed, eyes half-closed, his hands clasped across his immense stomach, as though trying to prevent its escape – suggested that he was deep in thought, which was always foreign territory for Lugg.

Eventually he gave the sort of loud, emphatic sigh which usually signalled we were passing an open pub and decided to speak his mind. 'We could have posted it, you know.'

'What are you suggesting, you old misery?'

'That blasted pot on the back seat. It's been from one side of the country to the other more times than a racing pigeon, thanks to the gypsies and then us. We should have tied it up with brown paper and string and stuck six pennyworth of stamps on. Let the local postman deliver it to that crazy old loon at Butcombe Manor.'

'Now, now,' I chided Lugg, though I knew he was generally impervious to chiding, 'calling her a loon is unkind. She's a lonely old woman who is clearly down on her uppers.'

'She could sell that big house.'

'I doubt very much that she could in today's market. Times are hard. Perhaps Lancelot sending the tankard back to her was a spark of filial charity.'

'Dunno about that,' snarled Lugg. 'She didn't strike me as a woman brimmin' over with motherly love an', as for the boy who ran away with the gypsies, well, he ran away with the gypsies, didn't he? Only time he came home was to break in and nick some of that fancy notepaper and the bits and pieces he needed from his printing press to make his dodgy hallmarks. Didn't announce hisself, didn't ask how the old bat was keeping. Could have left a pound note on the mantelpiece but didn't. Don't sound like there's much love lost there.'

'As usual, old chum, I will take your views on human nature under advisement,' I said, not wanting to admit that Lugg might be right for once.

I took a slight detour down a country lane – untroubled by traffic since Cromwell's New Model Army trooped along it – to Little Butcombe, in the faint hope that Mr Shadrach Lee and his family were still in residence. I felt it only polite to report that thanks to his help I had accomplished my mission and also, out of pure devilment, I might ask if his nephew Manfred was up for a re-match with Lugg, whom I had decided to promote as the Clapham Crusher, should there be any future engagements.

At some point in the future a sharp-eyed archaeologist might find traces of a campfire or a pit of buried rubbish, but other than a few tyre tracks in the grass, there was no obvious evidence that the gypsies had been there.

In Husbands Butcombe, however, Butcombe Manor was still there, though only just; for it seemed, though I knew it was impossible, as if bits of it had dropped off or faded away in the few days since we had first visited. Yet the main constituent, the heart, liver and lungs of the place, Lady Drinkwater, was very much still in command if not technically in residence, as she was out of the house and waving us to a stop before the Bentley was halfway down the drive. At the same time, she was pulling on an old army greatcoat over the two other coats she appeared to be already wearing.

''Ere she comes,' Lugg announced, 'rushing out to meet and greet us, no doubt just dying to return that ten-pound note you left as a deposit on the tankard. Tell you what, I'll bet you a tenner you don't get that back.'

'Have you got a tenner?'

'I will have,' he said confidently.

I applied the Bentley's handbrake to help Lady Drinkwater, who seemed determined to bring the car to a halt by applying the palms of her hands to its large headlights, or gig lamps as I liked to call them, and sheer willpower. She then scurried crablike around to my door and was shouting in the general direction of my right ear without waiting for me to wind down the window.

'Have you brought it back?'

'We have it here, all present, correct and vouched for,' I said, indicating the red silk bag on Lugg's knees.

'And it's not stolen goods?'

'Well, I don't have receipts, but I am assured it was bought legitimately and was sent to you via Shadrach Lee as a gift. A gift from your son Lancelot.'

I realized I was talking to an empty window frame and had to twist in my seat to continue the conversation as Cassandra Drinkwater was busy establishing herself in the Bentley's back seat. 'From Lancelot? How could I have known that?'

'You could have asked Shadrach Lee,' muttered Lugg.

'I have never seen the need to stoop to conversing with such people,' she said imperiously, pulling the greatcoat tighter and folding her arms. 'Now pass me that pot and drive me into Northampton.'

Lugg handed over the tankard in its bag and made to respond as she checked its contents, but I flashed him a warning glance as I started the engine and for once he took notice and, as he would say, buttoned his fat lip.

The drive into Northampton took place in complete silence, until we were in the town proper, and Lady Drinkwater began to give directions to the centre. We turned into a side road off Gold Street, and I did as I was ordered by the pilot in my rear-view mirror and parked at the kerb.

'I won't be long,' she said as she climbed out of the car, clutching the red bag to her chest.

We sat in silence after the car door slammed until Lugg asked, 'Where do you reckon she's off to?'

'To the pawnshop we passed two minutes ago round on Gold Street, unless I'm very much mistaken.'

'Well, would you credit it?' He relaxed back in the passenger seat and closed his eyes, Buddha-like.

'Yes, I would,' I said, 'unless I have totally misjudged her. Did you notice that she did not once – not once – ask about Lancelot, the son she has not seen for twelve years? Not even whether he was alive or where he was. All she wanted to know was whether the tankard was stolen goods or not, so she could cash in on it.'

'Maybe she's getting our petrol money.' Lugg opened his eyes which glinted with malice. 'Or she could be liquidating her assets to refund your deposit money . . .'

'I'm not holding my breath,' I said, drawing my wallet and extracting a ten-pound note, which I handed over with as much ill-grace as I could muster. It disappeared into Lugg's waistcoat instantaneously. 'And if she gets anything for it, it won't be as much as she's expecting.'

'You think those dodgy hallmarks will get spotted?'

'They may, they may not, but I have a feeling Lancelot rather wanted them to be.'

'You mean he's set her up?'

The Buddha expression had gone from Lugg's face. Now he was alert and, as always, prepared to admire dodgy dealing when he discovered it.

'It's a possibility – I put it no stronger than that as I am not a psychiatrist – that Lancelot is seeking revenge for a ruined childhood. Everything he cherished from his time with his real father had been taken away from him, including his beloved printing press, and consigned to the basement of that crumbly old house, gathering dust. I don't think he ever forgave her for that, but then I don't think she's an easy woman to forgive, and she admitted she had been a perfectly horrid mother.'

I restarted the Bentley's engine and treated Lugg to my best, loftiest smile.

'The Printer's Devil got the best revenge in the end, though possibly without realizing it.'

'With the gubbins for making those forged dies, you mean?'

'Not just that, my eagle-eyed friend, but I am sure you noticed that the machine mouldering away in the cellar at Butcombe Manor was a Stanhope Press from the 1840s, made by Thomas Cogger, of 3 Wardrobe Terrace, Blackfriars. Now that is a very fine maker's mark when it comes to printing presses, and I just happen to know a very rich newspaper proprietor who collects such things and who would pay several thousand pounds for such a piece. Far more, possibly several hundred times more, than dear old Cassandra will get for that silver pot.'

'You going to tell her that?'

'No,' I said, releasing the handbrake and steering out into the traffic, 'I don't think I am.'

AUTHOR'S NOTE

Albert Campion has had trouble with his memory before. From the start of Margery Allingham's thriller *Traitor's Purse*, Campion is suffering from amnesia following a severe blow on the head during an altercation with a gang of Fifth Columnists. He has not only forgotten who he is, but also the fact that he is engaged to Amanda Fitton. By the end though, he has recovered enough to foil a dastardly plot to undermine wartime Britain's economy and to marry Amanda.

As a fan of Allingham's work, I have always ranked *Traitor's Purse* (*The Sabotage Murder Mystery* in the USA) as one of my favourites. According to Margery's biographer Julia Jones (*The Adventures of Margery Allingham*, 2009), Allingham began planning the novel in the autumn of 1939, with the war barely two months old. She completed the book in mid-1940, coinciding with the retreat from Dunkirk and the fall of France, and it was published in 1941. Its plot of a mass counterfeiting of British currency might have seen far-fetched at the time, but after the war it was revealed that Himmler's SS had been actively planning exactly that.

I have felt free to take liberties with the 'Campion' family tree, as most of it is, probably deliberately, shrouded in mystery. It is known that Albert had an elder brother Herbert, a sister Valentine ('Val') and a nephew Christopher, as all are mentioned in the Allingham canon. There is no specific mention of a younger brother (Christopher's father) by name, so I have invented him.

Although Albert and Amanda had a son, Rupert, who features in several books, Margery never seemed convinced that Rupert could take over the 'family business' of detection and adventuring. Indeed, in a 1958 essay for *Time and Tide* magazine, entitled 'What to Do with an Ageing Detective', there is the suggestion that she was considering Christopher as his natural successor.

(The same essay, which revolves around imagined conversations between Margery and her characters, includes a wonderful exchange with the redoubtable Lugg where she asks him: 'If Albert has got older, why haven't you?')

In chapter five, Lugg refers to a previous incident with a 'crazed horsey woman', who is the rather frightening character Mrs Dick Shannon, in Allingham's cracking 1931 thriller *Look to the Lady* (another favourite).

In chapter twelve, when Campion describes the police arriving 'with commendable promptitude', he is paying a small homage to my old friend, the late Colin Dexter, who used the phrase in an early *Inspector Morse* novel but was asked to remove it by an editor. That rankled him for years. In chapter sixteen, the reference to the pharmacist daughter of the local doctor in Sturry is a nod to my most faithful supporter, Kinn McIntosh, with whom I share an interest in archaeology and a Yorkshire heritage, and who is better known as the crime writer Catherine Aird.

The Presscala Club, off Fleet Street, certainly did exist in the 1970s when I went to work in London. Though the more famous watering hole, El Vino's, was the 'in' place for journalists, the Presscala was popular with cartoonists and printers. Indeed, I was introduced to it (and several other watering holes) by a printer, Algy Wheatley.

For technical help, though any howlers are of my making, I am grateful to Christopher Austyn, formerly the head of the sporting guns department at Christie's auction house, who years ago gave me a copy of his book *Classic Sporting Rifles* (The Sportsman's Press, 1997), and I am forever thankful to Anne Lambert for instruction in matters equine.

Once again, I am indebted to Roger Johnson for his cartographic expertise and advice.

I would also like to thank those generous readers who have supported my stewardship of Mr Campion over the past ten years, especially those who have subsequently discovered the wonderful writings of his creator Margery Allingham.

Milton Keynes UK
Ingram Content Group UK Ltd.
UKHW040430140224
437791UK00007B/486